Convince Me, Viscount

A Very Fine Muddle
Book Six

Kate Archer

ARE YOU SIGNED UP FOR DRAGONBLADE'S BLOG?

You'll get the latest news and information on exclusive giveaways, exclusive excerpts, coming releases, sales, free books, cover reveals and more.

Check out our complete list of authors, too!

No spam, no junk. That's a promise!

Sign Up Here

www.dragonbladepublishing.com

Dearest Reader;

Thank you for your support of a small press. At Dragonblade Publishing, we strive to bring you the highest quality Historical Romance from some of the best authors in the business. Without your support, there is no 'us', so we sincerely hope you adore these stories and find some new favorite authors along the way.

Happy Reading!

CEO, Dragonblade Publishing

Additional Dragonblade books by Author Kate Archer

A Very Fine Muddle
Romance Me, Viscount (Book 1)
Be Daring, Duke (Book 2)
Stand With Me, Earl (Book 3)
Sweep Me Up, Baron (Book 4)
Write for Me, Marquess (Book 5)
Convince Me, Viscount (Book 6)

A Series of Worthy Young Ladies
The Meddler (Book 1)
The Sprinter (Book 2)
The Undaunted (Book 3)
The Champion (Book 4)
The Jilter (Book 5)
The Regal (Book 6)

The Dukes' Pact Series
The Viscount's Sinful Bargain (Book 1)
The Marquess' Daring Wager (Book 2)
The Lord's Desperate Pledge (Book 3)
The Baron's Dangerous Contract (Book 4)
The Peer's Roguish Word (Book 5)
The Earl's Iron Warrant (Book 6)

PROLOGUE

THE *TON* HAD breathed a collective sigh of relief at the end of the last season—all five Bennington ladies were now safely wed. Society no longer needed to proceed into each new year with a sense of trepidation and foreboding regarding what might happen next.

They'd all been rather shaken to witness the various goings-on of Lord Westmont's daughters.

How had Lady Beatrice managed to wed the one man in all of London who appeared to find her foolish?

Had Lady Rosalind actually arranged her own kidnapping to win the favor of the duke?

For what reason did Lady Viola turn up at a green at dawn, only to find her beloved ready to fire at three different gentlemen?

How had Lady Cordelia managed to set fire to the Duke of Castleton's staircase?

And finally, Lady Juliet—she'd advertised far and wide that she must wed a poet, and had instead wed a Corinthian who wouldn't know a poem if it hit him over the head.

All of these circumstances had been supervised by the dotty Miss Eloise Mayton—the spinster wearing widow's weeds and telling preposterous stories about the tragic endings of her many loves on the continent.

Matrons had frowned, lords had hidden their laughter, other

young ladies had fanned themselves—the Benningtons had taken London on a wild ride and London found itself relieved that the ride had finally rolled to a stop.

Of course, there was still the eldest brother, Viscount Darden, to consider. But then, he was a lord and bound to go about the thing in some sensible fashion.

The *ton*, unfortunately, was a little too blithe in their assumptions. That they anticipated the coming season as a sunny walk through a cheerful glen would only lead to chagrin when they found themselves blindly tripping down dark and windy paths.

They had nobody to blame for their naivete but themselves—if there was a Bennington left unwed, there was bound to be a scheme hatched.

CHAPTER ONE

Portland Place, 1807

CHARLES BENNINGTON IV, Viscount Darden, only son of the Earl of Westmont, was confounded by his father's letter. Though they had discussed the matter thoroughly when he'd been at home, it seemed the old soldier had done an about face.

The earl had been convinced he would not come to Town for the season. He'd been convinced that his household, not the least of which was his butler, had earned a rest in the countryside. Even the earl, always so oblivious to what went on around him, seemed to sense that it had been five mad seasons in which his daughters had launched themselves at an unsuspecting public.

Darden thoroughly agreed—not one of his sisters had seen fit to determine their future calmly and rationally. It had been a series of hurricane winds, crashing waves, blowing off courses, and shredded sails. Each one of his sisters' ships had eventually limped their way into a harbor, otherwise known as a church, but it had been exhausting.

This coming season was meant to proceed in perfect regularity—he and his valet would go back to the bachelor lifestyle they were both accustomed to. Rather than a house full of people, they would bring in a day maid twice a week to attempt to keep things in some kind of order and they would send out the laundry. They would employ a cook to make Darden breakfast and he could eat the rest of his meals at his club. His groom already lived comfortably in the stables and Darden had no need of a coachman as he drove his own phaeton.

He could come home at all hours and not find a footman or a butler peering at him. He could stay abed until the afternoon without anybody in the drawing room wondering if he were under the weather.

What else did a fellow need for his happiness?

Now, those genial arrangements were not to be. The earl had written that he would come to Town after all. A whole household was poised to descend upon them. His valet was to be bossed about by Tattleton and his groom would shortly find himself under Sandren's thumb in the stables.

If that were not confounding enough, one by one letters had arrived from his sisters. They were all opening their houses in Town too, and every single one of them wrote that they *looked forward to spending time with him.*

Cordelia had specifically told him she was not coming this year. Beatrice was not to come either, at least so Van Doren had said. Now they were all coming. What was going on?

"I am afraid I know what's going on," he muttered.

His valet, Richards, shook out Darden's coat and examined it for imperfections. "My lord?"

"They're all coming, Richards," Darden said. "Every last one of them."

This seemed to strike Richards rather hard. "All? Miss Mayton too?"

"My father does not mention it, but she will not be left behind."

Richards snorted. "You'll be spending any number of evenings listening to more ghastly goings-on or desperate doings."

Darden nodded. Miss Mayton really did choose the most ludicrous novels and then insist on reading them aloud. She favored an author named Richard Roydon and such were that fellow's deranged stories that Darden could only imagine Miss

Mayton was the only person who purchased his books.

"Miss Mayton's stories are the least of my problems."

"My lord?"

"Why are they really coming, Richards?" Darden asked. "Why, when half of them were not coming, have they decided to come? Why did every single one of them write to me that they looked forward to spending time with me?"

Richards did not answer these questions, though Darden suspected he knew the answer. It was the answer that had been hanging over their heads for years.

"That's right," he said. "For the past five years it's been all about my sisters and their romances and their alarming weavings and staggerings into a church. Now, their eyes are all turned toward me."

"No, my lord!" Richards said, sounding decidedly stricken.

"Yes, Richards."

"But the ladies' husbands, certainly they'd put their foot down at such a notion," Richards said, seeming to reach for any shred of hope. "Those gentlemen are your friends!"

"*Would* they put their foot down?" Darden asked. "As far as I can tell, those fellows are all clay in my sisters' various hands. I can just hear the cajoling and see the batting of eyelashes that went on to enact such a scheme."

"Do you suppose Miss Mayton is at the bottom of this?" Richards asked.

"I would assume so," Darden said. "Miss Mayton is always at the bottom of everything ghastly."

"What will you do?" Richards asked, his voice tremulous. "Were they to succeed…that would mean a wife. Then that would mean a housekeeper and a butler and a whole pile of people crowding out the servants' hall. We've been going on so pleasantly!"

Richards was right, they had gone on very pleasantly.

They would continue to go on very pleasantly.

After all, his sisters and Miss Mayton could scheme all they liked, but they could not propose to a lady for him and they could not drag him into a church.

Very naturally, he had every intention of marrying. He'd always intended it. It was just that his intention was like a far-off fence in the distance. Once one began walking toward it, one became cognizant that it was further off than one had thought.

"Do not fret overmuch, Richards," Darden said. "Five sisters and one matron are unlikely to outwit me."

Richards' hand shook as he hung Darden's neckcloth on a rack. Darden sighed. It would be nice if his valet had a little bit more faith in his abilities.

⟫⟫⟫✕⟪⟪⟪

MISS ELOISE MAYTON had always had the unique ability to ignore facts that she found unpleasant and adopt facts that were a deal more pleasant, even if they were not actual facts.

Her younger years on the continent had been rather fraught, but that did not trouble her too very much. She simply rewrote the story of her time there.

After all, was it not entirely likely that if she had ever met a Swedish count named Hans, that the dear fellow would have thrown himself off a mountain for love of her? Or that an Italian count might have dealt himself a deadly blow for love of her? Or a French poet might have hung himself for love of her? Or a Transylvanian duke might have impaled himself for love of her?

Had she actually met any of those fellows, she was certain there was a high probability of them dying of love for her.

That nobody had died of love for her would be the disappointment of her life, had she chosen to dwell on it.

Reality rarely intruded upon Miss Mayton's thoughts and when it did insist on raising its ugly head, she very quickly dismissed it.

Therefore, she found herself most uncomfortable to discover

a matter that could not be dismissed so easily. She had received a letter addressed to her in Somerset. It was the letter she'd been dodging for the past twenty years.

A person she'd rather not encounter was looking for her. It was not Hans or Gregorio or Phillipe or her Transylvanian duke. It was someone else altogether and she dearly wished that person would throw themselves off a mountain or stab themselves or hang themselves or even throw themselves off a parapet to be impaled by their own flagpole. Hans, Gregorio, Philippe, and her Transylvanian duke had found the decency to take themselves out of the world, why did this person not do the same!

Not one to wave the white flag before trying any number of ways out of a situation, Miss Mayton had thought long and hard about what ought to be done.

She was rather surprised when an ingenious solution did not immediately present itself. She was certain there was such a solution, however her mind had not yet grasped it. She would need time for it to come to her. She would need to elude the consequences of the letter until such a moment that she knew what to do about this unfortunate turn of events.

She had been determined to convince the earl to relocate to Town for the season. They had thoroughly decided they would not go, that they would stay quiet in the country. But now, they must go. They must get out of Somerset.

A mountain of letters later, her girls were united. She'd written to Beatrice, Rosalind, Viola, Cordelia, and Juliet, and successfully pointed out that if Darden did not marry soon he would become a confirmed bachelor and never marry. Five daughters urging the earl to come to Town, along with her own well-considered reasons for doing so, had swayed the earl.

As far as the earl understood it, his five daughters would be devastated if they could not once more find themselves all together at their father's table in Town.

Beatrice, living just at the neighboring estate, said they would go and they would take young Lily with them. Then of course, the earl had a new grandson to meet, as Rosalind had brought a healthy baby boy into the world.

Of all the reasons given in favor of going, no two facts could have overcome the dear old fellow so speedily.

His granddaughter was at an age when full conversations were possible and tended to be about the most charming subjects. Was the earl to give up discussions of where the sun went at night or why her stuffed bear could not talk out loud, or why there were never any cakes at breakfast? Was he to miss the little girl's speculations on such subjects?

Lily, being a good-natured sort of girl, hoped the sun had a comfortable bed to sleep in at night. She imagined her bear would tell her no end of secrets if he could talk. When she was grown, she would have cake for breakfast every day. The earl spent half the time wiping a joyful tear from his eye.

And then, a new grandson was on the ground! He had not even met the little chap yet but, by all accounts, he was a round and cheerful fellow.

If his two grandchildren were to be in London, then so would he.

Before they departed for Town, Miss Mayton had a long talk with the servants who would remain behind in Somerset. It was now their understanding that any unknown person inquiring about the family's whereabouts was likely a housebreaker and must be turned away instantly, with no information given out.

Housebreakers were overrunning the country and it was one of their preferred strategies. They would particularly inquire into the whereabouts of any lady of the household, as they would be interested to know where her jewels might be. Should the lord's servants encounter a stranger at the door, they were not to even breathe the address on Portland Place.

Miss Mayton did regret that she'd left the maids checking the locks on the windows and trembling over the notion of sly housebreakers, but what else could she do?

In any case, she and the earl were well away, having just

pulled into the yard at The Angel in Basingstoke.

They had made this particular inn one of their usual stops on their journeys to Town and had always found the proprietor a fellow of much good sense.

Just now, though, he did not seem full of good sense. He seemed downright distraught.

The earl peered out the carriage window. "What do you suppose is happening there?"

Miss Mayton was not entirely certain. The innkeeper was arguing with a gentleman, a fine-looking dandy, and they were passing a leashed hound back and forth between them.

The dog was black and had a forlorn look about him, as she supposed he might to have found himself in such a situation. Really, it was only his leash that was being passed back and forth. The dog itself had lain down between the two gentlemen as if he might as well rest while his future was being debated.

The lads who ought to be opening their doors and helping them down were too taken up with the scene to notice them.

"I suppose we ought to get ourselves out, Earl," she said. "As it does not appear anybody is coming."

"Always full of good sense, Miss Mayton."

With the earl's help, she descended to the yard and they made their way over to the scene that was unfolding.

The innkeeper, finally realizing he had guests arriving, cried, "Lord Westmont! My lord!" As he said it, he shoved the leash back to the gentleman.

The gentleman just as quickly foisted it back at him.

"My lord, I do apologize," the innkeeper said. "It is just that this fellow keeps forcing this dog on me. I don't keep dogs!"

"Neither do I," the man said languidly. "I did not mean to win him in a card game, but I did. Now my good fellow, I also did say that if you did not wish to keep him you might give him away or shoot him. What sort of inn is this, where a gentleman cannot seem to get rid of a dog?"

The dog in question growled though he did not get up.

"You hear what this gentleman says!" the innkeeper cried. "I can shoot him if I like. Since when is the proprietor of an inn to be going round shooting dogs? And this man, he is not even a guest of the inn!"

The gentleman looked around and said, "I see. One must stay here for one to get rid of a dog? You have a lot of rules, Proprietor." Turning to the earl, he said, "Mr. Beau Brummel, pleased to make your acquaintance. Lord Westmont, is it?"

"Yes, Westmont. Well, as to that, pleasant to meet you, Mr. Brummel I'm sure," the earl said, "Though, I really do not think you ought to force this dog on this poor man."

"I've got to force him on somebody," Mr. Brummel said. "Lord Bradley left him at my door and did a runner. Now, you can see for yourself that there are three of that animal's hairs on my coat already. I cannot live in such a manner." He turned his attention to Miss Mayton. "And this lovely lady is?"

"Ah, yes, may I present Miss Eloise Mayton," the earl said. "She is a cousin."

"Entirely charmed. My dear Miss Mayton," Mr. Brummel said with an eloquent bow, "may I condole on your recent loss."

Miss Mayton of course realized he'd noted her widow's weeds. As he had named her lovely and was charmed by her, she must clear up the confusion about that at once.

"Oh no, Mr. Brummel," she said, "I am not in mourning as most people think of it. You see, I experienced a series of tragic circumstances of the romantic variety while I lived on the continent. I wear the weeds in remembrance of my lost loves."

Mr. Brummel nodded. "Say no more, Miss Mayton. Hearts were broken."

"Yes, they were! Rather permanently."

"You find me in the midst of an unpleasant contretemps, my dear Miss Mayton. I pray you had come upon me in more genial circumstances, as I fear your opinion of me must be very low and I am crushed to know it."

Miss Mayton, having slayed no end of gentlemen in her imagination, had always found actually alive gentlemen less overcome by her. So, it was rather thrilling to hear that she was lovely, the gentleman was entirely charmed, and he was crushed by her alleged low opinion.

"Now, my dear Mr. Brummel," she said, "I am certain we can come to some sort of happy arrangement regarding your current difficulty."

"I won't shoot a dog," the innkeeper muttered.

"He is a hunting sort of dog, I imagine?" Miss Mayton asked.

"He is, Miss Mayton," Mr. Brummel said. "Lord Bradley says he is one of the finest in the land. I do not partake of the sport myself, as I find running round attempting to kill my dinner to be the sort of thing a man with no care for his clothes will get up to."

"Earl," Miss Mayton said, "Certainly Darden would appreciate such a dog. One of the finest in the land."

"Darden? But he is hardly ever at home…" the earl said weakly.

"Ah, but if he had a fine hound, he might very well be enticed," Miss Mayton said.

She had not the first idea if that were true, but Mr. Brummel must be assisted in this matter. He thought her lovely, was charmed, and was crushed.

"But Darden is always in Town, or at one of his friend's estates…"

"Never fear, Mr. Brummel," Miss Mayton said. "Lord Darden would be delighted to take custody of this fine specimen."

"Miss Mayton! You are everything gracious!" Mr. Brummel cried. "This courtesy will not go unrepaid. In a month's time, I am co-hosting a party with the prince at Carlton House. I will see that you, the earl, and Lord Darden are on the guest list."

Miss Mayton felt her cheeks go positively pink, which she supposed they had not done in twenty years. Mr. Brummel was very determined to see her again.

Goodness, she had not foreseen such a circumstance at her time of life.

But then again, the years had treated her very kindly. She *did* retain a certain girlish mien if her looking glass told her no tales.

It could not be mistaken—Mr. Brummel was determinedly flirting with her.

It would not surprise her if this was a case of instant love. She had long held the opinion that instant love was very common, if the love were true.

She pulled herself together and gave the dear man their address at Portland Place. After all, he would need to know where to send the invitations. And perhaps flowers or a note.

The gentleman handed her the leash and bowed. "Until we meet again, Miss Mayton."

Yes, Mr. Brummel. Until we meet again, good sir.

LADY MARIANNA TISDALE yawned as her maid fussed about with the unpacking.

Here she was, in Town to make her debut and fulfill her obligations. She would marry well and be a credit to her family. As a duke's daughter, she had always known her responsibilities. It was just so tedious!

She liked her house and her stables and her wood. She knew everybody in the village. She was very comfortable with all the servants and felt Norwood, their butler, had always had a soft spot for her. She positively adored Mr. Henderson, the duke's cook—that genial fellow had been slipping her cakes and biscuits since she was old enough to sneak down into the kitchens. Now, she was to go traipsing off to some new house.

What was the house like? Who was the cook? Who lived in the village? Would she like any of them? Would she even like whatever fellow she'd wed?

She felt as if she were on the verge of being tossed off a ship and left to float to some remote and foreign island to make her home there as best she might.

Her maid admired one of her dresses and said, "The gentlemen are certain to go wild over this one."

Marianna sighed. Her maid would enjoy the season far more than she would herself, she was sure.

"Melly," she said, "I cannot concern myself with just any gentleman. My father does not wish that I marry beneath me, so that leaves only two prospects—the Marquess of Mayfield and the Marquess of Wellerston, both destined to become dukes. A choice about as exciting as between marmalade and strawberry jam."

"You like both on your bread, but what if you don't like either of the gentlemen?" Melly asked. "What then?"

Marianna did not answer, as that question had continued to plague her. Her father did not seem to think that liking a gentleman had anything to do with marrying one.

She did not understand him. Marianna was certain that he and her mother had a rather torrid love in the early years of their marriage. They might be more settled now, but she'd heard the stories of her father's derring-do and romantic gestures, all to get her mother's attention.

As well, her mother had been a baron's daughter, so the duke had certainly not been thinking about rank when he'd chosen her.

As her father explained it, the two ideas could not be compared—her mother had gone up in rank upon their nuptials, but no party had gone down in rank. If Marianna was to wed below her rank, she would wake one day to find herself a lowly countess or viscountess. Or worse, a baroness.

"Well? If you don't like either of them, what then?" Melly asked again.

"I do not know what then," Marianna said. "Though I will find out soon enough. My father takes me to Almack's on Wednesday and claims both marquesses will be there. I rather think he's spoken to both sets of parents about a potential match."

Melly shook her head. "Tryin' to force yourself to like a fellow? The habits of lords and ladies can lead to some rum situations, if you ask me."

Though Marianna had not asked her maid any such thing, she rather agreed. It was a rum situation.

Nevertheless, it was *her* situation.

CHAPTER TWO

TATTLETON ONCE MORE found himself in Town, though Town was exactly where they were not meant to be. They were supposed to be going on quietly in the country this season. Yet, here they were!

It was Miss Mayton's doing, he was certain. Every ghastly thing that had ever occurred in this family had her hand in it.

And why had the maids who were to stay behind in Somerset come to him about a window lock that was broken and how it must be fixed against housebreakers who would come knocking at the door, looking for a lady's jewels? They'd heard that bit of nonsense from Miss Mayton. Why was she frightening the wits out of the servants?

Tattleton made his rounds of the drawing room, seeing it had been dusted properly. Only Lord Darden and that ridiculous dog Miss Mayton had picked up from somewhere were in it at the moment. They'd come so close to arriving to Town sans a stray animal of some sort, and then there he was. What was the lady thinking, foisting that dog on Lord Darden?

"Look at this, Tattleton," Lord Darden said.

Tattleton turned to see Lord Darden pick the dog up, as the dog seemed always to be lying down.

The dog drooped in his arms and then when Lord Darden attempted to set it on its feet, it sank down to the floor again. It was as if its legs were made of jellies and had no bones inside them.

"It hardly ever moves," Lord Darden said. "How is a hunting dog so lazy? Miss Mayton said his name is Artemis, but there does not seem to be much of the god of the hunt in him."

"Well my lord, if one receives a dog from Miss Mayton, what can one expect? It was bound to go wrong."

Lord Darden nodded as if he knew the truth of it. "Miss Mayton was gifted this dog by Mr. Brummel—what was that fellow doing with a dog bred for hunting? He strikes me as the type that would have some little puff of a thing to be sat on a sofa, just for the look of it."

Tattleton nodded gravely, though he was not personally acquainted with Mr. Brummel. He had heard enough about the fellow recently, though. Apparently, the gentleman was both charmed and crushed by Miss Mayton. Or so she said.

He could believe the crushed part at least—she had crushed him no end of times.

"Well," Lord Darden said, staring down at the dog, "there's not much to be done with him. I suppose if he ever bothers to get on his feet, somebody will let him out into the back garden."

"Of course, my lord."

"I'll be off to the YBC, if anybody is looking for me."

"You will be back for dinner, my lord?"

"I'm not certain," Lord Darden said. "I'll see where the day takes me."

"But the earl," Tattleton said. "He would wish it. I'm sure he meant to inform you of it before you went out. Lord and Lady Van Doren and the duke and duchess are to come for dinner."

"Are they?" Lord Darden said.

Tattleton thought it was asked in a suspicious sort of tone.

"And Miss Lily too, of course," Tattleton said. "I will entertain her while you dine. Benny and Johnny will run the table."

That, as far as Tattleton was concerned, was the real point of the evening. He was well aware that Benny and Johnny were not yet so skilled that they could pull off a service flawlessly, but he did not care. Not even if the Duke of Conbatten was forced to suffer through any missteps they would make. Tattleton was to be spending a good part of the evening with Miss Lily.

She was the most perfect little miss that had ever walked God's earth. What had she told him when last they'd met? She'd said if he ever went away, she would cry and cry. It was entirely true—if they were ever parted, he would cry and cry too!

"Tattleton," Lord Darden said, interrupting his pleasant reverie, "do you happen to be aware of any particular plot regarding me?"

"A plot, my lord?"

"A plot," Lord Darden said. "I think my sisters have wrestled their husbands into compliance and formed some sort of cabal. I think they wish to get me married off."

A cabal. Tattleton did not know anything about a cabal, but if there was one in the offing, he could bet he knew who was at the bottom of it.

It was outrageous that a cabal would plot to marry off a lord. If a matter were outrageous, there was only ever one direction to point.

"My lord," he said, "nothing of that nature has come to my attention. However, and I think I may be so bold as to be direct, if there is such a scheme being formulated, Miss Mayton is its author. She is always the author."

Lord Darden nodded. "So I thought too."

"I could not help but notice that Miss Mayton wrote an unusual amount of letters some months ago, and then suddenly we were coming to Town."

"Did she? Yes, I bet she did."

"And then," Tattleton continued, "before we set off, she saw fit to scare the wits from the maids staying behind. Some nonsense about housebreakers coming to the door and inquiring after a lady's jewels."

"Why would she do that?"

"It is my experience, my lord, that it is fruitless to wonder why Miss Mayton does half the things she does. All one can be certain of is that her efforts often precede a preposterous disaster."

The lord was thoughtful for a moment, ruefully looking down at his useless dog.

"Tattleton, will you be my eyes and ears in the house? Richards will keep an ear to the ground, but he cannot be everywhere you can be. He does not hear what you hear. He's a loyal lieutenant, but I need a general in my army. I've got to find out their plan."

Tattleton staggered back and grasped the mantel for support. Lord Darden had just inquired if he would be the general of his army.

He had, of course, always viewed himself the general of the household servants, with Mrs. Huffson as his lieutenant. But now, he was to be the general of the *lord's* army.

"Consider me engaged, my lord," Tattleton said.

"Excellent. Now, no detail is too small, no news is to be dismissed. I want to hear everything that is said, especially if Miss Mayton is saying it."

"Understood, my lord," Tattleton said. He briefly thought about saluting, but decided to wait for the moment they'd won the final victory against this cabal.

He did take Lord Darden's words to heart, though. No news was to be dismissed.

"My lord, as you wish to know everything that goes on with Miss Mayton, I regret to inform you that I am almost certain she believes Mr. Beau Brummel is in love with her."

Lord Darden sank down into a chair. "Brummel! What? No, she cannot."

"She can and she does," Tattleton said, reveling in the surprise the news had engendered. "Lady Rawley was here this afternoon and Miss Mayton told her how Mr. Brummel thought she was lovely and charming and was crushed that they'd not met under more genial circumstances, and then something about

Carlton House, I did not quite catch that last part of it. What I did catch, though, were blushes more suited to a sixteen-year-old!"

Lord Darden snorted. "I presume that's how she ended up with a dog who won't hunt. Well, I suppose that might take her mind off me for a few moments. As for Brummel—I don't really care for the fellow, so he's on his own with our lovesick matron. Brummel, what an idea."

"What an idea indeed, my lord," Tattleton said.

"Where has she gone off to this afternoon?" Lord Darden asked. "I hope she is not haunting the doors of Carlton House, hoping to get a look at him."

"She did not say, my lord," Tattleton answered. "She left in the carriage with Lord and Lady Van Doren."

"That's odd," Lord Darden said. "They haven't gone shopping—Beatrice could never convince Van Doren to shop with Miss Mayton. Or shop at all, for that matter. Perhaps they went to the park, though it is rather early."

"Perhaps, my lord. Rest assured, if she says anything about her whereabouts when she returns, you shall know it!"

MISS MAYTON SURVEYED the room. They had all agreed to meet at the Duke of Conbatten and Rosalind's house in Grosvenor Square—Beatrice, Cordelia, Viola, and Juliet, along with their respective lords.

The lords did not look ecstatic to find themselves there, but through their wives' careful management, they had all come.

Miss Mayton herself had put out the idea of a coordinated effort and now she must enact some sort of scheme to marry off Lord Darden. She did not particularly care if the lord wed this season or not, but it had got her to Town. Now, she was finding it slightly inconvenient, as she did find her head so filled with other more interesting things.

Ever since her stay at The Angel and her remarkable encounter with Mr. Brummel, she had left her problems in Somerset far behind.

Mr. Brummel thought she was lovely and charming, had been crushed to speculate that she might have a low opinion of him, and been determined to see her at Carlton House.

Fear not, Mr. Brummel, my opinion is far from low!

"I say, Miss Mayton," Lord Hamill said, "I noticed you no longer wear the widow's weeds."

Miss Mayton nodded graciously, glancing down at her bright blue dress. She had torn through her old dresses that had been left behind when she put on the widow's weeds and pulled out those that struck her as the most youthful. She did not deem those dresses sufficient for what was to come this season and would have a new wardrobe made, but they must do for now.

"I feel," she said, "that I have mourned long enough, Lord Hamill. It is time to rejoin the land of the living."

"I, for one, am glad of it," Beatrice said. "That color does something very well for your complexion."

Miss Mayton did not answer, but she had thought rather the same.

"Miss Mayton?" the duke said. "Perhaps you would like to start us off on this adventure?"

Miss Mayton nodded. She was perfectly aware that the duke would rather be anywhere else, but for the fact that he was clay in Rosalind's hands.

He'd been clay to begin, but now she'd borne him a son and she was held higher than any goddess. As well she should be, never was there such a gurgling and happy little baby as the chubby new marquess.

"I'll say nothing against this harebrained idea," Lord Van Doren said, "only because my opinions would fall on deaf ears and there is no point in wasting my breath. I am experienced enough with the Benningtons to know it is a lost cause. However, I do not see why we gentlemen have to be dragged into it."

Beatrice laid her hand on the viscount's arm, like she always did when she wished to calm the skittish horse that was Lord Van Doren. "It is a family affair, my darling."

"We all understand that we are here to help our dear brother Darden," Viola said. "He simply does not know how happy he can be when he finds the right lady. He's got too used to his bachelor lifestyle—it's becoming ingrained."

Juliet nodded. "Ingrained."

"And," Cordelia said, "we will need eyes and ears everywhere. We must ensure that dear Darden makes a good choice."

"That is so true," Juliet said. "We've all been lucky so far; we do not wish for Darden to ever regret his decision."

"I do feel a bit of a traitor though," Lord Hamill said to his wife. "Darden is my friend, and we are all members of the YBC. Except for Conbatten, who I am sure will be asked one of these days."

"I am breathless with anticipation," Conbatten said.

"And Van Doren," Van Doren said. "He is not a member either."

"You know you are welcome," Beatrice said. "Darden has asked you several times."

Van Doren shrugged, and everybody knew he would never join the YBC. Over the years, he had managed to make one friend—Lord Bertridge—and those two spent all their time talking over estate matters at White's. They were both very serious gentlemen who could not imagine joining a club dedicated to tomfoolery and shenanigans.

"You are in no way a traitor, my love," Juliet said to Lord Hamill. "Did you not bring Cordelia and Harveston together? This is no different, other than we do not yet know who the lady is who must make our dear Darden happy. I will write an ode about it and you'll feel ever so much better about the idea."

Whether Lord Hamill would be soothed by an ode on the subject remained a question very much up in the air, as far as Miss Mayton could tell.

She thought this group of people needed direction lest they go round in circles for the next hour. They could not dawdle in conversations going nowhere all the day long. She had other more weighty matters to think of. She had a wardrobe to plan!

"Now," she said, "Beatrice and Lord Van Doren and Rosalind and His Grace will dine with us this evening. Perhaps we start the scheme slowly and gently—just casual hints that it must be time to begin looking around at the various unmarried ladies of the *ton*. We do not wish to spook him."

Everyone nodded at this idea, and that was well. It was one of only two ideas she'd come up with.

"After dinner," she went on, "I will read to everyone from a new book I have secured."

"Delightful," Conbatten said.

"This book," Miss Mayton said, nodding, "may be very instructive to Lord Darden. It is called, *The Crafty Convolutions of Coldwood Castle* and it is about a duke who swears he will never marry. He is the guardian of his young nephew and quite naturally there is a gentle governess on the scene. Can this lady bring love into the duke's life, even though he's sworn he will never love anybody?"

"Excellent notion, Aunt, it sounds just the thing. Now, ought we to form our own club for this venture?" Cordelia asked. "Some name we can attach to our activities to make it official?"

"The society for finally chaining down Darden," Beatrice said, laughing.

"That is perfect," Miss Mayton said, not wishing to spend the next hour on thinking up names. "We will call it the SFFCDD for short."

"That's not exactly short," Lord Baderston said.

"But it is mysterious," Viola said. "If we are overheard, nobody shall know what we're talking about."

"I hardly know what we're talking about. Can we go now?" Lord Van Doren asked.

Goodness, Lord Van Doren could be more petulant than his

young daughter when she was crossed. At least dear Lily did not stick with her frowns for long, unlike the lord, who would frown all day if it were not for Beatrice.

Miss Mayton nodded, with what she hoped was a sympathetic expression, just as she did with Lily. "We meet again on Friday next. That will be after Almack's and we will have much to talk about. Who did Lord Darden dance with? What do we think of these ladies? Is there any lady in particular we wish to push along?"

All in the room nodded, though the lords' nods were rather reluctant and halfhearted.

"By the by," Miss Mayton asked, "does anybody know if Mr. Brummel ever attends Almack's? I do wish to thank him for that lovely dog. Artemis is turning out to be a treasure."

"He is turning out to be a carpet as far as I can see," Lord Van Doren said. "He never moves off the floor."

Beatrice laid a comforting hand on her husband's sleeve.

"Mr. Brummel often attends the patronesses," Lord Harveston said. "Though personally I never find much to say to the man—he's got all the substance of a hot air balloon."

Miss Mayton was rather staggered by that assessment. She comforted herself by remembering that Lord Harveston spent most of his time delving into arcane subjects no rational person was interested in.

"You will not have noticed Mr. Brummel at Almack's, Aunt," Juliet said, "as Father always takes you into the card room and Mr. Brummel seems to glory in coming in the doors at the last possible moment before they are barred against all comers."

"I think he does that so Lady Jersey does not pair him up with a slew of debutantes," Lord Baderston said.

Miss Mayton nodded. Finally, someone was talking some sense. Of course Mr. Brummel would not be interested in inexperienced young girls. He was far more allured by seasoned ladies who had retained their girlish looks.

CHAPTER THREE

THOUGH DARDEN WAS suspicious of why Beatrice and Rosalind, along with their husbands, were coming to dine, he could not very well say so. They were family, they were all in Town, why shouldn't they all come to dine? On its face there was nothing at all unusual about it.

It was just that now, when he was certain there was some plot against him, absolutely everything seemed suspicious.

Did he imagine it, or could Van Doren hardly meet his eye?

They'd gone into dinner, which was the usual adventure with Benny and Johnny manning the sideboard while Tattleton remained below stairs entertaining Lily. Or rather, being entertained by her.

"Dear Darden," Rosalind said, "I suppose you must be pleased that you are not rattling round this house on your own all this season? It is so tedious to be alone, I find."

"Naturally I am pleased to see Father," Darden said. "And Miss Mayton too, of course."

"Companionship is very pleasant," Beatrice added.

"Gracious yes," the earl said. "I always do find it so."

"Van Doren, you do find it so?" Beatrice asked her husband.

"Only your company, Lily's, the earl's, and Lord Bertridge's" Van Doren said. "If we are talking about large doses."

"I am certain Conbatten feels just the same," Rosalind said. "We are rarely apart."

Conbatten nodded gravely. "Not even in the bath."

Everyone at table looked in different directions upon hearing that statement. Darden was all but certain it amused the duke to say a thing that might shock. Especially since his wife did not seem to ever notice it was shocking.

"Not even in the bath," Rosalind said. "Though, when I was carrying our son, I did go off it and onto pickled vegetables for breakfast for a time."

"Fortunately," Conbatten said, "my duchess has since returned to my bath."

At that, nearly everyone at table leaned over their plates and gave what was left of their dessert a close examination.

Of course, not *absolutely* everybody. Miss Mayton appeared entirely unaffected upon hearing of the duke and duchess' personal habits.

"If only any of my gentlemen on the continent had managed to live," Miss Mayton said wistfully. "I am convinced we should have provided one another very genial company. But then, I must not be cast down about it. Those ships have sailed, as it were."

Darden nodded. Really, these people could not be more obvious. What a performance, talking of how tedious it was to be alone and the joys of companionship.

"In any case," Miss Mayton said, "it is never too late for love to come upon a person. I have often said so."

He stopped himself from laughing over Miss Mayton's speculations about love coming late, as he thought they were less about him and more about Mr. Brummel. Tattleton had informed him that she'd been mooning about the house all the late afternoon sighing and had topped it off with a visit from a modiste who came recommended by Lady Rawley.

Apparently, once Miss Mayton had decided to throw off her widow's weeds, she had also determined that she ought to have all new dresses. As her taste was not known for its restraint, he could only imagine what was to come of it. The last he'd seen of her before she donned the black bombazine, she'd worn an alarming purple taffeta dress and sprouted an enormous green feather in her hair. As she was a comfortably round person, she looked like nothing so much as an aubergine recently pulled from the ground and dusted off.

The only person at table who was likely not in on the plot against him, whatever the details of the plot were, was the earl.

It was not that the earl would fail to find favor in his son marrying, it was that nobody ever did like to trouble him on any matter.

"Now Darden," Rosalind said, "I suppose you will attend Almack's on Wednesday?"

He would really like to say no, and he'd like to mean it. Rosalind knew very well he could not, though.

The YBC had been staunch supporters of the patronesses and even engaged in charitable works in partnership with those ladies. Lady Jersey, in particular, would be entirely put out if he did not make an appearance at the first ball of the season.

Rosalind knew she had him trapped on the question. What exactly was their plan for Almack's?

He nodded, and Miss Mayton said, "We will all go, of course. Now I wonder, Earl, if we must play cards there? I feel, now that I have shed my widow's weeds, that I might like to dance."

The earl's eyebrows shot up, as did every other gentleman's at table. Darden pressed his lips together, all but certain that Miss Mayton was imagining Mr. Brummel would put himself on her card.

"Well now," the earl said, "of course, if you wish it, Miss Mayton. For myself, I suppose I can always get up a game of piquet with another fellow."

"That is settled, then," Miss Mayton said. "Now, as for this evening, I suppose the gentlemen will wish to take their port to the drawing room? We are set to begin a new story and I can tell you—it is riveting."

"Riveting!" the earl said. "That is what I always like so much about these stories. One imagines they are going this way, and then they go that way."

"They certainly go somewhere," Conbatten said in his usual dry tone. It was the tone Darden understood perfectly well, but which flew right over Miss Mayton's head.

She nodded graciously at the duke, in acknowledgement of his imagined esteem for her literary choices.

"I find, these stories always do point out some aspect of human nature," Rosalind said.

Did they? If they did, Darden had missed that completely. As far as he knew it, every single one of those stories was about a strange duke and an even stranger governess.

Nevertheless, if Miss Mayton had decided to read, there was really no stopping her. They dutifully took their port into the drawing room. It came as no surprise to find Artemis there, splayed across the carpet. He yawned at their arrival.

Did that dog ever even get up to eat? He'd really never seen such an inert creature who was still alive. He'd since learned that Brummel had got the creature from Lord Bradley, who'd claimed he was a skilled hunter and then dropped him off at Brummel's door and done a runner.

Darden expected Lord Bradley was laughing into his brandy to be rid of the dog.

They settled themselves in the drawing room, with Rosalind practically on Conbatten's lap and Beatrice sitting close to Van Doren so she might pat his hand consolingly when he seemed to be heading into temperamental territory.

"This story is called *The Crafty Convolutions of Coldwood Castle*," Miss Mayton said. "What we know from the description is that a duke has vowed he will never love, and therefore never wed. He is the guardian of his nephew, and that young boy will eventually become the next duke, as this duke will have no issue. Can the gentle governess bring love into the duke's heart?"

"I bet she does," Rosalind said. "A gentleman who thinks he cannot love will always find he is mistaken."

"It is in the admitting of the mistake that real joy can be

found," Beatrice said, nodding. "Giving over to the emotion is the true path to happiness."

Darden kept his expression neutral. He did not wish his sisters to know that he was onto their game, despite how painfully obvious they were. The true path to happiness indeed.

"Chapter one," Miss Mayton said.

The duke had advertised far and wide that he would never marry. As he was a man, he'd invented a very manly excuse for his vow. As far as the rest of the world knew it, he was a cold and unfeeling brute who could not feel any affectionate emotion.

The truth was far more terrible. He wished very much to love and be loved, but it was not to be. He harbored a dreadful secret that made marriage impossible.

What was he to do now, though? The gentle governess was everything lovely and gentle. She'd been making calf eyes at him for months! He was hard-pressed not to take her in his arms, and yet he could not.

"Duke," the gentle governess said, poking her charming head into his library, "should you wish to bid young Mortimer a good night?"

The duke waved her in, along with his dolt of a nephew who would become the next duke.

Mortimer bowed and said, "Goodnight, Uncle. I suppose I'll sleep like a log!"

Yes, of course he would sleep like a log. His nephew did everything with the cleverness of a log.

"I might even sleep late, I am that tired!" Mortimer said.

If only the duke were so lucky as to greet the night with such enthusiasm. As it was, night was his enemy. Night was the root of all his problems. Night was the difficulty. Night had robbed him of any chance at happiness.

Miss Mayton laid the book in her lap. "Now we are left to wonder, what is the duke's problem exactly and what can the governess do about it?"

"I suppose he's made a pact with the devil, or some such

nonsense," Van Doren said.

"Whatever his problems," Beatrice said, "I have every confidence in the gentle governess. Every gentleman deserves to be loved."

Darden nearly snorted at that. So this was to be his season—endless hints that he ought to begin taking a serious look at marriage and companionship. He supposed Miss Mayton had selected this book specially to make the point. If a duke who was afraid of the dark could find love, then certainly any nearby viscount could do it.

Their strategies would be irritating, but not insurmountable.

As long as that was all they were up to.

He would just need to keep his eyes wide open for any traps that might be set for him.

THOUGH MARIANNA WAS not at all enthusiastic over what the next weeks and months must bring, she was not quite as entirely immune to her new wardrobe of dresses as she'd led her maid to believe.

After all, where there was beauty, it could not fail to affect one's spirit.

Her mother, the duchess, had insisted on employing a certain Madame Renaud to compose her wardrobe. Let others bring in Mrs. Bell or Mrs. Bean, it was Madame Renaud who was deemed superior.

If Madame Renaud had a description she would apply to her creations, it must be "unstudied elegance." The madame had come, sized up Marianna with a practiced eye, and then given her verdict.

Her coloring was very fair, her hair the color of summer honey and her eyes a deep shade of blue. So many misguided modistes would lean toward pastels for the fair-haired. This was a mistake, apparently. Lighter colors would only wash her out and make her look insipid.

As for bows and fripperies, those accoutrements were even more insipid. No client of Madame Renaud's would appear in society as an overdressed confection of a fairy cake.

Marianna did not know if Madame Renaud was right, but she dreaded appearing insipid just as much as the modiste seemed to.

Glancing down at her gown as the carriage bounced along the cobblestones, she did not imagine there was anything at all insipid about it.

It was a deep violet silk with nothing to recommend it but its cut, which was quite recommendation enough. Melly said it made her eyes look even darker blue than they actually were.

It was lovely and it did give her some sort of courage. She supposed the knights of old may have depended upon their armor, but a lady had her silks.

"Well, my dear," the duke said from across the carriage, "both Mayfield and Wellerston will make an appearance tonight. It is to be your first look at them and you can begin to decide who you prefer."

"I suppose, my love," the duchess said to the duke, "both of these fellows are strapping young men ready to set a girl's heart aflutter?"

"What's strapping got to do with it?" the duke asked.

The duchess glanced over her duke's person, which was still a rather strapping specimen in his middle age, and said, "It had everything to do with it when I was Marianna's age."

"My dear," the duke said, "Marianna is my only daughter. You cannot condemn me for being determined to see her a duchess one day?"

"We'll see," the duchess said quietly.

Marianna said nothing to this discussion, though it so clearly highlighted the problem. Her father was not some beast of a duke, ready to force his daughter into an unwanted marriage. No, he was a loving sort and had his heart set on seeing her well-placed in society.

He'd been talking about it for as long as she could remember. Even when she'd been five or six, as he'd led her round the courtyard on her pony, he'd talked to her about becoming a duchess someday. She had delighted in the idea back then. It had seemed a pleasant fairytale. Of course, back then, she had not given a moment's thought as to who the gentleman involved might be. Really, the fairytale had been more about lovely places to live and lovely things to eat and there had been no gentleman there at all.

There seemed to be only two wishes the duke had ever held in his heart—that his son would produce an heir, and that she would become a duchess.

Her older brother Matthew had since married and he *had* produced an heir. Or rather, his marchioness had, though so much of the credit had seemed to go to Matthew.

That wish fulfilled, her father's attention was all on Marianna now.

How could she disappoint him in his lifelong wish? The discussions of it had gone on all her life. They'd gone on for so long, beginning when she was so young, that it was as if she'd agreed to it without ever actually agreeing to it.

She'd never outright and out loud disagreed with it, which seemed to amount to the same thing. By the time she had been old enough to question the idea, it had seemed too late.

"Here we are," the duke said as the carriage rolled to a stop on King Street. "The dragonesses await us."

"Kembleton," the duchess said, "do not frighten Marianna."

The duke laughed. "Never fear the patronesses, Marianna. After all, who are they? You are the daughter of a duke and will one day be a duchess. Your only pause should be over the king and queen. And the prince I suppose, if he ever becomes dignified. Everybody else can take a ticket and be noticed at your leisure."

Marianna was not one jot afraid of the patronesses, or the king and queen, or the prince. Her father's plans, though, were another matter.

DARDEN HAD GONE into Almack's and glanced round the ballroom. They were all there, his family, scattered round the room and all looking surreptitiously at the doors. No doubt awaiting his entrance.

He supposed he would be stared at all night. Every selection of dancing partner would be analyzed and discussed.

"Darden," the Marquess of Wellerston said.

Darden nodded in acknowledgement. He did not know the marquess well, having only just met him two days before at a rout. It was the fellow's first season and Darden was considering issuing him an invitation to join the YBC. He was friendly enough and he seemed up for fun. Some of the younger members had gone to school with him and had vouched for his propensity for shenanigans and tomfoolery.

"Well, I suppose that must be her," Wellerston said.

"Who?" Darden asked, not having the first idea of what the man was talking about.

"Lady Marianna Tisdale, daughter of the Duke of Kembleton," Wellerston said.

He paused, seeming to note Darden's confusion.

"Oh, you must not have heard. I did think everybody had heard it by now. Her father is determined she marry a fellow who either is or will become a duke. There's only the two of us now that Conbatten and Hamill have wed—myself and Mayfield. My father is all for it, though nobody has asked what I think about it."

Darden followed Wellerston's gaze. The Lady Marianna in question stood by what he took to be her parents.

She was achingly lovely. Tall and slim, her dress a deep violet setting off her hair like spun gold. That spun gold framed a face graced by high cheekbones and perfectly proportioned lips. She was all elegance.

"You might do a lot worse," he said.

Wellerston nodded. "She's a looker, I suppose. In the accepted way of things. Though, I prefer a petite brunette myself. Particularly Lady Jemima—I've known her forever, as she's from my county. I'd like to pick that lady up and carry her off."

"But you will pay your attentions to Lady Marianna?" Darden asked.

"I'll pretend to, for now at least," Wellerston said. "With any luck, Lady Marianna will be bowled over by Mayfield and I'll be off the proverbial hook."

"What does Lady Marianna think about all this?" Darden asked. "Certainly, she cannot be willing to be so managed."

"Apparently, she is," Wellerston said. "My father tells me she is determined to have me or Mayfield. She's determined to become a duchess and nothing else will do."

Darden watched the lovely Lady Marianna make her curtsy to Lady Jersey.

It was gracefully done. It was also beginning to give Darden an idea.

If one wished to ensure that one would not wed, one ought to chase after a lady who would under no circumstances wed that person. Lady Marianna was set on becoming a duchess. All he could offer was countess, and even that was far into the future. Becoming the wife of a mere viscount would not be up to her standards. He would be dismissed as a suitor instantly.

However, if his family believed that he was set on Lady Marianna, a lady who would not have him, they would leave him alone to nurse his disappointed hopes and turn their attention to next season.

"I'll do you a favor if I can manage it, Wellerston. I will secure Lady Marianna's supper, thereby relieving you of the duty."

"Good man!" Wellerston said.

Oh yes, he was a good man. Fortunately, he was not a *good enough* man for Lady Marianna Tisdale, daughter of the Duke of Kembleton and future Duchess of Somebody.

Hang on to your reins, dear sisters—your fox has slipped away and gone to ground.

CHAPTER FOUR

MARIANNA'S FATHER HAD discreetly nodded toward two gentlemen speaking with one another. "That's Weller-ston," he said.

"Which one?" she asked softly. She knew which one she hoped her father would say—he was a gorgeous man with dark hair and chiseled features. The cut of his clothes was exquisite but did not appear too studied. He was not a dandy, yet he was not a country bumpkin. He was something else, he was a London man. But more than that, he had a mien of confidence. There seemed a worldly air about him, was the only way she could think to describe it.

The other one was pleasant enough, she thought. Though he did seem…rather young. He was a bit gangly, as only a young man who was still growing into himself could be. She had seen enough of that process in her own neighborhood—there would be a series of years in which it seemed arms and legs had grown too long or the mind controlling the arms and legs had forgotten how to manage them properly. It was an unnamed awkwardness, and though it was unnamed everybody understood what it was—not still a boy, not quite a man.

Her father did not answer her, as his attention had been taken by some gentleman or other who wished to renew the acquaint-ance.

"I hope it's the one in the dark blue coat," the duchess said.

"As do I, Mama."

The man in the dark blue coat nodded to the other one and then approached Lady Jersey. That lady heard him out and then glanced in Marianna's direction.

Certainly, it must be Wellerston.

Though, he did look rather seasoned. It had been her understanding that Wellerston was just twenty.

Whether it was Wellerston or not, the gentleman was coming toward her and looked rather bold about it.

"Lady Marianna," he said, "Lady Jersey has given me leave to introduce myself and request to be on your card. Charles Bennington, Viscount Darden."

He executed a very well-done bow. Marianna sighed. She did not know anything about this Lord Darden, but that he was not Wellerston. He was a viscount, not a marquess.

She would force herself to look on the sunny side, though. He would be most pleasant to dance with.

In truth, it had not taken much forcing to look forward to dancing with this specimen of a gentleman.

She curtsied. "Lord Darden. May I present my mother, the Duchess of Kembleton."

"Your Grace," Lord Darden said.

He took Marianna's card and she was very surprised to note that he meant to escort her into the dining room to sample the patronesses' offerings.

She supposed she ought to be flattered. The truth of it was that she *was* flattered.

"Bennington?" the duchess said. "The name does strike me as familiar, Lord Darden. The duke and I have not come in for a season in years, and yet I feel like I know the name from somewhere."

If Marianna were not mistaken, there became a very slight pink to Lord Darden's cheeks.

He said, "I have five sisters who've come out over the years. I suspect that must be it."

He bowed and moved off. The duchess sighed. "He is not Wellerston," she said.

"No," Marianna said sadly.

"A shame. Bennington," the duchess said thoughtfully. "Goodness, I believe one of his sisters arranged her own kidnapping. At least, the Countess of Maybury wrote to me of it some years ago."

Marianna was taken aback by that idea. Who would wish to be kidnapped?

"She went on to marry a duke, so I suppose that was all swept under a carpet quick enough. It was Conbatten. Yes, she married Conbatten. Goodness, it's all coming back to me now—your father was unhappy about it. His first choice for you was Conbatten."

"And now we are left with the thin and gangly Wellerston," Marianna said. She surprised herself with the bitterness that had crept into her tone.

She'd never complained over her father's plans, as she did not like to be the cause of unhappiness.

But now that she was actually here, now that his plan was unfolding…

She felt rather cross about it, though she did not wish to feel cross.

Her mother patted her arm. "You are not a prisoner in a tower, my dear," she said softly. "We will see how this season plays out for you, but just remember that particular idea."

The duchess had hinted round that notion before. That she could defy her father if she wished to, and she would have her mother's support if she did.

Still, it was a rather frightening idea. It was not her father's anger she feared, but rather his deep disappointment. She had never disappointed her father and could not quite envision how it would be.

Before she could answer her mother's hint, Lady Jersey had swept up to them. "Duchess, Lady Marianna, may I present the

Marquess of Wellerston. I have given him leave to enter his name upon your card, Lady Marianna, as I understand the duke very much approves."

Marianna flushed to hear of her father's plan spoken of so openly. She had imagined it a very great secret kept in the family, but it seemed Lady Jersey knew all about it.

Absolutely everybody in England knew that Lady Jersey was a great talker. She had been nicknamed "Silence" as a jest regarding her habit of rambling. If that lady knew of her father's plans, then Marianna must suppose everybody in society knew of it.

It was so embarrassing!

Lord Wellerston did not look any less embarrassed than she felt as he fumbled with her card in an inept manner.

"Ah," Lady Jersey said, "and there is Lord Mayfield. I won't be a moment."

Lady Jersey strode off to collect Lord Mayfield. Marianna presumed he was to be dropped at her feet like a caught mouse who had been delivered by a well-meaning cat.

Lord Wellerston bowed and hurried away. Marianna pressed her lips together. Wellerston was tall and gangly, and now Mayfield was short and gangly. Neither had yet reached the fullness of their manhood.

The bitterness that had been creeping into her began to bloom. How could her father think to foist her on these two specimens?

She knew how, of course. He dreamed of his daughter becoming a duchess and it had blinded him to any other ideas. That was how.

Marianna reminded herself that they would not always be in such an awkward state. Both would grow to men. At some point.

Other gentlemen arrived with the blessing of Lady Jersey. They were all pleasant enough, but they were not destined to be dukes. And they were not as compelling as Lord Darden.

Why could life not be far more simple than it was?

DARDEN HAD NOT been idle while he waited his turn with Lady Marianna. He'd danced with a suitable number of ladies, all under the watchful eye of his family. But that was not all. He'd made it a point to mention to both Beatrice and Viola how taken he was with Lady Marianna.

Viola, in particular, had seemed to grasp the problem. She'd said, "Oh, but Darden, I have heard that she has two suitors— both to be dukes. I have heard that is her requirement."

Darden had laughed off the notion, though he knew it to be true. He'd said, "Nonsense!" as if he put little stock in the idea.

He'd then carefully watched as Viola made the rounds to her sisters, whispering in their ears and no doubt apprising them of this problem. Dear Darden was taken with a lady who would never have him.

Amidst that hilarity, Miss Mayton swam round the entrance of the ballroom like a shark on the lookout for drowning sailors. It had amused him to think that if Mr. Brummel fell into her clutches, that fellow would *wish* he was only a drowning sailor.

What on earth would Brummel make of the lady's dress? It was new, Darden was certain. If he'd ever seen such a concoction before, he would remember it.

Miss Mayton had garbed herself in a pale pink taffeta with an enormous matching bow buried in her hair. It was a style a twelve-year-old girl might find the height of sophistication, and it was entirely ludicrous for a matron of her age. She looked like a giant walking cake.

Brummel, the gentleman who preached restraint in dress as the most important quality in a person, would be hard-pressed to remain on his feet in coming upon the frothy concoction that was just now Miss Mayton.

Now though, it was time to escort Lady Marianna to the floor. He must appear to all his family that he was entirely taken with her.

She *was* rather marvelous to look at, so it was not such a leap to imagine that he would be taken with her. Really, had he been actually interested in marrying, well, she would have caught his eye instantly. He probably *would* have been taken with her.

"Lady Marianna," he said, extending his arm.

"Lord Darden," she said, lightly laying her hand upon it.

She was exceedingly composed for a lady just out. At least, in his estimation she was. He'd been banging around for seven seasons now and was well-used to the first-time out jitters one normally encountered.

She did not seem to view silences as things that must be filled with random observances.

Perhaps he was not to hear how well the room looked or how elegant the couples appeared or any of the other nonentities he was so used to hearing. He'd always thought there was a cadre of governesses out there somewhere who'd agreed on a list of comments any suitable young lady might utter, and so the young ladies uttered them.

"I would imagine you've heard certain rumors about me, Lord Darden," she said.

The comment was so direct he would not have ever seen it coming. He'd been wondering how he would sidle up to the idea that he well knew she would have no interest in him, but would she mind him hanging about through the season.

He had not even decided if he would tell her the cause of the ruse. But now…she was so direct.

"I will not claim that I have not," he said as the music struck up. "Though what I have heard was in no way damaging."

Lady Marianna laughed. "Goodness. No, I have not been condemned for improper behavior. Only singled out as the lady who would be a duchess."

As they waited their turn, he said, "It is that important to you? To find yourself a duchess?"

"It is important to my father, and therefore of significance to me."

That was rather a hedge of an answer. If Darden could read its meaning, he thought the lady herself was not so determined to become a duchess, but rather her interest was in pleasing her father.

"So you will carry on with it," Darden said.

"It is my father's wish."

Their turn came round, and Darden led her through the changes. Her dancing was exquisite. Whatever else the duke had been up to, he had not stinted on his daughter's dancing lessons.

"Well, we all know how fathers can be when it comes to their offspring's future," Darden said.

"Do we? I take that to mean your own father has some ideas?"

"Oh, well, of course he has his hopes," Darden said. "Though, he is a dear old soldier and does not apply any pressure."

Marianna laughed. "Apparently not."

Apparently not? What did she mean?

Seeming to note the confusion of his expression, she said, "Naturally, I do not know how old you are, but I must speculate that this is hardly your first season. Or your fourth."

Blast it, she was bold.

"I can guess from your expression that I've guessed rather low," Lady Marianna said, appearing very amused. "Fifth? Sixth, even?"

"Seventh," Darden said. He could not say why, but saying it aloud was somehow embarrassing, as if he should have been accomplishing something with his time.

He paused. He had accomplished something.

"Well, you see, I've been very taken up with founding a club," Darden said. "The Young Bucks Club."

Lady Marianna's brow arched just the littlest bit. "I see. Very good sense to be doing that now, else you might have been stuck founding the Old Bucks Club, which does not sound half so fun."

Old Bucks Club. Of course, he remembered Van Doren saying something similar when he'd founded the club all those years ago. He was still a young buck though.

Yes, certainly he was.

They spoke no more through the dance, and Darden was left with the uncomfortable feeling of not having been in control of the conversation. Or her view of him.

At the conclusion, Darden led her to the supper room. "As this is your first venture into Almack's, I hope someone has prepared you to be underwhelmed by what you will find on your plate."

"I have been warned," Lady Marianna said. "One of the ladies of my neighborhood described it as an absolute torture. I thought that ridiculous, by the by. After all, sour lemonade never killed anybody and dry cake can be managed."

She was a rather stalwart sort of lady, which Darden had not been anticipating.

He led her to a table and signaled a footman. He thought he better get to it, as Lady Marianna was only imagining dry cake. That dry cake was the highlight of the offerings and if it ran out they would be faced with day-old slices of bread.

There were some perks to having been around so long. The footmen were all very fond of him, as he sent them a Christmas present of a few pounds every year. Bertram, an old hand of the club, ran to get him what he wanted.

Darden noted Lady Marianna watching with interest as various desperate gentlemen vied for a footman's attentions, determined to secure dry cake. All but Conbatten seemed desperate, that was. He sailed in with Rosalind on his arm and simply gave the footmen a look and his bidding was done.

Having secured the dry cake, and Darden did feel a little victorious over it, he said, "Lady Marianna, you can only be unaware of our narrow escape. Had we not got hold of cake, we would have been staring at stale bread with just the lightest sheen of butter on it."

Darden did not know why he'd felt compelled to say so. He

almost had the idea that he needed to prove his worth in some way. As if to show that he could accomplish something after seven seasons in Town.

Lady Marianna laughed at the idea. "That sounds very like a trip with my father to the Highlands. We have a place there, very small and remote with very good fishing, and it can only accommodate a single footman and a maid. This leaves my father to manage the arrangements and he never orders enough food to be brought with us. We could buy it from the local village of course, but he inevitably gets into an argument over prices and comes back with nothing. He says those Scots are always trying to stick it to a duke and he won't have it. Though, since we inevitably end the trip surviving only on the fish we can catch, I rather think they do stick it to him."

Darden laughed. Really, she was very interesting to view such a trip with amusement. Another lady might be fanning herself and talking about how dreadful it all was and how it was a miracle they survived.

She was rather more sturdy. A bit like his sisters in that regard.

Darden stopped himself. What was he thinking?

He must stay on course, not be charmed by her!

In any case, what was so charming about his sisters now that they'd decided to meddle in his affairs? Nothing. That was what.

Darden reeled in his thinking to get back to the task at hand.

"Lady Marianna," he said, "I have an odd sort of question. A request, actually."

"Do you?" the lady said.

"Since you are set on becoming a duchess, and since I am in no way armed with such a distinction, I wonder if I might just hang about this season."

"Hang about, Lord Darden?"

"You know, dance with you, see you at routs, escort you round when appropriate, that sort of thing."

"Because you will not be a duke?"

"Precisely," Darden said.

"*Precisely* would indicate that I understand your meaning," Lady Marianna said. "Which I do not."

Darden paused. He had not been certain whether or not he would tell Lady Marianna the real cause of these machinations. However, it appeared as if he must.

"You see, I have five sisters," he said. "They are all married now, though it has been a rather exhausting road."

Lady Marianna nodded. "I understand one of your sisters arranged her own kidnapping?"

Darden was surprised she knew of it. He said, "Yes, that was Rosalind, but nobody talks about it now as she married Conbatten. The queen does not like it spoken of."

"Helpful to know," Lady Marianna said.

"And then there was Beatrice and the whole scheme with Van Doren. And of course Viola and all those duels, and Cordy setting a staircase afire, and Juliet almost marrying a schemer who wrote poetry in the Japanese style. But thankfully, she ended settling on Hamill."

Darden noted the look of surprise on Lady Marianna's features. He should have expected it—when he listed it all out like that, it *did* seem pretty surprising. Still, he must plow on and said, "What with all those situations, the attention has been firmly focused on my sisters. Now it seems the attention has turned to me."

Lady Marianna said nothing and waited for him to go on.

"All five of my sisters are scheming against me," Darden said. "They've dragged their husbands into it too, as far as I can tell. It is a regular cabal to get me into a church."

Lady Marianna nodded thoughtfully. "And you do not wish to find yourself in the vicinity of a church."

"Yes, that's it exactly," Darden said.

"If I understand you, then," Lady Marianna said, "you wish your sisters to believe that you are set on me, knowing I could never be set on you because of my circumstances."

"If it would not be too much trouble," Darden said, examining her closely.

Before Lady Marianna could answer what he realized was a rather strange request, a swish of pink taffeta nearly overset his glass of lemonade as Miss Mayton barreled past him.

"Mr. Brummel!" she cried, practically jogging to the other end of the room. "I had not the first idea we should encounter one another so soon after our propitious meeting at the inn."

Naturally, Miss Mayton had said this loud enough for everyone to hear it. And naturally, many a person in the room wondered what Miss Mayton had been doing with Brummel at an inn.

Darden's face must have paled, as Lady Marianna said, "Do you know that lady?"

"I do," he said. What he really wished to say was "Help me, most gracious Lord, I am afraid I do."

"Mr. Brummel looks rather frightened," Lady Marianna observed.

"As well he might," Darden muttered. Brummel was a drowning sailor and the pink taffeta shark was cruising right for him.

What transpired next, Darden thought he ought to be grateful he could not hear the entirety of. He heard enough though.

Miss Mayton waxed on about what a treasure Artemis was.

That dog was a treasure all right, if one wished for a dog who rarely moved. Van Doren had named him a carpet and he was not wrong. On occasion, Darden would find Artemis in another location, though nobody ever seemed to know how he got there. As far as he could understand it, the dog followed whatever sunlight was coming through the windows.

Miss Mayton went on to explain her throwing off of the widow's weeds and while Darden could not hear the precise details, he could see Brummel's expression well enough.

If he were to ever feel any sort of sympathy for Mr. Brummel, it must be at this moment. The fellow looked as if he'd been struck by lightning. Darden even noted him tugging at his over-complicated and over-starched knot as if he could not get enough air.

Not wishing to view the scene longer, he turned back to Lady Marianna. He said, "Brummel will be all right. Now, I wonder, could I hang about this season? Would you mind it?"

Lady Marianna looked suddenly serious. "Lord Darden, I think you well know that a lady has little control over who chooses to *hang about*. At least, in public places. I would not attempt to gain entrance to my father's drawing room if I were you, though. He would not like it."

It was not an unqualified yes. Nor was it a definite no.

He'd take it. After all, his sisters would not know if he'd been to Lady Marianna's house or not. He could always say he was going, and then go to his club.

All he need do to ward off his sisters' scheming was to follow Lady Marianna about like a lovesick idiot. They'd feel sorry for him. They might even attempt to turn him from her. But he would be steadfast in his admiration, and they'd give it up.

As for what to do next season if he were faced with the same problem, he'd figure that out when the time came.

He was not the founder of the YBC for nothing—let the shenanigans and tomfoolery commence.

CHAPTER FIVE

MARIANNA HAD ANTICIPATED a disappointing evening, and she'd not been wrong.

Oh, there had been moments when she'd forgotten herself and found herself unaccountably happy, but that had not lasted.

The lords Wellerston and Mayfield were entirely underwhelming.

Lord Darden, on the other hand, had been almost overwhelming.

At least, until he'd broached his scheme.

As it turned out, he'd not put his name down on her card because he found her pretty. He'd not taken her into supper because he was intrigued and wished to know her.

No, he'd picked her out as the only lady who could act as a shield against his sisters' scheming to see him wed.

She really ought not to like him at all. And yet she could not help herself, she did.

He really was so handsome and amusing. He was a man, a real man. Though, he had retained some boyishness about him that he somehow managed to make charming.

That club of his, for one. The Young Bucks Club.

As much as she would like to condemn it as foolish, she could not quite do it. He'd founded it himself, and there was something attractive about a gentleman so well-liked that a slew of other gentlemen would join his new club.

Yes, he was attractive and interesting and she liked him.

However, she was also stung by him. He had quite the nerve imagining that she would not mind being used in such a manner.

But then, she had not said no, had she?

"Well?" Melly said, brushing out her hair.

"Well what?" Marianna asked, though she knew perfectly well what Melly wished to know.

"The two gentlemen who's to be dukes," Melly said. "Was either of them up to snuff?"

"Not really," Marianna said. As she said it, she realized that once she'd been done dancing with both of those gentlemen, she'd not given them another thought. They'd been like biscuits on a tea tray. Not offensive or inoffensive. Just there and then gone, of so little import they were never thought of again.

"Berta says that the duchess is fretting mightily over your future happiness," Melly said. "You know, we do talk sometimes below stairs."

Berta was her mother's maid and Marianna certainly did know there was talk below stairs. Though, to categorize it as *sometimes* was putting the case mildly. She was convinced that, with all the listening at doors and the confiding to valets and lady's maids that went on, the servants knew the family better than the family knew themselves.

There were even times when the servants acted as go-betweens. Berta might tell Melly that the duchess was concerned that Marianna was not happy with the new music master. Marianna would confirm it to Melly, explaining that she'd been made uncomfortable by some of the man's comments, as if he were flirting with her. This would send Melly back to Berta, who informed the duchess. That particular music master was promptly dismissed.

Marianna could not even have said why she hadn't gone to her mother directly, but for the idea that her father had hired Mr. Jimson and so she ought to respect him. Even though she'd known from the first day that Mr. Jimson was a rogue.

Marianna could not imagine the talk that had gone on round the servants' table regarding *that* situation.

"My mother is very kind," Marianna said, not wishing to elaborate her thoughts just now.

Even if she wished to elaborate her thoughts on her mother's current concern, she was not certain of what her thoughts actually were.

"Was there any gentleman what did catch your eye?" Melly asked. "Like a fella who won't be a duke, but's a lord all the same?"

Marianna had no intention of answering that. There had been someone who'd caught her eye. But she had not caught his. Even if she were prepared to defy her father, there was nothing to defy him over.

She certainly did not wish for the servants to be mulling that idea over at table. Nor her mother, for that matter.

Chin up, Marianna. Your pride experienced a bee sting this evening, having been fooled into thinking a certain gentleman was intrigued and then being informed that he was not.

No matter. It was only a momentary prick and you did not give yourself away and embarrass yourself. Nor will you ever.

MISS MAYTON HAD risen early. It was not her usual habit to leap out of bed at the first opportunity. Especially not now that the girls were all out of the house and there was no planning and scheming to be done in the breakfast room.

She missed the girls terribly; they had been her constant companions these many years. After Juliet left the house and she'd found herself without that feminine companionship she'd so valued, it had been as if a fog had settled upon her.

But everything was different now. Everything was sunnier and more alive now.

She had since breakfasted and was in the drawing room with sewing on her lap so she might look as if she were doing something. She'd had the same piece of sewing for years and nobody had ever seemed to notice that while she held it in her lap quite often, she never actually did anything with it.

Nobody knew but for her maid, in any case. Both she and Fleur were wretched at sewing and Mrs. Huffson generally took care of anything that needed mending.

The bit of sewing she held was her theater prop so she might be left in peace to daydream about whatever was filling her head at any given moment. At this particular moment, her thoughts were overflowing with a certain gentleman.

Mr. Brummel had been everything gracious last evening.

She'd almost given up on seeing him. She'd strategically placed herself near the doors to the ballroom so that he might have the first opportunity to put himself down on her card.

She had trembled with anticipation regarding what he would think when he saw her out of her widow's weeds and into a new dress.

He'd be rather bowled over, she imagined.

The dress was perfection itself. It was an alluring confection, done in a lively pink taffeta to bring out the rosiness of her cheeks. It was new, and she had designed it herself over the modiste's objections.

Lady Rawley's own modiste, in fact.

Upon realizing she would come to Town, Miss Mayton had fired off a letter to Lady Rawley to express her availability to the acting troupe.

That had resulted in a letter communicating Lady Rawley's delight to hear it and already the troupe had all met together at the lady's house. This year's offering was to be *All's Well that Ends Well*.

As far as Lady Rawley was concerned, Shakespeare had not written a more preposterous play. Or as she had so aptly put it, "I can assure you that while my lord still lived, he would have *noticed* if a strange lady was in his bed. As well, once again we find the bard's treatment of women appalling—why does Helen put up with it? What exactly does she love about this Bertram?"

All the troupe were exceedingly gratified to hear of how Lady Rawley would set it all straight in their own rendition of the play.

Miss Mayton did consider Lady Rawley as having become a very good friend. She had of course been gratified that the lady had sent her own modiste when the need for a new wardrobe arose. But the seamstress was discovered to be so unimaginative! Her ideas had been deadly dull—all somber colors and conservative cuts.

Miss Mayton had taken the graphite stick and sheets of paper from the modiste and sketched out her own ideas. Then she'd clearly marked each drawing with the type of material to be used, taffeta was mostly preferred as it draped elegantly over whatever roundness had come upon her in recent years. She'd also specified the color of each dress and favored lively pinks, bright purples, cheerful greens, and sunny yellows.

No expense was to be spared in ribbons, bows, and buttons!

The modiste had been all aflutter until she'd drunk down a large glass of fortified wine to settle her nerves.

Miss Mayton had taken special care designing the gown she would wear to Carlton House, as it was bound to be a special evening. Perhaps the most important evening of her life.

That particular gown was to be done in a certain amount of yards of velvet she'd purchased years ago and had been saving for a very special occasion. She had instantly fallen in love with the material, and not less so when the proprietor of the shop had told her the shade was named parakeet green.

It was a rather heavy velvet, but she would count on the weather to abstain from too much heat, as she was certain it would graciously do.

There would be nothing somber or simple to be worn as she stepped into this new chapter of her life. It would be all vivacity and verve.

As the previous night had worn on with no sight of Mr. Brummel, Miss Mayton's spirits had begun to droop. Had she worn the alluring pink taffeta to no purpose?

She really should have had more faith in what the fates had in store for her. Very like a phoenix, her spirits had risen gloriously from the ashes. She'd not seen Mr. Brummel come in before the doors closed, but there he was in the supper room.

She supposed she had missed his entrance during one of her many visits to the ladies' retiring room. She'd been so bold as to add the tiniest bit of rouge to her cheeks and had felt a need to check in a looking glass that it had stayed where Fleur had put it.

Eloise Mayton well knew the signs of true love. One felt as if one's hair had been struck by lightning, and one was drowning but taking in more air, and one's heart sped up though one felt well.

Her hair *did* feel rather hot, and she *did* gasp a bit for air, and her heart *had* certainly sped up. As for feeling well, she had never been better in her life!

She'd made her way over to him in all haste.

Naturally, she'd begun her interaction with the gentleman by referencing the thing they had immediately in common—dear Artemis. The dog was an absolute treasure, so mild-mannered!

Mr. Brummel had appeared most gratified to hear it.

Then, she'd moved on to other subjects, such as her new dresses. She'd commented on the superiority of taffeta, she'd swished the skirt around to illustrate the point. She'd given Mr. Brummel every opportunity to express his admiration, but the dear gentleman had been too overcome to utter a word.

Entirely speechless. It had been more than she had hoped for.

Tattleton interrupted her pleasant reveries. "Miss Mayton," he said, carrying in a silver salver with a letter upon it, "this has just come."

Gracious. Could Mr. Brummel not even wait to see her? He must write the very next day? It was a bit forward, but then she would not hold it against him. He had found himself rather tongue-tied last evening. No doubt he wished to express his feelings when he had better composed himself. One who was very struck often found it easier to express ideas on paper rather than speech.

"Thank you, Tattleton," she said graciously.

As she reached for the letter, the butler cleared his throat and said, "May I inquire why Clara is writing to you from Somerset?"

"Clara?"

"Clara. The housemaid," Tattleton said. "If there is a problem with the lord's house, I would expect she write to either myself or Mrs. Huffson."

At this alarming communication, the dream Miss Mayton had been happily living in since her most recent encounter with Mr. Brummel popped like a bubble in a glass of champagne.

Thinking quickly, as she well knew Tattleton was a suspicious and nosy sort of person, she said, "Clara and I have other matters to discuss aside from the house, Mr. Tattleton. Matters of the heart, which everybody knows I am rather an expert in."

Tattleton nodded, though he did not look convinced, and handed over the letter. Before he left the room, he gave a withering glance to Artemis who was happily asleep on a sunny patch of carpet.

Now Miss Mayton was alone with the letter. A letter from Clara could only mean one thing.

She had a great urge to put it aside. After all, if she did not know a thing, she could not worry over a thing.

But no, that would not do. Turning a blind eye and covering one's ears so often *did* do perfectly well, but in this particular matter it would not do.

She must face it, though she so little liked to face anything unpleasant. She tore the letter open.

Dear Miss Mayton—

I am very glad you warned us of suspicious housebreakers coming to the door. As you did ask to be informed of such a terror so you might tell our Lord Westmont instead of informing Mr. Tattleton directly, I am writing to say it has happened! We are all mighty shaken over it and I had to drink some of the lord's sherry to steady my nerves. You're right to spare Mr. Tattleton the news, his nerves are so delicate these days that he might fall into an apoplexy to hear of it.

Just this morning, a stranger on horseback rode up, a nicely dressed gentleman, but we were not fooled! He insisted on knowing where you were. He even knew your name, criminals are that clever these days.

Not clever enough for us though. He was dressed in a somber black suit, like he was an undertaker. We reckon he bought it from a second-hand and imagined it would help him pass himself off as a gentleman.

We asked him his name and he would not say! He would only say that it was vital that he see you and he has been looking for you for a long time.

We didn't believe a word of it, told him nothing, and refused to even open the door. We was wonderin' if he'd tried to break it down when a very lucky thing happened. Lord Van Doren is always goin' on about how we don't got a need for two parrots in the drawing room, but he is wrong!

You know how Chester likes to shout 'murder' when he wants a biscuit or an almond? And then when Chester shouts, Jemina always shouts back 'Shut it, old man?' They did just that and kept shoutin' at each other like them two birds like to do when there's somebody at the door. I was peekin' out through the curtains and you should have seen the look on that housebreaker's face to hear them birds shoutin' at each other. He was downright terrorized.

I reckon that fella thinks we got a whole house full of madmen ready to murder him in here.

Anyway, he got on his horse real quick and rode off.

We are prayin' we seen the last of them and we gave Chester an extra biscuit.

I'm sorry to say it, but I'm gonna have another glass of the lord's sherry, I am that shaken up. If you could inform Lord

Westmont why the bottle is half empty, I'd much appreciate it.
Clara.

Miss Mayton laid the letter down. He'd been to Somerset. She'd got away just in time. And, if Clara's recounting of events was at all accurate, no mention of where she'd gone had been made.

Even if he guessed she was in London, he'd never find her here. It was too big a place to search and he certainly would not be on any of the guest lists for the places she would go.

If the season unfolded as she imagined it would, she would be off with Mr. Brummel and that fine gentleman would protect her. Naturally, he would be entirely understanding and sympathetic regarding the circumstances. When the time came to inform him of them.

Why could not some other people just go away? Why turn up now, when her life had just taken such an interesting turn?

IF IT WERE any other season, one of the last places Darden would have willingly gone was to Lady Hightower's musical evening. The lady herself was a cracking old matron, but the entertainment…

Hours together of one young miss after the next getting up to demonstrate the results of her youthful training at a musical instrument. It was a lady's version of an Oxford examination—the moment when one must prove what one has been doing all these years.

Sadly, it was about as interesting as an Oxford examination.

He'd been in the habit of sending Lady Hightower elaborate and heartfelt excuses expressing his devastation over missing the evening. He'd even done the same when his sisters were to play to wiggle out of it. He had been forever grateful he'd not been present for Rosalind's time at the pianoforte, which unfortunately was now referred to as *The Duchess' Dissonance*. At least, it was named that when the speaker could assure himself that Conbatten was not within a mile of the conversation.

Rosalind could not read a note of music and so just strung together bits of this and that tune she remembered and then slapped a name on the result—a travel through the world of music.

Darden had heard enough of these travels through the world of music to have privately renamed them travels to who knows where or why. It was not lost on him that Conbatten had moved his own pianoforte into what he called the 'family room.' The duke had specially designed a room to house every ghastly thing that had come from his wife's sisters—paintings, odes, and any travels through the world of music that might spring up to shake his walls. The duke might be indulgent, but he retained a healthy respect for his own sanity.

This season was not any other season, though. This season he had five sisters and their five husbands attempting to marry him off. Ten people! Eleven, if he counted Miss Mayton.

Really, considering the amount of mischief Miss Mayton could get up to, he should count her as *two* people.

That would make a dozen schemers, all looking to drag him into a church.

As he was certain that Lady Marianna Tisdale would be one of the ladies put to her Oxford examinations at the pianoforte or the harp, and equally certain that feigning love for the lady was the only thing that would save him, he had come.

"Goodness, Lord Darden," Lady Hightower said with amusement, "I am surprised to see you here. I rather count on your elaborate excuses each year—my butler finds them highly diverting."

"Diverting, Lady Hightower?" Darden asked, a snake of concern slithering up his spine.

"I should amend that," Lady Hightower said. "He finds them

hilarious. According to Bellforce, for several years now the servants have been inspired to play a game they've invented named *Devastating reasons why the lord cannot come*."

"Certainly not, Lady Hightower," Darden said, dearly hoping his face was not as red as a fall apple. He'd always thought his excuses particularly inspired, but apparently not as opaque as he'd imagined.

"Certainly so," Lady Hightower said, laughing. "It is a favorite at Christmastime. Last year's winner was our cook, who wrote his entry as Lord Nedrad. That lord could not come because he'd been swimming with sharks and now found himself sadly legless. Nothing less could have kept him away."

Now Darden was certain his face was red. No, it must be purple if the heat of it was anything to go by.

Nedrad. It was just Darden spelled backward! And anyway, he'd never written anything as unbelievable as a shark attack. What were those servants thinking?

"The timing of your sudden reappearance is interesting. None of your sisters will play tonight, so I must guess you come for another lady. Never fear, I will not pry into it."

He could at least be grateful that she would not pry into his reasons for coming. But a Christmas game invented from his excuses! He really ought to remedy whatever deficiencies in his written regrets had led to *that*.

"Go in, Lord Darden," Lady Hightower said in a kind tone. "Next year will be time enough for another entertaining paragraph of regrets."

Darden nodded. She really was a good-humored old girl.

Fortunately.

He spotted Conbatten and Rosalind instantly, the duke standing a head higher than anybody else in the room. He was not surprised. Conbatten was certain to attend Lady Hightower every year. It was unlikely he was at all interested in the performances that would soon assault his ears, but Lady Hightower had been somewhat of a mentor to him in his youth.

He made his way over.

"Darden!" Rosalind said, failing to keep the surprise from her tone.

The duke sighed. "Your attendance is unfortunate, Darden," he said.

"Unfortunate?" Darden asked. "Why?"

"Lady Hightower's servants will be left bereft that they did not receive an original and entertaining excuse for declining the invitation," the duke said.

"Oh, that's true," Rosalind said. "I hadn't thought. Did you know they even devised a game about it, Darden?"

"I have recently been informed," he said.

"Cook won the game last year—Lord Nedrad lost his legs to a shark," Rosalind said. "Is that not diverting?"

"Hilarious," Darden muttered.

"Now come, brother, what do you do here?" Rosalind asked. "It really is too odd."

"It's not odd," Darden said. "I enjoy music as well as the next man. I imagine Lady Marianna will play?"

This was all said very deliberately. He wished Rosalind to know, and therefore the entire cabal to know, that he was set on Lady Marianna. The faster they knew it, and understood it as a lost cause, the faster they might turn their attention elsewhere.

"I see," Conbatten said enigmatically.

"Lady Marianna *is* here, with her mother and father," Rosalind said.

"Where?"

"But Darden, Lady Marianna," Rosalind said. "Everybody has heard…"

Darden scanned the room. There she was. He might almost have missed her, as she was partially hidden behind a column.

Just as she'd been at Almack's, she was looking rather smashing. That gold hair of hers really was something, he'd never seen the likes of it. It positively glinted in the candlelight. He wondered what it looked like unpinned.

Then he reminded himself to stop wondering about things like that.

He left Rosalind and Conbatten and headed in her direction. He did not suppose Lady Marianna's father would be overjoyed to note him hanging about, but the important thing was Rosalind would see it. His other sisters would know he'd put himself to so much trouble as to attend a musical evening and then made a beeline to the lady. They'd all know it before the sun set on the morrow.

"Your Grace," he said bowing to the duchess. "Lady Marianna."

"Lord Darden," the duchess said. "I do not believe you know my husband. The Duke of Kembleton. Kembleton, this is Viscount Darden."

"Your Grace," Darden said.

"Viscount," the duke said. His tone sounded rather like he said, "Insignificant nobody who might as well be a grocer."

"Lord Darden is the eldest son of the Earl of Westmont," the duchess said, clearly attempting to gloss over her husband's rather instant disdain for a mere viscount.

"Never heard of him," the duke muttered.

"Father," Lady Marianna said quietly.

The duke shrugged and said, "Where is Wellerston? Or Mayfield? They ought to be here."

Well, well. The tales told of Lady Marianna seemed more than accurate. One generally could assume that any sort of gossip had been at least a little exaggerated, but not so in this case. The duke had only interest in the two marquesses of marriageable age and was not averse to publicly advertising that fact.

As Darden could practically feel Rosalind's eyes boring into his back, he knew he had to make further conversation to prolong the encounter. He could not allow the duke to drive him off so quickly.

"Lady Marianna, what instrument will you play this evening?"

"The pianoforte, Lord Darden," she said. "I have chosen a piece of music that is short and lively so that I am not forced to note my audience squirming in their seats."

"Goodness, Marianna," the duchess said. "Nobody will be restless."

It seemed Lady Marianna understood better what it was to sit through a series of young ladies playing than her mother did. Everybody *would* be squirming, and therefore highly approving of a short and lively piece.

"I am certain that whatever you have chosen will please," Darden said.

For whatever reason, this seemed to grab the duke's attention. "Don't be too pleased, if you don't mind."

Gad, the duke was a regular bull charging at fences in a pasture. No wonder Lady Marianna felt forced to go along with his plans. He would not be the sort who was easy to defy.

"Ah, there now!" the duke said, looking very suddenly cheerful. "I say! Mayfield! we are over here."

Darden noted Lady Marianna's cheeks pinken at this very obvious, and rather loud, gambit.

He turned and saw Mayfield trudging over. The fellow looked as if he were on his way to the hangman.

Clearly, Mayfield was not interested in the duke's plans. Wellerston was not, he already knew that. For all he knew, Lady Marianna was not either.

Darden imagined a few sets of parents had got together and decided between themselves what would be a good idea and now two marquesses and the daughter of a duke were being pushed together.

For the love of heaven, it was 1807—what were they thinking? It was as if they were still living in medieval times. Did they not imagine that their offspring might have some opinions on the matter?

Apparently not. He could bet that Mayfield had not come of his own free will. He'd been ordered to turn up and make himself pleasant, probably with the fate of his allowance hanging over his head.

He felt sorry for all three people involved. He sometimes forgot how good of a man his own father was—an occasion such as this reminded him of his luck.

The duke looked intently at poor Mayfield like he was a caught fish on a hook.

"My dear guests," Lady Hightower called. "If you will all take your seats. Now, it has become almost a running joke, but I once again beseech you to simply choose a chair, and not examine the placement of every single one of them as if you were intending on marrying it and making it your lifelong partner."

Darden nodded to the party and left Lady Marianna, the duke and duchess, and the poor captive Mayfield. He had stayed there long enough to convince Rosalind of his intentions.

He made his way to the sideboard and waved away a footman, pouring himself an exceedingly large glass of claret. He drank it down and poured another. Then he slid into a seat on the far end of the very last row and prepared himself to be lulled into a stupor by mediocre music.

CHAPTER SIX

ALL THE YEARS that her father had spoken of her becoming a duchess, Marianna had not once considered how awkward the situations around the idea would be.

Or considered how little the duke ever tried to hide his feelings.

He'd been downright rude to Lord Darden.

Marianna could not deny that she'd felt flattered that the lord made his way over to her so determinedly.

It was the stupidest thing in the world to be flattered by it. She could see very well why he did it. His sister, the Duchess of Conbatten, was in attendance. He wished to convince her of the ruse that he was set on the unattainable Lady Marianna.

Though, the truth was that if she had known nothing of the ruse, she would have been deeply flattered indeed.

And then poor Lord Mayfield. Her father had practically shouted at him to call him over. To say there was some foot-dragging was an understatement.

Before noting it, she had been wholly concentrated on how *she* felt about these machinations. Now it was brought to her attention that the two gentlemen involved had feelings of their own and were likely just as unenthusiastic.

Finally, Lady Hightower had called for the music to begin. Unlike her own idea of playing something short and lively, some of these other ladies went on for an eternity.

It was as if somebody had informed them that this was their very last chance at the pianoforte and they must squeeze every minute out of it that they could.

Just now, Miss Nesterling was moving very slowly through a very slow piece. It felt like slogging through a soggy dell, where one's feet were sucked into the muck at every step and it was a struggle to move forward.

Though she prided herself on her manners, Marianna had a great wish to take Miss Nesterling by the shoulders and throw her off the instrument. The lady was as lively as a funeral and Marianna was quite sure she'd just heard somebody groan behind her.

Somehow, the piece finally limped to its dreary end. Miss Nesterling, seeming very moved by her performance, stared down reverentially at the instrument's keys.

Gracious, the lady could not even rise and begone with any speed.

There was a subdued clapping and Lady Hightower hurried forward. "Very well done, Miss Nesterling," she said. "Now, we will hear from Lady Marianna Tisdale."

Marianna rose, determined to wake everybody up with a short and toe-tapping tune.

As she turned to the audience, she noted that at least one person needed more than a proverbial waking up. He needed an actual waking up.

Lord Darden was slumped, his empty wine glass resting against his chest and his eyes closed.

Marianna pressed her lips together to stop from laughing at the sight. He was in the very last row and it did not seem as if anybody had noticed.

Time to awake, Lord Darden.

She sat herself down, and her hands came down hard on the keys, racing along with speed.

She could play the piece in her sleep and was, therefore, free to look about her.

As soon as the notes rang out, Lord Darden startled awake and fell on the floor, overturning his chair as he went.

Heads turned at the racket. Footmen ran to assist the gentleman to his feet, right his chair, and take his empty glass away.

Marianna played on, determined not to give way to helpless laughter.

The lord was reseated and very determinedly straightened his cuffs as if nothing at all had occurred.

Marianna bit her lip as she neared the end of the piece. If the lord wished to convince his sisters that he was a besotted fool chasing after what he could not have, he might want to at least stay awake while the lady he was allegedly mooning over performed.

⌁

IF CHARLES BENNINGTON, Viscount Darden, had intended to bring any of his dignity with him to Lady Hightower's musical evening, he had clearly been remiss and left it behind in a coat pocket somewhere.

First, he was informed that Lady Hightower's servants had invented a preposterous game based on the various excuses he'd sent over the years. Devastating reasons the lord cannot come, they called it.

Then, he'd fallen asleep. That, in itself, would not have been the crime of the century. He would not have been the first fellow who'd fallen asleep at a musical evening.

But had it really been necessary to fall off his chair?

He'd been lulled to sleep by Miss Nesterling's plodding along, and then jerked awake by Lady Marianna's sudden pounding. He'd almost think the lady startled him on purpose.

He'd made such a racket in overturning his chair that absolutely everybody had seen him being helped up by a couple of footmen.

Lady Hightower had seen it. He supposed there'd be a new game in the offing in her servants' quarters—devastating reasons the lord fell off his chair.

Lady Marianna had seen it. And caused it for that matter. He was quite sure she'd been amused by it.

Her parents, the duke and duchess, had seen it. Darden was confident the duke thought it was what one could expect from a lowly viscount.

The other duke in the room, Conbatten, had only quietly sighed, while Rosalind had covered her mouth to stifle a laugh.

The entertainment was meant to be every young ladies' chance in the spotlight, but who had ended providing the most memorable performance? He had.

After all the ladies had taken their turn, he'd slipped out and went gratefully home.

If he had hoped that the news of his flinging himself off the furniture would not spread, and he *had* hoped it, that had been spectacularly naïve.

He'd just walked into his own club and Henderson had shouted, "What ho! The flying viscount is in the building!"

Darden had laughed. Mostly because he had to—he could not appear the bad sport to his own members.

Though, he was feeling rather the bad sport.

Hamill met him at a table and waved to a waiter to bring them some coffee. "It wasn't that bad," he said. "At least, I suppose it was not."

"If it were not that bad, I would not have just been named the flying viscount to the very great mirth of all who heard it."

"You know Henderson, he's fond of inventing nicknames," Hamill said. "They never stick, though—when was the last time we called Lord Bendringer 'Bad luck Bertie?'"

Hamill was doing his very best to downplay the results of his nodding off, but Darden knew the truth of it. There was nothing the *ton* liked more than a funny story. There was approximately zero possibility they would not rejoice over the tale.

However, that was not why he had sought out Hamill. He said, "I know about the plot."

Hamill paled just the smallest bit and Darden knew his estimation had been right. Hamill was the weakest link in the chain that was the scheme to get him wed.

"Plot?" Hamill asked, not very convincingly.

"The plot. To drag me into a church."

"Well, I would not say any dragging has been mentioned."

"What, precisely, has been mentioned? I can guess some of it, of course. It would have been Miss Mayton's harebrained idea, she would have convinced my sisters, who then put the screws on their respective husbands."

"Gad, you've guessed quite a lot."

"What haven't I guessed, though? What else is there to know? Come, Hamill. You may be married to my sister, but you are a YBC member first."

Hamill looked torn over that idea. Darden could not say whether membership in the YBC trumped marriage, but it seemed to have an effect on him.

"It's called the SFFCDD," Hamill said quietly.

"The what?"

"The Society For Finally Chaining Down Darden," Hamill said, his tone resigned.

They'd even named the thing. It was a society. This was worse than he'd thought.

"How exactly has a society been formed?" Darden asked.

"Well, there was a meeting, you see. At Conbatten's house."

A meeting at Conbatten's house.

He had to put a stop to it. The society must be disbanded.

"Hamill," he said, "I will brook no interference from my relatives regarding my personal plans. If I am set on a particular lady, the *society* is to stay out of it."

"You mean, Lady Marianna," Hamill said.

Darden nodded. It was imperative that this society of theirs be convinced he was set on Lady Marianna—the lady he could never succeed with.

"But Darden," Hamill said, "everybody knows she's to wed either Mayfield or Wellerston. She's to be a duchess."

"Nonsense," Darden said. "Ladies change their minds all the time. You should know that, having married one who had a spectacular change of mind."

Hamill sighed. It was a deep and sad sigh. "Jules will not like this situation. I bet she writes an ode about it."

Of course she would. If it had any grain of truth to it, it would be named *Ode to what were my sisters thinking?*

"And when, pray, is the next society meeting?" Darden asked.

"This afternoon," Hamill said. "We're to discuss who you danced with at Almack's. And I suppose what happened at Lady Hightower's house too."

"And attempt to turn me from Lady Marianna, I would guess," Darden said.

Hamill nodded sadly. "Probably."

"I won't be turned. You can inform the society of that fact and they can all go home. As for your part in this, remember you belong to the YBC—out of loyalty, you cannot tell anybody that I know about the society."

Hamill looked rather relieved at that directive. "Good," he said. "Jules would be very unhappy with me, and I never do like to see her unhappy."

With the smallest sigh, he almost whispered, "The one time I made her unhappy, she wrote an unhappy ode about it. I'll never forget it. Word to the wise, Darden—the color of one's bedchamber curtains is not as unimportant as you might think!"

Darden suppressed a smile. Jules was ruling over her lord with not a raised sword, but a raised pen ready to write an unhappy ode.

"We are agreed, then," Darden said. "You will report to me all the doings of this outlandish society and the society will be none the wiser."

Hamill had nodded, though he had a hunted look about him.

Darden was not surprised—he'd just been cornered into an uncomfortable box. He must twist and turn to somehow be loyal to both Juliet and himself.

He could not feel too sorry for Hamill, though. He, and Baderston and Harveston too for that matter, should have never allowed this ridiculous society to form in the first place.

Of course, if he was being realistic, Darden knew very well what a hurricane his sisters could be. What chance had their besotted husbands ever really had?

But that was their problem. His own problems had been solved, as far as he could see it.

TATTLETON, ONCE HE had put himself forward to do a thing, strode forward and did a thing.

He was currently acting as the general in Lord Darden's army and he had not been remiss in his duties.

Though, what he had discovered so far was alarming and confounding.

Miss Mayton had received a letter from Clara, and then she had left that letter lying on a table in the drawing room. She'd been called away by Fleur to examine some fripperies that had just been delivered. Like a schoolgirl, she'd run off giggling over it.

As Miss Mayton was suspected to be at the heart of the plot against Lord Darden, everything about her must be examined.

In the usual case of things, he would never dream of reading another's correspondence, but this was war!

Also, he was really wondering why Clara had written from Somerset. Had there been a fire they were trying to cover up? Were they shirking their duties and laughing behind his back? Or could it be surprising news, like one of those useless cats that roamed the house had actually managed to catch a mouse? Or perhaps it might be the happiest news of all, and he would discover that both of those diabolical parrots had suddenly dropped dead.

The idea of those birds lying in their cages with feet pointing to the sky did buoy his spirits for a moment.

What he had discovered in that letter was not anything he could have dreamed up. A mysterious man had been to the house, inquiring after Miss Mayton.

Clara may have been fooled into believing the man was a housebreaker, but Tattleton was a little more savvy than that!

A strange man in an odd black suit who had been looking for Miss Mayton for a long time?

Who was this man? Why was he looking for Miss Mayton? He could not be any of her long-lost lotharios—they were all dead, if any had ever actually lived. And why was Miss Mayton avoiding this person? Was that the real reason they'd had to come to Town for the season when they had not planned on it?

And what was Clara thinking of, drinking the lord's sherry!

This stranger searching for Miss Mayton did not seem as if he could have anything to do with trying to get Lord Darden married. However, this man had something to do with something mysterious. He must get to the bottom of it.

In the meantime, there was to be a dinner this evening. The earl had informed Lord Darden that his presence was needed. Lord and Lady Baderston and Lord and Lady Harveston were to attend them.

Lady Viola and Lady Cordelia were to be under their roof once more. He really did miss the young ladies, even though they were currently scheming against Lord Darden. He missed always hearing laughter coming from above stairs or in the drawing room. He missed when one of them would call him a darling for doing some little favor or other.

He missed the ode Lady Juliet always composed for his birthday, even though they were always dreadful. He had a portrait of himself that Lady Viola had painted hung in his quarters. At least, he'd been told it was himself. He even missed the excitement of whether Lady Cordelia would knock over a candle and set the house afire during her spirited renditions of Desdemona's final moments.

But he must not get sentimental. He was a general now and must be all discipline.

Tattleton would be Lord Darden's eyes and ears. If any hint was dropped that he could take to the lord, it would not slip by him.

Mrs. Huffson bustled into the servants' hall with a bit of sewing which, as usual, Fleur had claimed she couldn't manage.

"I understand we are to have a full house tonight, Mr. Tattleton," she said genially.

"Indeed, Mrs. Huffson," he said. "It is time that the general prepares for battle."

"Goodness, it is only a dinner," the housekeeper said.

Poor Mrs. Huffson. She was so terribly naïve—she never saw what was really going on. A battle would commence, and Tattleton would lead the charge.

⇶⟨⟨⟨

Miss Mayton once more found herself in a meeting of the SFFCDD at the duke's house on Grosvenor Square. There was so much on her mind that she wished to be in her own drawing room with her bit of sewing so she might spend hours thinking of it.

Her situation at this moment was a case of both best and worst. Mr. Brummel, quite naturally, was in the best category. That other gentleman who'd been so bold as to knock on the earl's door in Somerset was clearly the worst of her situation.

If anything could have diverted her at this moment, it was the brief visit of the young marquess. What a chubby and gurgling little thing he was! He was all bright eyes and taking everything in. Little did he yet understand what doting parents he had, and what a soft situation he'd been born into. Very few landed on the bedsheets with such a comfortable future assured.

Rosalind had brought him in and shown him all round, under the proud eyes of the duke.

"In a few short years," Beatrice said, "he will be a playmate for Lily."

"He's a fine-looking chap," Van Doren said. "If we might proceed with this charade now? Lest we be still sitting here as those few short years pass by?"

Beatrice snorted, as she always did find Van Doren's original brand of wit very amusing.

"Miss Mayton?" Conbatten asked.

She suppressed a sigh. She'd put together the SFFCDD as a diversion, but now she was saddled with seeing it through.

"I suppose," she began, "we ought to discuss Almack's."

Viola nodded solemnly. "Our dear brother was very struck by Lady Marianna Tisdale, though I did inform him that she was to wed either Lord Wellerston or Lord Mayfield. He called my saying so nonsense."

Rosalind nodded vigorously. "He was just the same at Lady Hightower's musical evening. We were most surprised to see him there, and certainly he came because Lady Marianna would play. He went straight to her side."

"Though," the duke said, "he scampered off pretty quickly at the end of the entertainments."

"Well, he would do. He fell out of his chair at a most inopportune moment," Rosalind said, laughing. "He must have drifted off and just tumbled out of it. I suppose he did not wish to discuss *that* with Lady Marianna."

"I don't see that there is much to be done," Lord Hamill said. "Darden is set on a lady who will never have him. Perhaps we just give it up until next year?"

The lords Harveston and Baderston nodded vigorously in agreement. The ladies in attendance, however, stared at each other in some amazement.

"Give up?" Viola asked, seeming entirely confounded by the thought.

"What an idea," Cordelia said.

Van Doren snorted. He pointed at Hamill. "He's new."

The duke pressed his lips together to suppress a smile at Van Doren's astute observation.

"My darling," Juliet said to Hamill, "the Benningtons never just give up."

"I was afraid that would be the case," Hamill said.

"We must only decide how to proceed," Rosalind said, "now that we understand that dear Darden will not be turned away from Lady Marianna. After all, it cannot be hopeless, can it?"

"I should say not," Cordelia said. "Just think what straits we were brought to with Conbatten. Did we give up then?"

In case Lord Hamill didn't know the circumstances, Conbatten said, "They certainly did not give up. Not before a rousing kidnapping."

Rosalind smiled at the duke. "It was rather rousing, was it not?"

The duke nodded indulgently, although Miss Mayton had always thought that Conbatten privately viewed the kidnapping gambit as a rather foolish idea. He'd somehow seemed to blame her, as if it had been all her idea. It was very unfair, as it had only been partly her idea.

"And then, Harveston and I nearly killed ourselves to be together," Cordelia said. "We were positively injured."

"Baderston came close to killing three different gentlemen defending me," Viola said.

"I nearly dropped dead in pursuit of Beatrice," Van Doren said. "Nobody knows what I went through."

Beatrice patted his hand, which must be meant to confirm his heroics. As far as Miss Mayton could ever see, all that gentleman had done was charge into the house like a madman one evening and demand Beatrice marry him. She still did not quite understand it.

"If we are agreed that we will not give up," Miss Mayton said, "and we are also agreed that Lord Darden is quite set on Lady Marianna, well!"

"Well what, Miss Mayton?" Lord Harveston asked.

"Well we must only arrange it that she weds him," Miss Mayton said. Goodness, for an intellectual, Lord Harveston was a bit slow to the mark.

"How, though?" Lord Harveston pressed.

"He's new, too," Van Doren said, pointing at Lord Harveston. "Else he would know it will be some preposterous idea."

"What idea?" Lord Baderston said, a note of trepidation creeping into his voice.

"We do not yet know," Viola said to her lord.

"We know it will be preposterous, though," Van Doren muttered.

"As a beginning, I think we should all get better acquainted with Lady Marianna," Rosalind said. "Then, she will see how genial it would be to join the family and it will give her courage to defy her father."

"But what if she does not actually prefer Darden?" Hamill asked weakly.

This was cause for more amazed looks. "Goodness, Hamill," Juliet said, "who does not adore Darden?"

CHAPTER SEVEN

SINCE THE START of the season, Marianna and her mother had a special teatime each day to sort through the endless invitations coming their way. And, they *were* endless. It seemed everybody in the world wished to say that the Duke and Duchess of Kembleton, or the duchess and her daughter, had come to their entertainment.

The duke did not interfere in these deliberations too much. He'd only given the directive that they were to accept invitations where they might find the lords Wellerston and Mayfield in attendance. As he did not know with any specificity which entertainments that might be, it was a suitably vague directive and they did not take it much into account.

This particular afternoon's piles of letters were turning out very odd indeed. First, they'd encountered a note from Lady Harveston addressed to Marianna. The lady would be pleased to call upon her at the duchess' next at-home day.

It would have been correct for Lady Harveston to await the duchess' card before informing the household that she would soon arrive to present her own. The duchess did not hold anything against Lady Harveston, but she'd not had any particular plan to call upon the baroness.

The duchess had concluded that Lady Harveston must be running some charity or other and would wish the duchess to become involved. Any charity got a boost when a duchess threw her hat in and those running such a concern could become exceedingly bold in their desperation for success.

That idea did not support what was discovered next, though.

There were other notes arrived for Marianna—Lady Van Doren, Lady Baderston, Lady Hamill, and finally, the Duchess of Conbatten.

Though only the Duchess of Conbatten had the societal right to approach the house without having been approached first, it seemed that was of little consequence to the Bennington ladies. Every single one of Lord Darden's sisters had written that they looked forward to seeing her at the duchess' at-home day.

What did it mean? Was this part of the scheme to push their brother into a church? Though Lord Darden had imagined that following about an unattainable lady would put them off it, perhaps they were willing to take bolder steps.

Perhaps they thought of outlining the problem and requesting that Marianna say something definitive to drive him off, so they might steer him toward another more suitable lady.

She really did not like to be in the middle of this family…whatever it was.

"Goodness," the duchess said, "I had, of course, noted Lord Darden's interest in you."

Marianna smiled. "Though he could not stay awake for it and ended by falling on the floor."

The duchess waved her hands. "Oh, that had nothing to do with you, my dear. That was all Miss Nesterling. Gracious, that young miss could lull to sleep a wild elephant—I had a deal of trouble keeping my own eyes open."

Marianna did not answer. She agreed, but was well aware that while it was perfectly fine for a duchess to make such scathing pronouncements, it was not so acceptable for a young lady just out to make them.

"No, Marianna," the duchess continued, "these missives from all of Lord Darden's sisters can only mean that he has told them that he holds you in some regard. There cannot be any other reason they all write at once and pretend to be oblivious as to the social conventions."

Marianna suppressed a sigh. Naturally, it would seem to her mother that could be the only reason. She knew better though.

She said, "Of course we cannot be sure of their purpose, if there even is a purpose. Perhaps they have all formed a charity together and mean to arrive in force to make their case."

The duchess was pensive. "Perhaps. In any event, Lord Darden certainly is a fine specimen. I only say, there is no shame in becoming a viscountess, eventually to be a countess. What matters is where your heart takes you."

Marianna smiled. Where her heart would take her. Goodness, she had an idea of where it might have taken her, but that idea was all for naught.

Marianna Tisdale was simply a pawn in the handsome Lord Darden's battle with his sisters.

Oh, but if she were not a pawn, what would she think then? Something entirely different, she was sure.

"I suppose we will wait and see what these ladies have to say for themselves," the duchess said.

"So you mean to admit them?" Marianna asked.

"Heavens, yes. I am fascinated by this gambit. Now, the hour grows late and I ordered the carriage for a turn round the park. And Boudicca to be saddled too, as I did assume you would like to ride. We'd best go up and change."

⇛⇚

DARDEN HAD BEEN feeling as if there were no comfortable place to be at this very moment. At home, Miss Mayton was always lurking around and who knew what schemes she was harboring. If that was not uncomfortable enough, she took every opportunity to inquire about Mr. Brummel.

He'd already told her he did not know the gentleman with

any sort of intimacy and that he was not a member of the YBC.

That information had not slowed her down. She brought up making Brummel a member several times, though it was out of the question. She also brought up other things. Other ghastly things, like what did he suppose Mr. Brummel's opinion was regarding a bright-colored velvet named parakeet green?

Of course he did not know, though if he had to guess he would have said Brummel's opinion of anything colored parakeet green would have hovered somewhere between offended and feeling faint.

At the same time, the YBC was an uncomfortable location too. It had always been his haven, and it would be again at some future moment. At this particular moment, though, every time he walked in, he was cheered as the flying viscount.

He had Nero saddled and rode off to the park. At least there he might trot along and have some time to think without being harassed about parakeet green velvet or flying off a chair. Two of his sisters were coming for dinner and he did not know what sort of gambit they had in mind, other than to know it must be something.

In any case, Nero could use some extra exercise outside of what he was getting from the grooms. He looked a bit fat and Darden was all but certain he'd got into the oats again.

He'd been named Nero for his debauchery anywhere near oats. He'd kick down a stable door to get to them, and once there he'd make himself sick eating them. The stable hands had firm instructions to keep the store of oats in the annex built for the purpose and to ensure that Nero's stall door, which had been reinforced, was firmly closed.

He was a crafty creature though. Last spring he'd eaten a vast quantity before he was stopped and he'd almost died. He'd not died, but what had come out of him as a result of that adventure had been rapid and astounding.

For all that, Nero was a very fine specimen and when it was time to get four legs moving, he did not disappoint.

Once in the park, Darden steered his horse along the carriage road.

It was beginning to crowd up, it was that time of day when the *ton* cruised round looking at one another. No matter, all he need do was tip his hat and carry on thinking. Nero would dodge any vehicle or animal that needed to be dodged.

Just as a carriage was making its way round him, a voice said, "Lord Darden."

The carriage had slowed, and he did too. He knew the voice and was startled at its effect on him. It gave him a little shiver.

He reined in. "Lady Marianna."

She accompanied the carriage from atop her horse, a fine-looking mare of sixteen hands. The duchess was inside the carriage, her head popping out the window.

"Your Grace," he said.

At least, he hoped that was what he said. Lady Marianna was stunning in her riding habit. It was a very dark green fitted coat of worsted wool with gold buttons on the bodice and cuffs. It had a Parisian flair to it and the dark color set off her golden hair, which was just now peeking out from under her hat.

"A fine-looking horse, Lord Darden," the duchess said.

"His name is Nero, and I'm afraid he's a bit run to fat at the moment," Darden said. "He is rather debauched when it comes to oats, hence the name."

Why was he blathering on about Nero? No lady cared how his horse felt about oats.

For some reason, Lady Marianna and the duchess laughed.

"My daughter rides Boudicca," the duchess said, "the uncomfortable thorn in Nero's side."

That *was* an unfortunate coincidence. Queen Boudicca had bravely fought off the Romans under Nero when they'd annexed her father's lands.

"Fortunately, this Nero is only interested in conquering oats, not the Iceni people."

"Lord Darden," the duchess said, "we have been recently

flattered to receive several notes from your sisters."

Darden meant to move his mouth to say something, but nothing came of it. He was speechless. Why? Which sisters? What were they doing?

"All of them, in fact," Lady Marianna said. "Lady Baderston, Lady Harveston, Lady Van Doren, Lady Hamill, and the Duchess of Conbatten."

All of them! Cold icicles slipped down his spine. All of them.

"They mean to call at our next at-home day." Lady Marianna said. "I speculated that they must be involved in some charity and wish for my mother's backing."

Lady Marianna stared meaningfully at him.

What were his sisters doing? Aside from their meddling, they could not just inform a duchess they were unacquainted with that they planned to arrive. Well, Rosalind could, but the rest of them had no right to.

"Charity? Yes! That might very well be it," he said. "Ladies do become…overenthusiastic. About their charities."

"What is the charity, Lord Darden?" the duchess asked.

"The charity? Well, it is hard to say. I know Rosalind, the duchess, does some work with schools for the disadvantaged. The queen favors it, I understand. So maybe that's it? Or perhaps it is a newer venture put together by Juliet, Lady Hamill."

"That, or some other scheme we do not yet know of," Lady Marianna said, with an arched brow.

Yes, that was indeed more likely. A scheme he did not yet know of. A diabolical and preposterous scheme, if he knew his sisters at all.

Giving out the idea that he was set on Lady Marianna was supposed to drive the society to chain him down into nonexistence. It was not supposed to prompt all of his sisters to visit Lady Marianna.

Why were they going? What was the plan?

"In any case, Your Grace," Darden said, "there is not the least cause to admit them. They really will not mind it. They will not think a thing about it."

"Not admit them?" the duchess said, laughing. "Gracious, I cannot think of anything more diverting than to admit them and hear what this is all about."

Darden felt the blood drain from his face and was certain no gentleman had ever appeared more pale outside of his own coffin.

"We'd better carry on, Marianna," the duchess said to her daughter. "Your father has some idea of going to the theater tonight and will wish for an early dinner. You know how out of sorts he gets when he is in a theater box and hungry."

Lady Marianna nodded to him and urged her horse forward. "Lord Darden," she said.

"Pleasant to see you again, Lord Darden," the duchess said.

"Your Grace, Lady Marianna," he said, bowing from his saddle.

He could have sworn the duchess had an amused look before she sat back in the carriage.

Darden turned his horse and headed back to Portland Place. His sisters were intent on visiting Lady Marianna. The duchess was intent on receiving them.

Two of those very sisters were coming for dinner.

Considering the clumsiness of their attempts so far, he had every expectation that he'd gather some kind of clue as to what they meant by acquainting themselves with Lady Marianna.

With any luck, they had the idea that they'd pressure the lady to cut him loose so he might be pushed and prodded in another direction.

Perhaps Lady Marianna would refuse the request and they'd all see their machinations were hopeless. Or she might even agree to it, and then he could simply refuse to be driven off or pretend he was laid low by it.

Though his thoughts should have been wholly on his sisters and their plans, his mind did drift here and there.

Had any lady ever looked better atop a horse? He could not imagine it to be so.

Perhaps it was just the smallest bit of a shame that Lady Marianna *was* unattainable.

His mind had drifted to such a degree that he hardly remembered directing his horse to Portland Place. Perhaps he hadn't. Nero would be set on getting back to the stables to check on the availability of oats in his stall.

A groom took his horse and Darden jogged up the steps. He met Tattleton in the hall and said, "Tattleton, keep your ears wide open this evening. I wish to hear anything of my sisters intending to call upon Lady Marianna Tisdale. They believe me set on the lady, though she would never have me. That ought to have put them off their plans, but somehow it has not."

To his surprise, the butler saluted him.

Darden bit his lip as he ran up the stairs. It seemed that when Tattleton had agreed to be his general, he'd taken the task on quite literally.

MARIANNA HAD NEVER been so embarrassed in her life. They had simply gone to the theater, it should all have been very regular.

There was nothing at all regular about the situation she now found herself in.

Her father had invited both Lord Mayfield and Lord Wellerston into his box and then engineered them into sitting on either side of her.

It was such a public display of his plans!

Of course, by now, all the *ton* would have become apprised of his idea that she was meant to wed either Wellerston or Mayfield. But to sit between them so publicly. It was humiliating.

Worse, she could see very well that the lords were feeling just the same. Lord Wellerston's cheeks were on fire and Lord Mayfield pulled at his neckcloth as if he were choking.

When it had become apparent what her father's arrangements for the evening were, Marianna instantly understood that the duchess had not had any idea of it. It was one of those rare occasions that her mother appeared annoyed with the duke.

Marianna was annoyed too, though she did not like being annoyed with her father.

She could not help it though, she was annoyed and irritated and embarrassed. It was as if her father did not take her feelings into consideration at all. She kept her back ramrod straight and her eyes firmly on the stage. She could not bear to view anybody's notice of this absurd situation.

Lord Mayfield suddenly said, "Lord Darden took you into supper at Almack's, Lady Marianna."

She nodded her head, though she could not imagine why he should comment on it.

"He's a jolly fellow, is he not?" Lord Mayfield said. "I cannot think of a person who does not admire Lord Darden."

From her other side, Lord Wellerston leaned forward and said, "He *is* a rather jolly fellow. I also cannot think of anyone who does not admire him."

"And he's founded his own club," Lord Mayfield said. "That is rather something, is it not? I am not a member myself, but I've heard it's very jolly."

"I have heard the same!" Lord Wellerston said. "I hope to become a member. As it is so jolly."

As the conversation went on, it dawned on Marianna what this nonsense was really about. They were both hopeful that her head had been turned by Lord Darden, which would conveniently let them off the hook they were just now on.

This was a fine situation. Lord Darden was using *her* to decoy his sisters away from their ideas and Lord Mayfield and Lord Wellerston were using *Lord Darden* as a decoy away from her father's ideas.

"Perhaps I should become a member of Lord Darden's club too!" Lord Mayfield said. "For the jolliness."

The duke leaned forward from behind them. "I think we've

all heard enough about the falling-down viscount for now," he said.

Both lords looked abashed and fell to silence.

Marianna hoped the theater lights were dim enough to camouflage her burning cheeks and her eyes bright with tears that she refused to let fall.

Absolutely nobody was interested in Lady Marianna Tisdale. Not Lord Wellerston. Not Lord Mayfield. Not Lord Darden. Every gentleman in her sphere was only looking to get away.

She was not herself interested in either of the lords who sat by her side, but she could not help but be stung by their obvious desperation for her to look elsewhere.

Lord Darden had stung her with his plans to hang about her, only to fool his sisters. Now these two lords had stung her from either side.

It was too many stings for a lady's pride to bear.

TATTLETON MANAGED THE sideboard and directed the footmen. He'd been doing the task for so long that it was no great matter to put his full attention on what was being said at the table.

He was listening intently for any clues that Lord Darden might not have picked up on. Anything at all that might be helpful to him.

Just now, Lady Cordelia and caught her sister's attention and said quietly, "We ought to say."

Lady Viola had nodded gravely back.

Say what? What did they ought to say?

Fortunately, he was not to be kept in suspense for long.

"Darden," Lady Viola said, "we are planning to call on Lady Marianna on Tuesday."

Lord Darden narrowed his eyes. "So I've heard," he said. "I saw Lady Marianna and the duchess in the park and they mentioned it."

"Well they would, wouldn't they?" Miss Mayton said to no point whatsoever.

"Father," Lady Cordelia said, "Darden has found himself quite taken with Lady Marianna Tisdale."

"Has he, eh?" the earl said. "Has a hook finally caught the bachelor fish, then?"

"There is a difficulty, unfortunately," Lady Viola said. "Lady Marianna is a duke's daughter and it seems she is intent on becoming a duchess herself."

The earl laughed. "We cannot help her there, I'm afraid."

"Now naturally," Lady Viola said, "we have tried to explain this to our dear Darden. On its face, it can seem an insurmountable difficulty."

Lord Darden waved his hand. "Nonsense. Now, I do not know what it is you intend on communicating to Lady Marianna. I can only speculate that you wish to influence her in the hopes that she will kindly drive me off. I will not be driven off, though. You are wasting your time."

"But that is just it, Darden!" Lady Viola said. "We do not wish her to drive you off at all. We wish her to consider what a joy it would be to join our family. We are all exceedingly genial, you know."

"Yes," Lady Cordelia said, "what is becoming a duchess compared to *us*?"

Tattleton staggered and grabbed hold of the sideboard to steady himself.

It was his understanding that Lord Darden had put it about to his sisters that he was admiring of this Lady Marianna *because* it could never come to pass.

Now they were determined to make it come to pass?

Tattleton glanced at Lord Darden. He looked very like a cornered fox as the hounds circled and guns were drawn.

"Of course, we understand that becoming a duchess is her father's wish, but she may be inspired to defy him," Lady Viola said.

"Papa," Lady Cordelia said, "you would not mind being defied over such a small matter, would you?"

"Oh dear," the earl said, "do not ask me such a question. I should not like to comment on what another father may think or do."

"What do you say, Harveston," Lady Cordelia asked her husband. "If we have a daughter, I am certain you would not mind if she wedded a viscount, even if you had a future duke already picked out."

"Well, I—"

"I will not even ask Baderston," Viola said, smiling at her own husband. "He is far too reasonable to object to it."

"I—"

"There, you see? It is settled," Lady Cordelia said.

Tattleton could not see what was settled. Neither one of those lords had been allowed to say anything at all!

"No, it is not settled," Lord Darden said. "I would ask you to refrain from meddling into my affairs."

"That seems fruitless," Miss Mayton said.

"Our aunt is right, Darden," Lady Cordelia said. "We adore you too much to refrain from meddling."

"Not meddle to assist our dear brother?" Viola said. "What an idea."

Tattleton was staggered. What was Lord Darden to do about this latest development? It was very hard, if not impossible, to turn the ladies of the family away from any notion they'd become set on.

He'd once read of a terrifying sort of weather called a tidal wave that could strike in far-off places. The endless ocean would come inexorably ashore, running over anything it encountered. Nothing could turn it round and it would only recede of its own accord. Nobody understood when it would come or why it did so, only that every living being would be powerless against it.

The Bennington ladies' plans were often very like it.

The dessert plates had been cleared and Miss Mayton said, "I suppose everyone will like me to read this evening?"

"Ah, the duke who's got some kind of difficulty with the dark," the earl said jovially. "Indeed, I am very interested to know what his problem is."

Tattleton was not very interested to know what that duke's problem was. There were problems enough right here in the room.

CHAPTER EIGHT

D ARDEN SAT IN the drawing room with his port. His second glass, in fact.

Tattleton had seen how he had fared at dinner and had been ready to refill his glass as soon as he'd emptied it.

He'd got himself into a very fine muddle. It had seemed a foolproof plan—convince his sisters that he was set on a lady he could never have and thereby put an end to this society for chaining him down.

Now, they were determined that he would have the unattainable lady.

The duchess had indicated she would receive them and then…my god, what would they say to Lady Marianna? It was too awful to think of.

"Now," Miss Mayton said, opening her book, "what we know so far is the gentle governess is in love with the duke who swears he cannot love anybody. That, of course, is only a façade, a mask he wears to cover a more difficult problem, though we do not yet know what that problem is."

The gentle governess poked her head in the library door. "Your Grace, young Mortimer is here to bid you goodnight."

The duke nodded and his idiot nephew barreled into his library. "Goodnight, Uncle. I shall sleep like a baby, I am that tired."

The duke suppressed a sigh. It was well he did, for if he al-

lowed himself to sigh it would be an endless sigh to end all sighs.

"Tell me, Mortimer," the duke said, "what is it you do all day that makes you so tired all the time?" the duke asked.

He did not hope for a rational answer, but he'd grown weary of hearing the same thing every night. His nephew was that tired that he'd sleep like a log, or the dead, or a baby, or a rock.

Mortimer appeared thrown off by the question, which was hardly surprising. Mortimer was thrown off quite often.

"Well, Uncle, I suppose I walk around. And I eat things. And I see things. Sometimes I ride my pony, which will really wear a person out."

The duke nodded. "And all the breathing that must be done on top of everything else, I suppose."

"Yes! That too. I hadn't even thought of that," Mortimer said. "But it's true—I breathe all day long."

The duke had a great wish to throttle his idiot nephew. If only he himself could be "that tired" from merely existing on the earth.

As it was, he was never "that tired." He was always restless. Sometimes he didn't sleep at all. Or worse, sometimes he did and was left to wonder what had happened.

If the gentle governess knew his secret, she would never love him! Nobody could.

He was deeply in love with the gentle governess and could not bear to ever view her look of disgust when she discovered what he really was.

He was doomed to go through life alone. Then, when he'd reached the end of his time, Mortimer would take the mantle and assume the dukedom. That was, assuming the imbecile didn't wear himself out with all the breathing he did all day.

How could life be so cruel?

Miss Mayton laid the book down. "Now we know the duke longs for the gentle governess' love, but he is afraid of what she will think when she discovers his secret."

"Gracious," the earl said, "this tale is really keeping the mystery going! I wonder what it could be that tortures the duke at night? And poor Mortimer, I don't like to agree with the duke's assessment, but he does seem rather a dolt."

Darden could not care less about Mortimer. Mortimer could fling himself off the Dover cliffs for all he cared. And, considering the sharpness of Mortimer's intellect, the boy might well make the mistake. Then he'd be *really* tired.

The more pertinent question was what was Darden to do about his sisters?

What if they went too far with their words and practically declared for him?

He might find himself in a church with the very lady who was supposed to keep him out of one.

The idea gave him a sort of sick feeling that he could not name unpleasant or pleasant.

Should he just tell his sisters it was all a ruse from the start?

It would set them scheming again, but whatever scheme they came up with could not be worse than the one they'd dreamed up at the moment.

It might be the way to go. He must just think it through logically. And talk to Hamill about what his sisters planned on saying.

⟫⟫⟫✦⟪⟪⟪

MARIANNA AND THE duchess surveyed the drawing room. It was their at-home day and the cards would be rolling in. Five cards in particular would arrive—Lord Darden's sisters.

The duchess had been specific in her instructions to the kitchens—there were three-tiered trays of sweets and savories of every description placed elegantly round the room.

"Fit for a duchess' drawing room, I'd say. Well done, Norwood," the duchess said.

Their butler nodded gravely. His eyes drifted toward the

tiered tray of individual savoy cakes. He knew them to be one of Marianna's favorites and Marianna knew them to be distinct. Cook had explained to her that it was a particular skill to make them so small without drying them out. Very few could do it creditably.

She smiled and nodded at Norwood. They had known one another so long that they could speak volumes without speaking at all. Her acknowledgement would be communicated to Cook. The savoy cakes had been noted and were appreciated.

They heard the sound of carriage wheels roll to a stop outside.

"Goodness, somebody wishes to arrive at the earliest possible moment," the duchess said. "I hope it is Lady Hightower, I always find her so amusing."

Minutes later, Gavin, their most senior footman, came in looking as grave as a churchyard. Marianna had noticed that he'd taken on that particular mien ever since he'd been named first footman. She presumed he was practicing for when he would be a suitably grave butler.

He cleared his throat dramatically. "The Duchess of Conbatten, and the ladies Harveston, Baderston, Hamill, and Van Doren and…Miss Eloise Mayton, Your Grace."

Miss Mayton? The lady in pink taffeta who had seemed to frighten Mr. Brummel at Almack's?

Her mother bit her lip to stop her amusement. "Do show them in, Gavin."

The six ladies filed in, spread out in a line, and curtsied. In unison, they said, "Your Grace. Lady Marianna."

The duchess went forward to greet them. It was quickly identified who was who, as the duchess did not know any of them in particular. Though, it had been no great matter to determine the identity of Miss Mayton. Despite calling herself a miss, she was decidedly a matron. She was also dressed decidedly alarmingly in a frothy concoction in a startling shade of purple.

The duchess said, "Do come in. You are all very welcome."

Norwood directed the tea service as it rolled through the door on a spectacular silver inlaid cart. Their butler would serve the tea, as had always been tradition in the duke's household. The duchess was well aware that it was her purview to do it, but she thought the notion rather tiresome.

Her mother did not conform to any idea she found tiresome.

Gavin reappeared. "Lady Hightower and Lady Rawley, Your Grace."

The duchess nodded. "Marianna, do entertain the ladies while I greet Lady Hightower and Lady Rawley."

After her mother had turned toward the door, Lady Baderston said, "Might we steal you away to a quiet corner? Over there, perhaps?"

Lady Baderston had nodded toward an alcove in the corner of the room, set with a sofa and several chairs.

Marianna murmured her acquiescence, though she was rather surprised by it. She did not know why these ladies had come, but whatever their reason, they did not seem inclined to dally over it.

They sat themselves cozily in the alcove as Norwood managed the tea from his cart before moving off to assist Lady Hightower and Lady Rawley. One of the junior footmen brought round a tray of cakes, and while most of the ladies declined, Miss Mayton was very enthusiastic and took more slices than one might have predicted.

"The duchess was very good to allow us to crash in like this," Lady Harveston said.

"She might have refused," Lady Hamill said, "but then, we *were* very determined."

"Goodness," Miss Mayton said, "when my girls are determined, there is little that can stop them."

"May I inquire why I have been singled out for this honor?" Marianna asked, curious as to what they would say about this en masse visit of five sisters and a matron wishing to converse in a quiet corner.

"Of course, you must already know it," the Duchess of Conbatten said.

"Naturally, she does," Lady Baderston said.

"I believe she may be attempting to be discreet in pretending not to know it," Miss Mayton said. "Some ladies do, I understand."

"I really do not know," Lady Marianna said.

"Ah," Lady Baderston said. "Discretion. That is rather charming. Sisters, Aunt, it is left to us to get to the point."

"Our dear Darden," Lady Hamill said.

"Now," the Duchess of Conbatten said, "we are well aware that you are meant to become a duchess, and of course, our dear brother could not offer you that. But we thought, what if Lady Marianna saw how genial we all are?"

"Exceedingly genial," Lady Harveston said, nodding. "You would really enjoy becoming part of our extended family. It is such fun."

"Such fun," Lady Van Doren said. "My sisters are all very talented and entertain us no end. You have not heard anything until you've heard Ros play her travels through the world of music."

"Or one of Jules' odes," Lady Baderston said.

"The odes are very moving," Miss Mayton said.

"And Viola could paint your portrait," Lady Harveston said. "Conbatten already has one and I can assure you he values it—he even built a room for it."

"And let us not leave out our aunt," the Duchess of Conbatten said. "She very often reads to us some riveting stories."

"That is true, I cannot deny the charge," Miss Mayton said.

Marianna was silent through this list of delights one might experience in a Bennington household. What on earth could she say? Lord Darden's plan was to throw off his sisters by claiming that he was set on Lady Marianna Tisdale, though the match was impossible.

Apparently, they did not seem to think it impossible? Did they speak for Lord Darden or only for themselves?

"Oh dear," Lady Van Doren said, seeming to note her confusion. "We may have come into this with too much directness. We often do, you see."

"I hardly know what to say, in truth," Marianna said.

"Well, it is not necessary that you say anything at all," Lady Hamill said. "You might just think things over. I can assure you, thinking helps quite a bit. At one time, I almost talked myself into marrying a poet writing in the Japanese style. But then I thought about it and married Hamill instead."

"Did you?" Marianna asked, not having the first idea how such a thing might have come about.

"And then," Lady Baderston said, "we did inquire of our father how he would feel if he'd been defied over who we chose to marry."

"Our dear Papa did not seem the least put out about the idea," Lady Harveston said.

"All we can say, really," Lady Van Doren said, "is that Darden is the dearest brother living."

"We all feel it," Lady Harveston said.

"All of us," Lady Baderston said.

"The lord is so genial," Miss Mayton said. "It is entirely natural that his sisters adore him."

And so the next twenty minutes were spent extolling the virtues of Lord Darden, his father the earl, and a full accounting of the estate in Somerset.

Marianna was rather surprised by the number of birds, cats, dogs, and even a goat, who were members of that estate's household. Particularly that there was a parrot who screamed "murder" when he wished for an almond, and then another who shouted "shut it, old man" in response. Now, apparently, there was another dog soon to join the family. Miss Mayton named him a treasure that had been gifted to her by Mr. Brummel.

Of course, the various wildlife haunting their halls would be the least of Marianna's surprise this afternoon. She had not imagined that Lord Darden's sisters would be determined on a match. However, they most certainly were.

They'd ended with inquiring into her social schedule. Seeing Lady Rawley in the room, Miss Mayton had explained that she was part of that lady's acting troupe. All the sisters hoped she was planning on attending the performance as it was two days' hence.

She would indeed attend. Her mother had known Lady Rawley since they were girls. The duchess said that every year she received letters from friends outlining the hilarity of the evening. The theatrical was reliably absurd, but Lady Rawley was such a darling that nobody held it against her.

Finally, Lord Darden's sisters had taken their leave. Though, not before Miss Mayton and Lady Rawley had an enthusiastic reunion and explained to everyone that in two days' time they would bring them *All's Well that Ends Well*.

At least, that was what Shakespeare had named the play, Lady Rawley had said enigmatically.

As far as Marianna was concerned, she could not say whether this visit from Lord Darden's sisters had ended well or not. It was terribly confusing.

They were very bold. Really, they were wildly inappropriate. For all that, though, Marianna could not help but be charmed by them. They certainly were making a rather heroic effort to secure their brother's happiness, however misguided that effort was.

It was misguided, was it not?

Lord Darden had not somehow changed his mind, had he?

MISS MAYTON HAD been very satisfied with their visit to Lady Marianna. She felt that she and her girls had successfully pointed out all of Lord Darden's good qualities and extolled the charms of the Bennington family in general. Why marry some young marquess when the delights of the Benningtons awaited? The girl would be a fool to do anything other than wed Lord Darden.

That accomplished, her mind had turned to her own situation. She had acquired a wardrobe for this new stage of life she'd entered, but there were so many bits and bobs still to be purchased!

Sandren had driven her to shop after shop. A ribbon here, a bonnet ordered there, a pair of gloves purchased at the next place. Perhaps the highlight was the pair of shoes she'd ordered for the party at Carlton House. They were delightful silk ballroom slippers in a shade very close to parakeet green.

Now she'd stepped into Rundell and Bridge to examine the jewelry. It would be expensive, but she had plenty of money set by, far more than anybody knew. She'd had the idea that an emerald would really set off her parakeet green velvet. Once the idea had got into her head, she could not get it out again.

She found Mr. Rundell himself at the counter, showing Conbatten a trayful of sapphires.

"Your Grace!" she said. "I had not imagined finding you here."

"Miss Mayton," the duke said. "I am often here. It is my decided opinion that my duchess cannot have enough jewels. At this moment, I have noted a lack of sapphires in her cases and thought to remedy the situation."

"Ah, very sensible," Miss Mayton said. She really could not imagine why Lord Van Doren remained so against arranged kidnappings, it had worked out marvelously for Rosalind—the duke was besotted with her.

"What, pray, brings you here this afternoon?" the duke asked.

"Well you see, I have had a dress made, it is in the shade of parakeet green, and I thought I might find an emerald to wear with it."

"Parakeet green?" the duke asked.

"Just so. It is very vibrant."

"I can well imagine."

"I'm to wear it to Carlton House. Dear Mr. Brummel has

insisted I be invited."

"Has he?"

"Oh yes, ever since I rescued him from an uncomfortable situation, he's been quite taken with me."

The duke narrowed his eyes just a fraction. "Would this be why you've thrown off the widow's weeds, Miss Mayton?"

She could feel herself blush, but there really was no fooling the duke. Very little got by Conbatten. "I find myself in a new chapter, Your Grace."

"I see," the duke said enigmatically. He turned his attention to the tray of sapphires. "That one," he said, choosing the largest of them. "Have it set in platinum and surrounded by these other medium sized stones, and then the smallest on the outside. I would like a leaf and branch pattern connecting them all. Put the whole tray aside, sketch the design, and send it to me for approval."

"Yes, Your Grace," Mr. Rundell said, taking away the tray.

Miss Mayton had become captivated by a lovely emerald necklace that would be just the thing to set off a parakeet green velvet gown. It was simple, which would suit what she was going for—not a girl, but still retaining girlish looks.

A sudden pounding on the window snapped her from her reverie.

"Eloise!" the voice shouted.

She felt her heart nearly stop. Perhaps it had not just nearly stopped but stopped altogether. She slowly turned. There he was. Him. At the very window.

Alongside the panic, her thoughts were that he looked so much older than last they met!

He was here. How had he found her? How would she get away?

"Miss Mayton?" the duke asked.

She snatched up her reticule. That rogue might think he had her trapped, but she would not allow it. It was her opinion that when there was not a way around, then one must go through.

She darted out the door, shoved the man to the pavement, raced to the earl's carriage, and threw herself in. "Go, Sandren! Go with all haste!"

Sandren, appearing very alarmed, did pause for a moment. "You haven't stolen anything?" he asked.

"No! Now go! Go this instant," she cried. She'd take the reins and drive herself if she knew how to. They must get away!

Sandren snapped the reins and the carriage set off.

The man had no chance of catching her, fool that he'd been to alert her to his presence.

She turned and looked out the back window.

Her heart sank a little further than it had already. The duke had collared the man and was dragging him into the shop.

Lord have mercy upon me. The Duke of Conbatten was to hear it all now.

If she knew that scurrilous rogue who was working so hard to find her like she thought she did, he'd tell the duke every last detail.

Those details might be rather hard to explain away, even for her.

The question was, what would the duke do with the information?

Always willing to soothe herself, Miss Mayton began to hope the duke would not do anything at all. Perhaps the man's preposterous story would not even be believed. After all, it *would* seem wildly improbable.

She must just invent a reason why some deranged stranger was shouting at her on the street and accusing her of things.

Certainly, she could think of something.

Though she was cheered by these musings, she did still find herself rather out of breath upon reaching Portland Place. That sprint to the carriage had knocked it out of her. She'd not actually run anywhere since she was a girl.

The wide-eyed groom helped her down to the pavement.

As she made her way to the doors, she called over her shoulder, "That was nothing at all, Sandren. Nothing at all to wonder over."

Mr. Tattleton opened the door and she charged past him. "I am going for a rest, Tattleton," she said, heaving in breaths. "I am not at home to anybody. Nobody at all!"

She climbed the stairs, though at this moment each rise seemed like a Swiss Alp. Reaching her bedchamber, she collapsed gratefully into a chair.

What an afternoon.

CHAPTER NINE

TATTLETON WAS WELL-USED to the eccentricities of Miss Mayton, but this was something new.

She'd come into the house as if she were running for her life and claimed she was not at home to anybody. In general, she was at home for anybody who cared to turn up on their doorstep at any time of day or night. Further, he'd certainly never seen her move so fast. He was determined to get to the bottom of it.

He told Benny and Johnny he was going for a walk, and then ignored their looks of surprise. They knew perfectly well that he did not favor strolling round with no destination or purpose in mind.

Tattleton made his way to the stables and requested a private interview with the coachman.

Sandren led him into his quarters and, just as the last time he had ventured thus, the place was neat as a pin. He had no idea how the coachman managed it. How did he keep bits of hay from setting up shop in every corner and crevice?

"You'll want to know what Miss Mayton was up to, I reckon, Mr. Tattleton. I'll not tell any tales, I'd like to know it too."

It was evident that Sandren did not understand what Miss Mayton had been up to, but had recognized that she'd been up to something.

"Perhaps if you can tell me where you went and what you observed, we might be able to get to the bottom of it," Tattleton said, rubbing his chin.

"Where didn't we go?" Sandren said. "Miss Mayton did her shopping all over Town. The last stop was to Rundell and Bridge."

"The jewelers?" Tattleton asked. What on earth was she doing at a jewelers? The earl did not give her an allowance that would afford the purchase of jewels.

"Aye," Sandren said. "Now, I can't say what went on in that shop, but all the sudden I hear a fella shout, 'Eloise.'"

"That is her given name!" Tattleton said.

"Aye. And so I turn and what do I see? Miss Mayton comes out of the shop like she was an arrow launched from a bow, tackles the fella to the ground, jumps in the carriage, and orders me to get going. I asked, you didn't steal anything, did ya? 'Cause it seemed hard to believe she would, but why else would she push a fellow down and run for her life?"

"Indeed, why push a man down and then run?"

"She says no, she didn't steal anything and orders me to set off and so I do. I did get a glance behind me to see if the fella was a-chasin' us, but he weren't. The Duke of Conbatten had him by the collar."

"The duke!"

"Aye. And that's all I know of the thing, Mr. Tattleton. 'Cept when we got here, she told me I wasn't to wonder about it."

"I bet she did."

"That's a bad business, to my mind. You can't force a person not to wonder if they're set on wondering."

"You certainly cannot," Tattleton said. "If a person begins to wonder over something, good luck trying to stop it. At this moment, I find I am prepared to wonder over this matter for as long as may be necessary."

Whatever this situation was, and Tattleton had a very good idea that this man who had shouted Eloise was the same who had knocked on the door in Somerset. Who was he? What did he want?

The Duke of Conbatten had grabbed hold of the man. That meant the whole truth of the situation would come to light.

Perhaps Miss Mayton's unfortunate hold on the Benningtons was nearing a satisfying end.

He'd had his suspicions all along. Now they would finally see what she was!

Of course, he was not altogether clear on what exactly Miss Mayton was, but they would all soon find out!

❧

DARDEN HAD GONE to the YBC to find Hamill. Fortunately, jests about the flying viscount had begun to fade. Henderson had moved on and named Lord Dunston "Doddering Dunston" for a late-night drunken episode involving several falls on the pavement.

Hamill was playing cards and Darden unceremoniously dragged him away.

Finding a quiet corner, he said, "Apparently, my sisters intend on calling on Lady Marianna with some idea of supporting me in my suit. Can you stop them before Thursday?"

"Thursday?" Hamill asked.

"Yes, Thursday. That is Lady Marianna's at-home day."

For some reason, Hamill was looking rather green.

"Uh, some bad news on that front, old boy," he said.

"What? What bad news?" Darden asked.

"The lady's at-home is on Tuesdays. Yesterday."

"What!"

Hamill nodded sadly.

"They went already? What happened? What did they say to Lady Marianna?"

Hamill squirmed in his chair. "Well, all Jules said was it was very pleasant, and they talked about what a swell fellow you were, and how the earl was so genial, and how the estate in

Somerset was very pleasant, and…"

Hamill had trailed off, which Darden did not think a good sign at all.

"And what?" Darden said, in a dark tone that rather surprised him.

"And that *your* earl wouldn't mind if *he* were defied over one of *his* daughters' choices of a husband."

"They went that far!"

Hamill sighed. "Come, now. You knew they would go that far."

"No, I only *worried* that they'd go that far," Darden said. "My god, what must Lady Marianna be thinking of all this?"

"Now, Darden, is it really that bad that she understands your feelings?" Hamill asked hopefully. "A gentleman might even find it convenient. Instead of having to surprise the lady when you declared yourself, she'll be ready for it."

"That's the problem!" Darden nearly shouted.

Seeing he'd gained the attention of some of the gentlemen at other tables, he lowered his voice.

"It was all a ruse, Hamill. Do not you see? I intended to put my sisters off by claiming I wished to attain the unattainable lady. Lady Marianna has known all about it since the beginning."

Hamill spent some moments taking that idea in. "So, you're *not* set on Lady Marianna?"

"As I said, it was just a ruse to throw my sisters off my trail. Naturally, if I had reached that moment in my life where I was prepared to consider marriage, well, she is very pretty, and she's got a wit about her, and a certain style, and that smashing hair. Of course, it would be the most usual thing in the world if she were in the running."

"But she's not in the running now?"

"There is no running to be in now." Darden raked his hair. "What would she have thought of this visit from my sisters, though? She might think the ruse is off, that I'd somehow grown feelings, she might expect…what am I to do?"

Hamill shrugged. "You could marry her, I suppose. You could do worse."

He could do worse. That was exactly what he'd said to Wellerston.

But he was not ready to wed. The decision was so…lifelong.

The question of when he would be ready had presented itself to his mind on occasion. But so far, it remained the far-off fence.

It was true what he'd said to Hamill, though. If he had been ready to take the monumental step, Lady Marianna would be in the running.

No, the truth was not even that. She would be well ahead in the running.

There probably would not be anybody else in the running.

But he was not ready, and Lady Marianna would never have had him if he was.

That. That right there was the answer. Did it really matter if Lady Marianna believed his sisters and began to think that his feelings had changed? That his hanging about was no longer a ruse?

No, it did not matter. Because Lady Marianna was determined to honor her father's wishes and wed either Wellerston or Mayfield.

At least, if she had not been somehow convinced to defy her father.

No, his harebrained sisters could not have convinced a sensible lady to reverse a decision she had no doubt given careful consideration to. She would wed Wellerston or Mayfield.

He could not, at that moment, account for the sinking feeling that came over him.

He supposed it was having put her in such a situation. It was her first season and he'd dragged her into a ruse she had no business being in. It had been self-interested on his part, he could see that now. He was even more afraid it had crossed into ungentlemanly territory.

Aside from that, it seemed just a shame that a woman like

Marianna should be wasted on such untested youths. They were both still boys, really. They were reaching for manhood, which they would get to eventually, but they were not quite there yet.

He ought to know—he clearly remembered being in their shoes. Swaggering around, attempting to convey that he knew more than he did, and all along feeling like he was floundering in a sea of older men who were cognizant of the fact that he did not know much.

"This is what I say, Darden," Hamill said. "If Lady Marianna knew all along that you were claiming you were interested as part of a ruse, then I suppose she won't be put out about anything your sisters might have said to her. She might even think it funny."

"Funny?"

"Of course, Jules won't find this funny," Hamill said. He looked rather stricken over that idea. "She won't like that she was fooled. None of them will."

"I suggest you do not mention it, then," Darden said.

Hamill nodded. "I don't like to keep things from Juliet," he said. "On the other hand, she might write an ode about this. She might even write more than one."

"I must just think of a way to approach Lady Marianna. Perhaps I joke about it, and then she can joke about it too," Darden said thoughtfully.

"Whatever you propose to do, think it up before the morrow."

"Why? Why must I settle on something by the morrow?"

"Because tomorrow is Lady Rawley's theatrical evening and Lady Marianna is going to be there."

Darden snorted. "Lady Rawley's theatrical? I have no intention of attending it."

Hamill fiddled with his cup. "I think you'll find your sisters have pressured the earl to come, in support of Miss Mayton and Lady Harveston, who both have parts to play. It seems they have equally convinced the old soldier that you must come too. I'm pretty sure he'll be informing you of it."

Darden sat back. "They are diabolical. My sisters are positively diabolical."

Hamill shrugged. "But lovely all the same," he said. "Jules could set the house on fire and I'd likely only notice how pretty she looked doing it."

"She's got you wrapped round her finger, Hamill."

"Yes. Yes, she does."

⇥⟫⟩⟨⟪⇤

MARIANNA'S FATHER HAD not deigned to attend Lady Rawley's theatrical evening. He'd said it sounded absurd and it was not likely to see the likes of Wellerston or Mayfield. He would not be dragged away from his cards unless there was a chance that one of those two gentlemen would turn up, which he was certain they would not.

She was glad her father would not attend. Lord Darden's sisters had assured her that their brother *would* turn up, and she did not know what she thought about it. Other than to be grateful that she would not have to witness any rude behavior toward the viscount from her father.

As well, she could not help the simmering resentment that seemed to be growing in her heart over her father's plans. The theater, and its accompanying humiliations, had seemed to let something loose within her.

She had begun forming opinions she'd never dared hold before.

Marianna was well aware that her father loved her and wished the best for her. But she was not a pawn to be moved round a chessboard! She was a thinking and feeling person. Had he lost sight of that?

All of this was heavy on her mind as the carriage made its way to Lady Rawley's house.

Her mother pulled the invitation from her reticule. "Listen to this, Marianna. This evening is sure to be vastly amusing."

Her mother read the paper.

In this exciting new idea of All's Well that Ends Well, *more aptly renamed* All's Well that Ends Appropriately, *it SEEMS as if things proceed as expected, until the final question must be answered. Will Bertram accept Helen as his wife? Will it be as usual, or will a righteous lady claim her power? (Heads are spinning as the innocent rise up!) All will become known in the most dramatic terms in a final revealing moment.*

Cast:
Helen played by the incomparable Lady Margaret Rawley
Diana played by the indomitable Lady Cordelia Harveston
Bertram played by the indubitable Lady Agatha Montfried
The French King played by the indispensable Mrs. Jemima Robinson
The Italian prostitute played by the ingenious Miss Eloise Mayton

The duchess folded the paper and tucked it back into her reticule. "Goodness, Lady Rawley is very bold indeed. An Italian prostitute? What is an Italian prostitute doing in this play? And one wonders how she convinced Miss Mayton to agree to such a role."

"Miss Mayton seems a very genial lady," Marianna said. "But perhaps not overburdened with caution?"

"Or a drop of sense, I imagine," the duchess said. "Gracious, that reminds me that I never told you of the amusing conversation I had with Lady Rawley and Lady Hightower when they came to our at-home. Naturally, Lady Hightower made hay over Lord Darden falling asleep and falling off his chair."

"Which we decided was entirely Miss Nesterling's fault," Marianna said, smiling.

"We were right about that—Lady Hightower thought just the same. But here is something amusing—it seems Lord Darden never comes to her musical evening. Rather, he has been in the habit of sending elaborate regrets. They are *so* elaborate that Lady Hightower's servants have invented a game inspired by them."

"A game?"

"It is called *Devastating Reasons the Lord Cannot Come.*"

Marianna giggled in spite of herself. It was too ridiculous.

"In any case, Lady Hightower is certain Lord Darden came because a certain lady would play and she was equally certain the lady was you. Lady Rawley was practically swooning over the idea. It seems everyone but your father views him as quite the catch."

Marianna turned her face away. She was beginning to think she might have to tell her mother about Lord Darden's ruse, as the duchess seemed to grow rather fond of him.

It was as if the duchess had dismissed her duke's plans out of hand and had forgotten all about Lord Mayfield and Lord Wellerston. She was beginning to wish she could do the same. She was beginning to wish she could take on her mother's stance, say no to her father, and brace herself for whatever thunder and lightning was the result of it.

For all that, though, she did not wish to tell her mother of Lord Darden's ruse. For one, it was embarrassing, and for another, the duchess would be furious that her daughter had been dragged into such a thing.

"I believe Lord Darden is a confirmed bachelor, Mama," she said. "He is in for his seventh season, after all. He is only being friendly, I am sure."

In truth, Marianna thought it might well be the case that Lord Darden never intended to wed. Seven seasons and he was still dodging the idea must say something.

The duchess sniffed. "His sisters think otherwise, it seems to me."

Of course, it had seemed so to Marianna too. But she did not know anything for certain. Lord Darden's sisters were in all likelihood misguided. They'd been fooled by the lord's ruse and had simply not reacted the way he'd predicted they would.

But they'd said so much, and so directly! It seemed outlandish that they would have dared it unless they had informed the lord that they would.

There was the slightest chance he'd changed his mind about the ruse. Not a large chance, but a chance, nonetheless.

What a muddle.

"Ah, here we are. Let us proceed in and discover what an Italian prostitute is doing in Lady Rawley's drawing room."

HAMILL HAD TOLD no tales—Darden's sisters had assured that he would be boxed into attending Lady Rawley's theatrical. Darden had been informed by the earl that he must indeed attend, as it had become very nearly a matter of family honor. Both Miss Mayton and Cordelia were regular members of Lady Rawley's acting troupe and they could not be let down.

Once the earl was convinced, it had been an easy leap to supposing Darden must be convinced too. Or, as the earl had said, "Sometimes one must put aside one's own preferences in support of one's family."

Support of one's family, indeed.

Nevertheless, there had not been a way to slip out of it. His father was so lenient with him and rarely questioned anything he did. If the old soldier asked him to attend an evening, he could not see throwing down the gauntlet over it.

If the description of the theatrical and what he saw upon entering the drawing room did not deceive him, it would be absurdity piled atop absurdity.

Lady Rawley as Helen, Cordelia as Diana, and Miss Mayton as, heaven help her, an Italian prostitute, were all dressed identically. Long black veils hid their faces and long gowns protruded with the signs of a baby on the near horizon, only the ladies' various heights and widths giving them away. Why all three ladies were costumed to appear as if they were carrying a child, he could not imagine. Perhaps the hapless Bertram was soon to be the father of three?

Lady Agatha, who was to play Bertram, was dressed as some sort of medieval dandy who had accidentally donned a skirt instead of trousers. There were medals pinned all over the front of her coat, as if Bertram had performed heroically in battle.

Mrs. Robinson played the French King, and it was clear that the troupe had carefully examined a portrait of Louis XIV. Where would they have even located such a wig? The lady was drowning under a mass of long black curls as if a kraken risen from the deep sat upon her head.

"Father, Darden," Viola said, striding up to them. Lord Harveston accompanied her, as of course he must attend. His wife was poised to tread the boards as Diana.

"Earl, Darden," Lord Harveston said.

Darden narrowed his eyes at Viola, as he did not see her own husband anywhere. "Where is Baderston, pray?"

Viola looked momentarily flustered, but recovered herself. "Oh, well he is devastated to miss it, of course. But he had an important engagement. With someone or other."

Darden for the smallest moment thought the earl must realize he'd been bamboozled into coming. With the exception of Harveston, who could not possibly wiggle out of it, there was not another son-in-law to be found. Nor were there any sisters. Where was all this support for the family they'd talked about?

"Well," the earl said genially, "I suppose he's sorry to miss it. We will be sure to tell him all about it when we get the chance."

Darden sighed. His father was such a good old soul. It was usually something he appreciated, but just now he'd prefer the earl to be a little more suspicious!

"Oh look!" Viola said. "There is Lady Marianna. I do so adore her. Father, you must be introduced to Lady Marianna."

Before the earl could indicate his joy or otherwise at the notion, Viola had flown off to retrieve the lady.

Darden glanced behind him, and then wished he did not. Viola was practically dragging Lady Marianna and the duchess to their party.

Subtlety was not Viola's strong suit.

Lady Marianna was looking very well, as it seemed she always did. Her golden hair glowed in the candlelight and her delicate features were so pretty! Her dress was restrained, as seemed to be her preference. It was a deep green silk with no decoration, but it was cut to perfection. Just now, she appeared a goddess in a garden of blown peonies.

She really was divine to look at, though he turned away so he would not be caught out staring.

Darden turned to Harveston, who would know perfectly well what was unfolding just now.

Harveston would not even meet his eye, the traitor.

"Your Grace, Lady Marianna, may I present you to my father, the Earl of Westmont," Viola said.

Darden could not help but notice two things—the duchess appeared vastly amused by Viola's machinations and Lady Marianna appeared mortified.

"A pleasure to know you, Your Grace, Lady Marianna," the earl said.

Lady Marianna curtsied. Her mother said, "Do call me Duchess, Earl."

"Very kind," the earl said.

"Father," Viola said, "all of my sisters, and our aunt too, have been talking about how much we adore Lady Marianna."

"Ah, I see," the earl said. "Well I do not suppose there is any reason why you wouldn't."

Poor Father, what on earth was one to say to such a statement?

The duchess wore a small smile. "Earl, my house was graced with a visit from all your daughters and Miss Mayton. It was quite the entourage."

Another thing the earl could not hope to answer with any sense.

Lord Iverson interrupted them from the front of the room, calling out, "Dear ladies and esteemed gentlemen, if you would be so kind as to take your seats."

Darden had never been so happy to hear from Iverson as he was at that moment.

At least, he'd imagined all embarrassment must come to an end when the play was set to begin. Embarrassment for him, anyway. What would occur onstage was another matter.

What happened next, though, he could hardly explain.

There was some hurried urging from Viola that the duchess and Lady Marianna must come with her, and at the same time she had him firmly by the arm. Very firmly.

Before he had a moment to understand her intent, he was practically thrown into the first row and found himself sitting next to Lady Marianna, with the duchess laughing into her handkerchief on the lady's other side.

Viola was to his left. She patted his arm and whispered, "You know you can always count on your sisters, dear brother."

Those sisters he was assured he could count on were positively diabolical. It was not that he minded being seated next to Lady Marianna, not in the least. But he would not wish the lady to get any ideas!

Still, here he was and she had a subtle scent of violets. He had a great urge to lean over toward her, though he did no such thing.

"Here we are," Lord Iverson said, "at another of Lady Rawley's wildly creative theatrical evenings. Gracious, it seems only yesterday that we gathered here last year to be bowled over by a new version of *Hamlet*. This evening, our dear Lady Rawley brings us *All's Well that Ends...Appropriately*. Yes! She has changed the name of *All's Well that Ends Well*. I am on tenterhooks to see what our esteemed thespians have in store for us."

Lord Iverson led the applause as Lady Rawley graciously bowed her head.

Darden only hoped this *evening* would end appropriately, though he had not much hope of it.

CHAPTER TEN

MARIANNA WAS HARD pressed to ignore that she sat so close to Lord Darden. His arm had brushed her arm and she had been surprised by the way it made her feel.

All along, she had been entirely uninterested in both Wellerston and Mayfield. She had, if she were to be honest, been uninterested in the entire season. She'd wished to be at home, with everything and everybody she knew. She wished to be strolling to the village and chatting with Mrs. Rightwell, the mistress of their modest haberdashery, or calling to Mr. Tidwell that she hoped his cow was recovered, or slipping a coin to naughty little Jimmy Sedkin.

There had been a strong attraction to Lord Darden because, after all, he was the most handsome man in any room, but that had not seemed to lessen her longing for home. Now, there was something about touching his person that made her wish to throw off ideas of home and think of new ideas.

Very new and scandalous ideas.

She was certain her mother would be shocked to know what thoughts drifted through her daughter's mind just now. She was rather shocked herself and grateful that the one thing a person could keep forever private were their thoughts.

Marianna put her attention to the stage, determined to forget that Lord Darden was by her side.

It must be granted that Lady Rawley was a great help in that regard. Never in her life had Marianna witnessed anything so distracting.

Lady Rawley, Lady Cordelia, and Miss Mayton were all disguised, their protruding waistlines giving the idea that all three were with child. They stood in a line and all three had their hands clasped behind their backs.

Lady Rawley stepped forward. "It is I, Helen!"

Lady Agatha, playing Bertram, staggered back. "What? Helen! No! You hath died. You're supposed to be dead? Why aren't you hath dead?"

"Silence!" Lady Rawley's Helen shouted. "Though we all three hath the appearance of carrying a child, only one of us hath carries a child and that child is *your* child! That same lady wears your ring."

"She hath weareth my ring, did you say?" Bertram cried. "Then it can only be my dearest Diana! It can be no one else! I giveth Diana my ring on the night that we hath…that we…well, you know what we did! This is a dream cometh true!"

"Silence!" Lady Rawley shrieked. "Recall that you hath proclaimeth to all and sundry that you would only be married to the woman who carried your child and weareth your ring. Hath you the steadfastness to stand by it?"

"Yes, yes I do!" Bertram said, clapping his hands together. "I am rid of *you* and I hath Diana as my own! I hath won the game! I am the winner!"

"Silence!" Lady Rawley shouted.

For a lady who kept yelling about silence, Marianna thought Helen did not seem very inclined to the state.

"You fool," Lady Rawley went on, pacing the stage like a caged tiger. "When you thought you hath lain with Diana, I toldeth her you were already wed and convinced her to switch places with me. Then, unbeknownst to *her*, and to you too you great big buffoon, *I* hath switched with a prostitute I found down the street. It hath been a double switch!"

"A double switch?" Bertram asked.

"A double switch!" Lady Rawley shouted triumphantly. "You are now wed, Bertram, to an Italian prostitute!"

Bertram held his head in his hands. "No! It cannot be! Hath it? Yes? Is it possible? No! It cannot be possible!"

Bertram suddenly fell to the floor. "Yes. Blast it, I hath known she seemed too experienced!"

Marianna's mother let out a sound that was very like a hiccup. She knew perfectly well it was the duchess' attempt to stifle hysterical laughter.

"Silence!" Lady Rawley shouted at the now despondent Bertram.

At what Marianna hoped was the last call for silence, all three ladies threw off their veils and cloaks. Lady Rawley as Helen and Lady Cordelia as Diana removed the pillows round their waist to reveal that they were not, in fact, with child.

Miss Mayton, daringly playing the prostitute who'd been found down the street somewhere in Naples, remained with her pillow in place and held out her hand to show the ring.

"I donteth carry your child nor weareth your ring," Cordelia as Diana said.

"And I donteth carry your child nor weareth your ring," Lady Rawley as Helen said.

"I do-ith carry your child and do-ith weareth your ring," Miss Mayton cried. "Me benedica, I hath become a proper lady now! My life of…past other things I used to do for a living…hath come to an end! I will liveth in the lap of luxury and groweth very fat from your table, caro signore."

As Bertram wept, all eyes onstage turned to the king, played by Mrs. Robinson. She clutched her belly and heaved with laughter. "That is good, very goodeth indeed. I hath never liked Bertram and now he's married to an Italian prostitute! Now, my two good ladies, Helen and Diana, you will chooseth from among my courtiers any you wish to wed."

"We can chooseth for ourselves," Lady Rawley cried triumphantly.

"It hath be our decision," Lady Cordelia said.

Her mother leaned close to Marianna's ear and whispered, "Remember, it hath always been your decision too."

"Gracious me," the king said jovially, "If I am not mistaken, this hath been a case of all's well that ends appropriately."

There was a moment of silence while the audience took in what they'd just witnessed and slowly became cognizant that it had come to a blessed end.

As the applause began, Marianna said, "That was astonishing."

Lord Darden erupted into laughter over the comment. "I cannot think of a better description."

"Are all the theatricals so…well so…like that?" Marianna asked.

"Highly likely," Lord Darden said. "In the last I attended, Romeo and Juliet hath lived happily ever after."

Marianna laughed. "As they always should have. Really, the two of them were annoyingly idiotic."

"As Shakespeare's doomed lovers often are," Lord Darden said. "I recall that they named their firstborn son Romiet, so their idiocy lived happily on."

"Ah well, I suppose Shakespeare's cronies played a game about it—devastating reasons the couple cannot live."

As she had imagined, this reference to Lady Hightower's servants inventing a game about his excuses caught Lord Darden off guard. He recovered himself. "I suppose the whole world now knows that Lady Hightower *and* her butler never believed any of the regrets I've sent over the years."

Marianna giggled. "They invented a game, it is funny, I thought."

"It is, rather," Lord Darden admitted. "It seems I am to be the subject of jokes all season. The members of my club named me the flying viscount, for reasons you can probably guess at."

Marianna bit her lip. "I do not suppose you can be blamed for becoming suddenly unseated at Lady Hightower's musical evening. The piece was a bit slow."

"And long."

"Yes, yes it was."

He'd turned to talk to Marianna and was near enough that she could smell his scent. It was manly, as if pine needles and woodsmoke had intertwined. She restrained herself from leaning closer.

Lady Viola stood and said, "Your Grace, Lady Marianna, do not move an inch. Lord Harveston has been sent to the sideboard to get you refreshment. You can stay jolly right where you are, Harveston can be trusted to make up a well-done plate and choose the best wine. Darden, you will stay and entertain the ladies."

Though Marianna had got an inkling of how bold and managing Lord Darden's sisters could be, it seemed there was no length they would not go to.

She heard her mother positively snort on her other side.

What did it mean, though? Did Lady Viola act with her brother's blessing, or did she act because she'd fallen for his ruse and thought she was helping him though he did not wish to be helped?

"Lord Darden," the duchess said, leaning round Marianna, "do ask Lord Harveston to leave my plate on the table, I will return in a moment. I must go and congratulate Lady Rawley for this evening's entertainment."

Lord Darden nodded. "As you wish, Your Grace."

As she rose, the duchess laughed and said, "And it *was* entertaining."

Marianna had no doubt that her mother would seek out Lady Rawley, but she also felt as if her departure was conveniently timed and she was being managed in some fashion.

Left sitting alone with Lord Darden, she was determined to be direct. She must have answers to the questions swirling in her mind. She said, "My lord, your sisters are making a concerted effort to bring us together. I am afraid your ruse has not had the effect you had hoped for."

Now she waited. What would he say to it? Was it possible he'd say it was no longer a ruse?

She could hardly breathe and suddenly her dress felt too tight. It was as if there was not enough air in the room.

"I am glad you brought it up," Lord Darden said, "as I wished to bring it up myself but was not certain how to approach it."

What did that mean? Say what you mean!

"My sisters, well they are…let us call it determined. Now, mind you, I should have seen it would be so. After all, were I looking toward marriage, you would of course have been in the running."

"In the running?" Marianna asked. She felt at once disappointed and insulted. In the running?

"Well, in a manner of speaking. You know what I mean," Lord Darden said.

"Do I?" she asked. "I had not known that a gentleman looking to wed viewed it as a horserace."

"A horserace? No, that is not it. What I mean is, had I been looking to marry, of course I would be looking in your direction. Why wouldn't I?"

"How gallant," Marianna said, not quite keeping the bitterness from her tone.

"And had that been the case, it would have been all up with me," Lord Darden pressed on, ignoring her insult. "You are to marry Wellerston or Mayfield, after all. So it really is just as well…"

"We'll see what I do," Marianna said.

Lord Harveston returned with a plate of cakes and jellies and a glass of wine. A footman behind him carried another plate.

The lord glanced at the empty chair beside her.

Marianna said, "Lord Harveston, my mother requested you leave her plate on the table, she will return for it."

Lord Harveston nodded and set down her own plate, handing her the glass of wine.

"I do thank you, my lord," Marianna said, working to keep her tone pleasant. She rose and said, "I will go and give Lady Rawley my congratulations."

She did not turn to take her leave of Lord Darden but left him sitting alone in his chair.

He could sit alone for all eternity, thinking about his ridiculous horserace.

She would have been in the running, indeed.

⤜⤛⤚⤙

DARDEN HAD BEEN left with the awkwardness of sitting alone after Lady Marianna had taken her wine and stalked off without even a nod to him.

Harveston had looked at him quizzically, but rather than attempt to explain the unexplainable, he'd just shaken his head.

Harveston moved off and not a moment later, Lady Marianna's mother returned. She did not sit but took up her glass of wine from the small table.

"I see my daughter has left you on your own, Lord Darden."

"Ah, yes, I believe she has gone to convey her congratulations to Lady Rawley, Your Grace."

"Is that all she's done?" the duchess asked.

It was rather direct, what on earth was he supposed to say to it?

"I ask, because it seemed to me, at least from a distance," the duchess went on, "that her departure was rather curt."

Even more direct.

"I imagine, Your Grace, that Lady Marianna finds me an irritating sort of person."

"Hm," the duchess said. "I doubt that is it. Well, we'll see what she does, in the end."

The duchess moved off and Darden was left to ponder the lady's words. They were in the same vein as what Lady Marianna herself had said. She'd said, we'll see what I do. Now the duchess was wondering what her daughter would do.

What did it mean? Did it mean she would not have Wellerston or Mayfield?

The idea that she would refuse her father's directives and choose for herself buoyed him up in some strange way. It was not as if it would have any effect on his own plans…at least, he did not imagine so. But then, it oddly felt as if it might.

That idea had been like an itch scratching at his brain—what if, what if, what if.

If she refused Mayfield and Wellerston, it might affect him.

It *would* affect him. That was what the itch kept pointing out.

But how had it happened? Where had this itch come from? Seven seasons in and he'd not been itching once.

He supposed if anybody were to prompt an itch in his brain it *would* be Lady Marianna. Still, it felt as if it had snuck up behind him with no warning.

In the carriage with the earl, he said, "Father, how did you know that it was the right time to consider marriage?"

The earl laughed. "Oh, I never knew it was the right time to think about a wedding, gentlemen seldom do."

"But then, how…"

"I only knew it was the right time to secure your mother. I remember wondering how many ladies like her would come along. And then I realized, probably none at all. Was I to be a fool and allow her to slip through my hands? Or was I to march forward with the thing? As you know, I marched forward."

Darden sat back. It did make sense. His father had not ever decided to marry, he'd just decided he'd best not allow a particular lady to get away.

What if Lady Marianna would actually consider him? What then?

He'd been thinking about her quite a lot over the past days. He'd fooled himself into imagining that he'd been thinking about her because of the ruse. He'd assured himself that he'd been thinking of her because of the cat and mouse game with his sisters. But really, what did Lady Marianna's golden hair and her clever wit and her scent of violets have to do with the ruse?

Sitting next to her this evening, well, he'd hardly managed to keep his eyes on the play. He'd spent most of it glancing down at her delicate hands folded in her lap and having a great urge to slip one of his own hands between that delightful pairing.

He sighed. "If I *have* encountered such a lady, I think I've made a terrible mess of it."

The earl laughed long and deep. "Gracious, you must not let that stop you. You'd hardly be a Bennington if you hadn't somehow made a mess of it."

That was true. All along, he'd been confounded over his sisters' various methods of arriving to an altar. It had been one near disaster after the next. Why should he be any different?

If he wished to pursue Lady Marianna, and he was very speedily realizing that he did, he must not be put off by this setback.

It had been a rather dire mistake to talk about her being *in the running* if he'd been inclined to wed. She had not liked that at all. It was a stupid thing to say, implying that there might be a whole gaggle of ladies racing alongside her, waiting for him to make his choice.

Yes, very stupid indeed. She must think his opinion of himself was as big as all England.

But then, if she did not have any ideas about him, why should she have cared about it? All he had to do was clear up that he was not so against marriage as he'd thought and that there would have only been one woman he'd consider and there was no *in the running* and never had been.

That was not so much to clear up, was it?

"Darden," the earl said, "I must guess the lady you think of is Lady Marianna?"

Darden nodded.

"I see," the earl said. "She is the one who is meant to wed one of two gentlemen chosen by her father?"

"Yes, Wellerston or Mayfield. They're both to be dukes."

"Ah," the earl said. "Perhaps, then, you might wish to ingratiate yourself with the duke. If he is to be disappointed, that might soften the blow."

The earl was right, of course. But how to ingratiate himself with the old gentleman? The duke very clearly did not approve of him. He did not even know much about him, other than he was a lowly viscount prone to falling out of his chair in the middle of a musical evening.

"Perhaps we might hold a dinner," the earl said. "We'd have to schedule it for a month from now to have any chance of him and anybody else we include to have an opening on their calendar."

"I very much doubt an opening on the duke's calendar will garner his acceptance of an invitation from me," Darden said.

"No, but he's got a wife, does he not? The duchess seemed very inclined to like you. I can assure you, Darden, that if a wife wishes a husband to attend a thing, that fellow will find himself attending a thing."

"That's true," Darden said. "My sisters' husbands have turned into limp macaronis. Even Van Doren is managed."

The earl nodded, as if he'd never expected any other result. "We address the invitation to the duchess and then we see what she does with it. In any case, the delay will work to your advantage. As you hinted, you have some ground to make up."

Darden nodded. It was very odd, but now that he'd decided that he would pursue Lady Marianna, it felt the most natural thing in the world.

What had he been doing, pretending at this ruse and swearing he was not ready to wed? It had almost become a habit of some sort—he did not like peach jam, thought piquet was headache-inducing, would always take claret over Canary, and would prefer not to wed at this moment. He'd thought about *not* marrying so many times that it had seemed an immutable fact about him.

But the very idea that Lady Marianna would wed Wellerston or Mayfield, or any other man, made him feel a little sick.

Now that he'd let his thoughts loose on the subject, all sorts of ideas that had been hiding somewhere raced to his notice. He imagined unpinning her hair and helping her out of her dress and a few other things he'd never tell a living soul.

The marital fence, which had always been in the distance, was right in front of him. Very suddenly, it seemed an easy jump. For him, anyway. His father was right, though, he had some ground to make up.

Invitations to a dinner would go out. He would invite the duke, the duchess, and Lady Marianna. Other than that, it would be a family affair, with all his sisters and their husbands. He'd need some propping up in the duke's eyes and his family would be more than willing to do it.

More immediately, he must gather together his sisters, and Miss Mayton too. They must be brought to understand that his pursuit of Lady Marianna had been a ruse but was a ruse no more.

It would be a convoluted sort of explanation, but they were Benningtons. They would understand him perfectly.

CHAPTER ELEVEN

MARIANNA HAD MUCH rather have stayed at the house, alone in her bedchamber to brew and stew over Lord Darden. Her mother would not allow it, though.

Now that Lord Darden's sisters and Miss Mayton had called upon them and gained entrance, it was their duty to return the call upon each one of the ladies. Six different calls to six different houses.

At least, she'd thought it would be six. As it happened, Miss Mayton did not host an at-home and then Lady Hamill resided with her in-laws so they might consider themselves excused there unless her duke and duchess were to call upon them.

Still, four was plenty to get through.

Lady Van Doren's at-home was the first on the list and Marianna was all too aware that the house sat directly across the avenue of Portland Place from Lord Darden's residence.

Would he call upon his sister? If he did, what stance should she take with him? She'd left him very abruptly, a bit rudely, at Lady Rawley's theatrical. He'd earned it, she thought. Her hopes were disappointed, she was stung a thousand times over, and she was determined that nobody should know it. There was little worse for a lady than disappointed hopes, other than publicly known disappointed hopes.

And, she did have disappointed hopes. All along, she'd not allowed herself to think too much into the future or whether she would do her father's bidding.

Now that there was no question of her needing to defy her father over a certain viscount, she realized she very much wished there was.

She was also confused. Lord Darden had told her that if he were interested in marrying, she'd have been in the running. Hardly a declaration or a flattery, but not a dismissal either.

What did it mean? Did it mean it was her bad luck not to be coming next season, or the next, or the next?

Lord Darden had been in Town for seven seasons, what on earth was he waiting for? What if she wed nobody this season and came back next year? Would he be ready then? Or would she foolishly come back season after season and he was never ready.

Or worse, he thought he was not ready and then found himself bowled over by some lady. That was probably the likeliest conclusion. Marianna guessed there had been no end of gentlemen over the years who were determined to stay a bachelor, but then met a lady who upended all their ideas.

Perhaps that was what stung her the most. She would not be the lady that prompted him to throw over all his ideas to secure her. She supposed she was pleasant, but not compelling enough.

"Marianna," the duchess said, as they walked to Lady Beatrice's door, "I do believe you are turning into a brooder."

Marianna forced a smile. "Certainly not, Mama."

"Well, chin up, my girl. I feel confident things will work themselves out."

Marianna did not inquire what things her mother referred to.

They were admitted to Lady Van Doren's drawing room and found their hostess with two of her sisters—the Duchess of Conbatten and Lady Hamill.

Marianna had a passing thought of how approving her father would be of those two sisters—one was a duchess, and one was a marchioness who would assume the mantle sometime in future. It was precisely what she was meant to be doing herself.

"Your Grace, Lady Marianna," Lady Van Doren said. "How

pleased I am to see you here. Do make yourself at home."

"I will send word across the street," Lady Hamill said. "Our aunt and Darden will wish to hurry over, I am sure."

Marianna hoped she kept her features composed. Encounters with the Benningtons were like trying to steady oneself on the deck of a rolling ship on high seas. She had wondered if she would encounter Lord Darden, and then found herself at once disappointed and relieved to find him absent. It had never occurred to her that he would be sent for.

But sent for he had been. Marianna faced the windows overlooking the avenue and watched a footman run across it and knock on the door.

Perhaps Lord Darden would be told she was here and not wish to come. Perhaps he'd send one of his outlandish devastating reasons he could not come.

Lady Van Doren poured the tea and said, "We understand from Viola that you attended Lady Rawley's theatrical. I was very sorry to miss it, but my lord cannot abide theatricals."

The Duchess of Conbatten laughed. "The truth of it is, Van Doren cannot abide much, with the exception of his wife and daughter. We are fond of him in our own way, though, as he adores them both."

Marianna had no idea what she was meant to say to that, and she supposed her mother did not either.

Lady Hamill had seated herself and said, "Viola told us Lady Rawley's latest play was positively smashing. She said our Miss Mayton and Cordelia were particularly inspired."

Marianna hid the amusement from her features and looked to her mother to see what she would say about it.

"It was the most original thing I can ever remember seeing," the duchess said.

There was a sudden fracas to be heard, coming from the street. Marianna looked out.

Her breath caught. There was Lord Darden, looking as wonderful as ever.

But what on earth was he doing? He seemed to be wrestling with a black dog and pulling on its collar. Miss Mayton was there too, running round in circles as if that would be of some assistance.

Lady Van Doren looked over her shoulder. "Goodness. The canine carpet has decided to get on its feet. I did assure Van Doren that he would at some point. James," she said to a footman, "do go out and assist Lord Darden with…whatever he is doing with that dog."

James nodded and hurried from the room. Marianna heard the front doors open. As the footman ran out to help, the dog broke free, ran toward the house, and then disappeared from view.

In a moment, it had bounded into the drawing room and trotted directly to her, tail wagging.

Marianna peered closer at the dog. "Artie?"

The dog yelped in response. Lord Darden ran in, straightening his coat.

"Your Grace, Lady Marianna," he said, bowing. "Please excuse my dog. He's never run off. Or run at all, for that matter."

"What in the world has got into him, Darden?" Lady Hamill asked.

"Is this, by any chance, Artemis?" Marianna asked.

"Yes, that is his name," Lord Darden said.

The dog glanced behind him and growled at Lord Darden, then laid his head on Marianna's lap.

Marianna's mother could not control her mirth over the situation. "Heavens, Artemis has resurfaced. The hound who would not hunt."

"Yes, I gathered that rather speedily upon becoming acquainted with him," Lord Darden said ruefully.

"How did you come by him, though?" Marianna asked.

"Miss Mayton gave him to me," Lord Darden said, just as that lady came in, huffing from all the circles she'd run.

"Miss Mayton," Marianna's mother said, "pray, how did you

come to acquire this animal?"

Miss Mayton's face grew very red and Marianna was not sure if it were caused by her recent exertion, or whether the matron blushed.

"Dear Mr. Brummel insisted I have him," she said. "Our Mr. Brummel won him in a card game from Lord Bradley."

Marianna's mother snorted with laughter. "This is too amusing. Lord Fellowston gave him to my duke, who pawned him off on Lord Bradley, who pawned him off on Mr. Brummel, who handed him over to Miss Mayton, who gifted him to Lord Darden."

"What is wrong with the dog, if I may ask," Lord Darden asked. "Until just now, he's hardly moved."

"And that, Lord Darden," her mother said, "is precisely what is wrong with him."

"Artemis could never be convinced to run with his pack," Marianna said. "The huntsman would lead them toward the wood, and he'd slip away and make straight for the house. Whenever he could get in, he took himself to the fire and had a nap."

"He *is* very skilled at napping," Lord Darden said.

Artemis growled, then licked Marianna's hand and wagged his tail.

"I was rather fond of his hijinks," she said. "Unbeknownst to my father, I let him in the doors whenever I could."

"No wonder he is so fond of you," Lady Hamill said.

"Ah, the mystery of how he was always getting inside is solved," Marianna's mother said, clearly enjoying herself.

"I believe he has made his preferences known, Lady Marianna," Lord Darden said, "if you would care to have him back."

Marianna looked down at Artemis, who looked up at her with soulful eyes. "Oh Mama, do you suppose I might? I really did miss his incursions into the drawing room and he is no trouble—he only wants to be warm and sleep."

"Of course you must have him, if Lord Darden is certain he

can bear to be parted with him."

"I can absolutely bear it, Your Grace."

"This is really too amusing," her mother said. "Artemis has come full circle and is back with us. The duke will be positively confounded. He'd been so pleased when, as he put it, he'd unloaded that useless dog on Bradley."

"He will not be angry, though?" Marianna asked.

"Do not worry a thing about it," her mother said. "He will see the humor in it. Once I explain it to him."

"I suppose this is an amusing story I might relay to our dear Mr. Brummel," Miss Mayton said.

Lord Darden made to sit down in the chair next to Marianna's. Artemis growled at him and he moved one over.

"Gracious, Aunt," the Duchess of Conbatten said, "you will have so much to tell Mr. Brummel when you see him at Carlton House. You must also describe Lady Rawley's theatrical and your turn as the Italian…the Italian lady."

And so, Miss Mayton went on to describe how she prepared for the role of Italian prostitute for her current listeners. It seemed she had approached the earl's cook, who had spoken with an Italian wine merchant, and that was where she'd got the phrases "Me Benedico" and "Caro signore."

"Mind you," Miss Mayton said, "knowing how important veracity is to any performance, I did consider interviewing a prostitute. But then I thought, where does one find one?"

"Nobody knew," the Duchess of Conbatten said.

"We even asked our husbands," Lady Hamill said, "but they did not know either."

Marianna well understood that her mother would be doing everything she could to suppress her laughter. She did not dare even glance at the duchess, or she would be in helpless fits herself. She knew perfectly well from her brother that even if these ladies' husbands had never visited a prostitute, they certainly knew where one could be found.

She was beginning to think that it was pointless to envision how a certain thing would unfold. She'd had ideas of a staid drawing room and should Lord Darden be there, deciding what stance she should take. How should she present herself?

As it was, she'd got Artemis back and Miss Mayton had just explained the difficulty of discovering where one might locate a prostitute.

As for Lord Darden, well it was apparent that Artemis was against him. She'd probably be well-served to bow to the dog's superior judgment. As it was, her own judgment had got her nowhere.

Miss Mayton found herself all aflutter. Another meeting of the Society for Finally Chaining Down Darden was set to commence.

That, in itself, would not have set her nerves quavering, but there were two aspects of it that did.

One, she had not seen the duke since she'd looked out the back of her carriage window as she'd made her escape from Rundell and Bridge. She'd not encountered him since the frightening day she'd made her escape from that man.

What she'd seen out that carriage window was the duke collaring that awful person.

What had happened after she'd got away? What had been said? What would the duke say?

Every day since that terrible day, she'd jumped at the door knocker, certain he would come for an explanation. She'd done her very best to think of happier things, like Mr. Brummel, but the idea of facing the duke kept creeping back in.

His Grace had not sought her out. She knew she'd have to face him eventually though. She'd spent the morning practicing a brave, and yet innocent, expression in her looking glass.

The second reason her nerves were all a-jangle was that Lord Darden was here. The society was supposed to be a very great secret! How had he found out about it? Was he incensed? Did he know it had been her idea?

It must have been one of the husbands that spilled it: her girls would never let out a secret. One of those men had cracked under the pressure.

Lord Darden appeared strangely sanguine, which she could not account for. He was an easygoing sort of lord, but even an easygoing person might find themselves a bit put out to discover that a society had been formed to chain him into holy matrimony.

The duke entered his drawing room with Rosalind on his arm. He was, as always, inscrutable.

He nodded to all in attendance and said, "I suppose we ought to get started. Miss Mayton?"

"What?" she cried. "What are you asking?"

With a small smile, the duke said, "To begin the meeting?"

"Oh, that, yes," she mumbled. Gracious, that fellow knew how to give a person a fright.

Lord Darden stood up. "I think it best if I begin this society meeting."

His sisters were all smiles and trying to put a good face on it. Their husbands, but for Conbatten, squirmed in their seats.

"As you are well aware by now, I have uncovered the details of this new-formed society you've thrown together."

"For your benefit, dear brother," Viola said.

"We have your best interests at heart, Darden," Cordelia said.

"Indeed. Well, I have a few things to inform *you* of that you are not yet cognizant of. One, I knew something was going on from the moment you all sent me letters that you would come to Town. Two, it was not all that difficult to get to the truth. Three, I had devised a ruse to throw you all off my trail. The ruse was that I was set on Lady Marianna Tisdale. Knowing she will wed either Wellerston or Mayfield, I presumed you would give up your efforts for this year, at least."

A ruse? What was Lord Darden doing, thinking up ruses?

"A ruse!" Juliet cried.

"You cannot mean it," Cordelia said. "We adore Lady Marianna."

"Yes, well I did not anticipate that you would ignore the idea that she was to wed a future duke."

"Oh, of course we did," Beatrice said.

"Nothing would have stopped us once we became convinced that you were set on the lady," Juliet said.

"*They* ignored the facts," Van Doren said. "Though I pointed out the problem many times. Does anybody listen? No, they do not."

Beatrice patted Van Doren's hand. Though Van Doren seemed irritated that nobody had listened, Miss Mayton knew perfectly well that he was pleased as Punch to be found right.

"Now, here is where it gets a bit complicated," Lord Darden said. "I began with a ruse, and Lady Marianna knows all about it."

"She knows?" Cordelia cried.

"Poor dear Lady Marianna, to be so used like that!" Juliet said.

"Yes, well, it was not the best idea I've ever come up with," Lord Darden admitted. "However, it gets even more complicated. I have decided that my pursuit of Lady Marianna should not be a ruse, after all. It is, in fact, no longer a ruse."

Miss Mayton found her head spinning. There was a ruse, and now it was not a ruse?

"So," Rosalind said slowly, "really all it means is that we are back where we started."

Conbatten stared straight at Miss Mayton, "It appears we have been wildly bamboozled."

Why was he looking at her? What did he mean by that?

"Does Lady Marianna know it is no longer a ruse?" Beatrice asked.

"No. That is a difficulty," Lord Darden said. "Among other things."

"What other things?" Cordelia asked.

"Well," Lord Darden said, looking decidedly uncomfortable,

"I may have said something unfortunate at the theatrical. Before I really knew my own mind, you understand."

"How unfortunate?" Lord Harveston asked.

"Um, something along the lines of *had* I been looking for a wife, she would have been in the running."

"The running!" Juliet cried.

"Dash it, that was bad," Lord Hamill said.

"Oh, Darden," Viola said. "Was she meant to understand that she might compete with other ladies to win? As if it were some sort of contest?"

"She called it a horserace," Lord Darden said, hanging his head.

"Gracious, Brother," Beatrice said, "you have made a mess of it."

"All too predictable," Van Doren muttered.

"I must agree with Van Doren's assessment," Conbatten said. "Lies and schemes very predictably lead to difficulties."

Miss Mayton fiddled with her fan. The duke was looking at her again. What did he know?

"Now," Rosalind said, "why are we all hanging our heads and looking downtrodden? This is only a setback, after all. We must just decide what to do about it."

"Agreed," Juliet said.

"But what is it we should do?" Cordelia asked.

"Aunt?" Viola said. "You always have such splendid ideas. What should we do?"

All eyes turned toward her. Especially the duke's eyes, and he was looking very amused. Why? What was he thinking?

"Hm," she said. "There is Lady Bloomington's masque coming up. I suppose something might be done there."

"Darden could wear a costume that signals his intent!" Cordelia said.

"What about Romeo?" Rosalind said.

"No, she hates Romeo," Darden said. "She thinks he's stupid."

"Poor Romeo, he did so well until the end," Cordelia said.

"I know what it should be," Viola said. "Darden must be Beowulf. He slays the monster Grendel and the monster could be the idea that Lady Marianna should marry for title. Darden will slay it."

"It's something, I suppose," Darden said.

"Darden," Beatrice said, "you must know that we'd all adore informing Lady Marianna that the ruse is no longer a ruse, but that really should come from you."

"Yes, I believe so," Darden said. "I must just find the right moment."

"It is always the right moment," Conbatten said, staring at Miss Mayton, "when one wishes to clear up any misconceptions in their history."

Miss Mayton fanned herself with such vigor that her fan flew from her hand. What did he mean with all these hints? Did the duke intend to torture her into some kind of breakdown?

Lord Darden retrieved her fan and Miss Mayton took in a long slow breath. She would not allow him to do it. She would deny, and then deny again. If there were a strange man attempting to locate her, then he was just some deranged individual who had become fixated on her for his own deranged reasons. Nothing more complicated than that.

She must turn her eyes toward the future. She would set her sights on a certain well-dressed gentleman who had found himself beguiled by her at a certain inn.

That was where happiness could be found, not in looking backward or over one's shoulder.

"It is settled then," Juliet said. "The battle plan 'Darden unravels his ruse' is underway."

CHAPTER TWELVE

TATTLETON PACED THE drawing room. He had been faced with some mysteries during his time shepherding the Bennington family through this world, but this seemed to be the mystery to end all mysteries.

There were so many disparate parts to it, he could not put it together.

Miss Mayton had run from a man outside of Rundell and Bridge. That man had known her given name. Tattleton was certain it was the same man who'd turned up looking for her in Somerset. After all, there could not be two men seeking out Miss Mayton. As it was, it seemed rather surprising that there was *one* man intent on finding her.

Then, Sandren had told him that the Duke of Conbatten had collared the man on the pavement. The duke had got hold of the mysterious man.

Tattleton had waited for all to be revealed, but nothing had been revealed!

Then, a note had been delivered to him, and it had been done slyly. A boy wearing no livery had bided his time until Tattleton opened the front doors to take some air. The boy had sidled up to him and whispered, "From His Grace, the Duke of Conbatten, tell nobody."

Tattleton had practically flown indoors to read the missive, certain it would reveal all. It had only said, *Do inform me, confidentially, if any unknown gentleman with a foreign accent arrives to the house. Conbatten.*

A foreign accent! Now the mysterious gentleman was a foreigner? Clara had not mentioned that in her letter to Miss Mayton that had described the strange man at the door. He supposed he should not be surprised—Clara was what one might call a flighty and unobservant creature. She had once not noticed sparks from the fire smoldering on the drawing room carpet because she was so intent on paying attention to the blasted parrots who were clearly trying to bring her attention to it with squawking and flapping their wings.

Of course, there was one bright spot in all this. Tattleton could not help but be cognizant of the honor of the duke requesting his help. A duke of the realm required Horace Tattleton's assistance. The note had not mentioned anything about becoming the general to the duke's army, but had it been a longer missive it surely would have.

He now found himself a general of a *duke's* army. What next? Would the prince need his services? He could not imagine the circumstance, but then he could not have imagined this circumstance!

He felt pride swell in his breast. Should that mysterious foreign fellow turn up here, Tattleton would tie him to a chair and deliver him to the duke.

Tattleton felt, with this new responsibility to the duke, that it was more urgent than ever to discover what was really going on.

He was becoming convinced that the dog Miss Mayton had got from Mr. Brummel and then foisted upon Lord Darden was somehow a part of it.

All along that dog had barely moved, except to drag itself to whatever area of the drawing room carpet was catching the sun at any given hour. They would set out food for it in the servants' quarters and it would be eaten, but nobody ever saw him eat it! It would just be gone in the morning, as if the dog's ghost drifted down the stairs in the middle of the night and emptied the bowl.

The maids had been dusting round the creature for weeks!

But then suddenly, the wretched canine was up on its feet, practically knocked over Miss Mayton, and shot out the door. Lord Darden had gone after it, but it had somehow got away and went straight into Lady Van Doren's house.

It had never returned.

As a usual thing, Tattleton would be delighted to know that one of the animals that had come into the house had gone out of it again, to be seen no more. But this exit was too suspicious.

Lord Darden had returned to the house without the wretched dog and said, "It turns out, there was a mystery to Artemis' origins and habits. Apparently, all the lying around he does is not as foreign an idea to others as it has been to me."

There was a mystery to that dog's origins. And there was something foreign about the dog. Were the mysterious foreign man searching for Miss Mayton and the mysterious foreign dog she'd brought into the house somehow connected?

It seemed all too likely. But how?

And then, as if all of that was not enough to make a person's head spin, Lord Darden said Tattleton need not worry about reporting to him anything he'd heard anymore. The society to chain him down was unmasked, the ruse was over, and it was no longer a ruse.

How? Why? Did the mysterious foreigners—the man and the dog—have something to do with that turn of events too?

He was gravely disappointed to find himself retired as Lord Darden's general. He had, in the privacy of his heart, imagined all sorts of dramatic and very public denouements. Various outcomes might lead to the pivotal moment when Lord Darden announced to all—"Tattleton was the one who led me forward. He was indispensable for his incisive judgments and acted as my general."

Though, that very thing might happen still, with the duke conveying his public congratulations. Perhaps that was how the Prince of Wales, or even the king or queen, would become aware of the existence of Horace J. Tattleton, butler to the highly-placed.

If only he could provide the duke with some vital piece of information!

Mrs. Huffson bustled into the servants' dining hall.

"Ah, there you are, Mr. Tattleton," the housekeeper said. "Oh dear, you look very on edge. Now, I will suppose it's the idea that we're to have two dukes at table. I suspect you've just got used to having one."

Tattleton, had he been less discombobulated over current events, might have been flabbergasted by the housekeeper's words. Instead, it felt like just one more mystery that must be unraveled.

"Mrs. Huffson, you find me entirely in the dark. What extra duke is poised to arrive?"

"Goodness, the earl has not had a moment to inform you of it, I expect. Apparently, invitations are to go out to the Duke and Duchess of Kembleton, and their daughter, Lady Marianna Tisdale. All the rest of the Benningtons and their lords are to be included too, so that will bring the Duke of Conbatten. Two dukes."

Lady Marianna Tisdale was the ruse that was no longer to be a ruse. What did it mean? That very lady had visited Lady Van Doren's house when the mysterious foreign dog had made a run for it and never returned.

How was it all connected?

"I have a headache, Mrs. Huffson."

"Ah well, the dinner is not for some weeks. I am sure Cook will handle things splendidly and it will all come off without a hitch.

Tattleton rubbed his temples. Nothing the Benningtons had ever done in their lives had come off without a hitch.

MARIANNA HAD SPENT a quiet night the evening before, reading in the drawing room with Artemis at her feet.

Her mother and father had gone off to a card party and she was perfectly satisfied to stay behind.

At least, she had initially been satisfied. As the night wore on, though, she became less so.

Of all the beings living in the world, the last she had imagined might affect her feelings and opinions was Artemis.

And yet, the dog had affected her mightily as he lay content on a soft rug, gently tugging at the blanket on her knees until she gave it up to him. After he'd secured the blanket and stared at her until she covered him with it, he occasionally yawned to indicate his complete satisfaction with the arrangements.

It occurred to her that Artemis had managed his situation far more expertly than she had her own. The poor dog had been passed from hand to hand with no say in it. Rather than take what was being forced upon him, he'd bided his time and waited for his opportunity. When that opportunity had come round, he'd not hesitated a moment.

Artemis had heard Marianna's voice, or the familiar sound of the carriage wheels, or the coachman's sonorous tone. He'd heard something that served as a beacon home. He'd acted boldly to relocate himself to precisely where he wished to be.

Then he'd settled in and demanded a blanket to ensure his happiness.

Artemis had not allowed himself to be buffeted by the winds of fate indefinitely.

Once those thoughts were upon her, a newfound courage rose up in her breast. She could not imagine where it had been hiding, but there it was. Her courage told her it was her life to manage as she saw fit. If Artemis could take hold of his destiny, then certainly, she could direct her own.

At that moment, she knew what must happen next. She must get herself home to the countryside with everything familiar surrounding her. She wished to leave Lord Darden and his stupid ruses and horseraces behind. She would walk to the village and have those comfortable conversations she'd been having for years. She would retire to the bedchamber that had been her own since she left the nursery. The house would be a warm blanket surrounding her and it would help her forget that this season ever occurred.

She would go home, and she would take Artemis with her.

Now, she had knocked on her father's library door. The moment had come when the duke must be acquainted with these ideas. He would not be happy to hear of her new-found opinions. He would likely be shocked to discover that she actually had opinions. She did not like to make him unhappy, but it must be done.

Last night, she had finally realized that allowing herself to be pushed in a direction she did not wish to go was not just weak, it was wrong. It would end up making nobody happy, including her father. If she ended miserable in a loveless marriage, he would discover it eventually. Then he would reflect and he would regret the pressure he'd applied.

The duke was at his desk. Marianna said, "Father, I would speak with you on a serious subject."

The duke laid his papers down. "Has something been said? Have Mayfield or Wellerston declared themselves?"

Marianna sighed. She sat down in front of the desk and said, "They have not, nor will I give them the opportunity to do it."

Before her father could protest, and he did seem on the verge of it, Marianna hurried on. "I won't be moved. I wish to return home to the country and I will come back next year and see what happens then."

"Next season?" the duke asked, looking incredulous. "Would-be dukes are not falling out of trees, you know. Both Mayfield and Wellerston might have engaged themselves by then."

"I would say I highly doubt it, but if so, I wish them luck. They are both boys and have no business thinking of a wedding just now. Further, I wish you to understand that it is very unlikely

I would consider them next season or any season that follows—I do not like either of them. I do not dislike them, I just do not like them in any particular manner."

Her father waved his hands as if to dismiss the idea. "As to liking a fellow, that can grow, naturally."

"Father, this is my life, I have to live it, and I will make the decisions about it."

"But we did make the decisions about it!" the duke said. "We've been talking about you becoming a duchess since you were a little girl! It was the plan all along!"

"*You've* been talking about it and it has been your plan. I have been remiss in not challenging the idea. Now, I wish to go home."

"That is out of the question," the duke said. "Even if I agreed to it, which I do not, we've loaned out the house for another month. Remember? Lord and Lady Mendleban are there."

Marianna paused. She had entirely forgotten the Mendlebans. Their daughter, Lady Harrow, lived a half mile off from their own estate and had just given birth. Lady Harrow had plenty of room for her parents, but the Mendlebans were not overfond of their daughter's husband and felt some distance between them would keep things smooth. As the duke had known Lord Mendleban since they were boys, the house had been offered for their convenience. They would have arrived three days after the family had departed.

"Well then, I will stay here," Marianna said, "but not go out anywhere. I will read a lot of books until I can go home."

Her father was getting rather red in the face. "Go read a book now. In your room, if you please. I will speak to your mother about what's to be done."

Marianna nodded. Strangely, she did not find his discomfiture as frightening as she had imagined she would. It was as if once her courage had decided to make an appearance, it could not be turned round. She felt more relieved than anything else.

She nodded and turned toward the door.

"And take that stupid dog with you!" the duke said.

Marianna smiled to herself. Little could her father know that it had been the stupid dog that had prompted this new turn of events. The duke would go positively mad if he understood that Artemis, the dog he got rid of that had somehow come back, had pointed out to his daughter that she ought to take the reins of her life in her own hands.

No matter. She felt very free at the moment. She had a heart to heal up, as it had been stung in this town, but she was free.

There might not be anything with Lord Darden, but there would not be anything with Lord Mayfield or Lord Wellerston either.

She would not become a duchess, and she was glad of it.

DARDEN HAD SPENT the evening before at home with the earl and Miss Mayton. It was very unlike him, he should have wished to be at his club, but he could not muster up the enthusiasm for it.

Once he'd decided he would declare for Lady Marianna it was all he could think about. He could not keep his mind on cards, or keep up with jokes, and he had no interest in drinking himself under the table. Since that was generally all that went on at his club, he did not go.

They'd had a quiet dinner and then Miss Mayton had read to them from the dreadful book she was just now engaged in. Darden's mind had wandered all over the world and back. At one moment, he was seeing Lady Marianna on the morrow at Lady Bloomington's masque. Then they were alone in a bedchamber. At the next, he was imagining them side by side years from now with children at their feet.

A wife and children! Who was he turning into?

He supposed it did not signify, as whoever he was turning into he was not sorry about it.

As far as Miss Mayton's story was concerned, he'd only taken in half of it. It seemed the gentle governess was determined to discover the mystery of the duke's secret and would stay up all night to see what went on.

Darden supposed the duke had sold his soul to the devil and had a nightly otherworldly encounter with that creature. He had no idea what the gentle governess was supposed to do about it. All he did know was that his father was on tenterhooks over it.

Now, the time for the masque had come. Lady Bloomington, as was her wont, did things in her own way. It was a ball, but a ball like no other. Sideboards were set up in various rooms. There would not be a sit-down supper, but rather footmen would circulate all evening with trays of champagne and little bites to eat that the lady called her entremets.

Darden let several of those trays go by in favor of the champagne. He downed his glass.

"Now, Lord Darden," Miss Mayton said, "do be careful. Even I have been taken by surprise from the effects of so much champagne being handed to me."

Darden was well aware that she had. One was not likely to forget a drunken matron stumbling round in widow's weeds.

He once again examined her costume for this year's masque. He did not understand what she had been thinking, but of course he rarely did. She was dressed as a girlish milkmaid. It was extraordinary—the puffed sleeves and frills belonged on a girl of fourteen.

"I suppose Mr. Brummel will not wish to miss this evening," Miss Mayton said, clearly searching the crowd for him. "I wonder how such a one as Mr. Brummel will have disguised himself."

Miss Mayton turned to stare at him, and he felt forced to provide some sort of answer.

"I can only speculate," he said, "as I am not an intimate of that gentleman. I would suppose he would wear a domino he has had his tailor do something with."

"Ah yes, that would be very like him."

"Very like who, Miss Mayton?" the earl asked, having not paid any attention to the conversation until that moment.

"Mr. Brummel, Earl," Miss Mayton said, blushing up to her eyebrows.

"Oh, that fellow," the earl said.

Though the earl had not said much, it was clear enough to Darden that he was growing concerned about Brummel. He did not perhaps know that Miss Mayton was infatuated with the fellow. He certainly could not guess that Miss Mayton imagined the feelings returned. Nevertheless, he suspected enough to give him unease.

"Well, Miss Mayton, shall we seek out the card room and leave the young people to it?" the earl asked.

Miss Mayton appeared rather hilariously shocked to hear of herself not included in the young people they were to leave to it. "Earl," she said, "I think I would rather stay in the ballroom. Now that I've thrown off my widow's weeds, I would very much like to dance."

"Ah, I see," the earl said. "Of course, no harm in that."

"I will stay by Lord Darden," Miss Mayton said.

Darden smiled and nodded, but wished she would not. He was intent on watching the door for Lady Marianna. He must get his name on her card in all haste.

He could not be ludicrously dressed as Beowulf for nothing.

As the earl made his way to the card room, a ghostly figure approached them. It was the size of a lady, but the face was entirely obscured.

"It is me! Viola."

"Goodness, dear," Miss Mayton said. "I would not have known."

"Now, I have come to ask my dear brother a very great favor," Viola said. "There is to be a waltz to open the masque and Baderston does not know it. Might you spin me round the room so he can see how it's done?"

Darden nodded.

"Excellent," Viola said. "Baderston said he does not mind watching me waltz, but was very hopeful he might only have to view me at such a dance with either you or old Lord Jumberling."

Miss Mayton said, "Oh dear, but what if Lady Marianna is free for the waltz?"

Both Darden and Viola laughed. He said, "Lady Marianna is a stern duke's unmarried daughter—she will not be free for the waltz tonight or any other night."

He spun Viola round in the hold that so many matrons fanned themselves over to better make his point.

"Oh yes, I see what you mean," Miss Mayton said. "But then I suppose Mr. Brummel enjoys the waltz."

Darden pressed his lips together to stop from laughing. It would give him great pleasure for Brummel to know he was meant to be waltzing with his milkmaid admirer of a certain age.

He put himself down on Viola's card, cheekily writing down *Her brother, per Baderston.* He once more looked toward the door. "I must think Lady Marianna is coming, wouldn't you, Viola? She did say she was coming?"

"She is here already. Goodness, I had imagined you'd already secured her for a dance."

"Here? Where?" He'd kept a sharp eye on the door, how had he not seen her?

"She is on the far side of the ballroom with her mother, the duchess. She wears a reddish-brown velvet dress and the mask of a fox, it's very charming actually. Goodness, I did think you would know her. I recognized her by her long blond braid. Her mother is wearing a medieval court dress with a wimple."

Dash it, he'd not recognized her. How stupid of him. He had assumed that as a young lady just out she would choose a costume that highlighted her beauty, not hidden it.

But then, Lady Marianna was not like any other lady.

"I am off," he said, striding across the ballroom.

CHAPTER THIRTEEN

T HE DAY BEFORE, Marianna had been sent above stairs, accompanied by Artemis who'd been delighted with the idea. She'd informed her father that she would not wed Wellerston or Mayfield. He was, as expected, very aggravated and would need time to get used to the idea.

According to her maid, the duchess had been summoned to the duke shortly thereafter and the door to the library closed. The conference had gone on for the better part of an hour. Then, her mother had come into Marianna's room and Melly had hurried out of it.

"Is he terribly disappointed?" Marianna asked her mother.

"Oh yes, he always is when he does not get his way," the duchess said, not looking the least bit alarmed over it.

"I did not like to do it," Marianna said. "But I am determined that from now on I will decide for myself."

"Brava. That is precisely what I have hoped for."

"I know you did, and you attempted to convince me. But in the end, Artemis made me see it."

The dog in question was just then stretched out on the rug in front of the fireplace, having dragged one of Marianna's Kashmir shawls off the back of a chair and settled on it. The duchess looked at the hound quizzically.

"Mama, Artemis took his fate into his own hands and he refuses to give up what he wants. Last evening, he decided he must have the blanket that was across my knees and there was no turning him from it until I gave it up. It occurred to me that I ought to at least have the same amount of courage as the hound who won't hunt."

The duchess slapped her hand over her mouth to stop her laughter. Then she said, "Gracious, perhaps do not tell your father that anecdote. He already does not like that dog."

Marianna smiled in answer. She certainly would not lay her recent revolt at Artemis' door.

"Tell me," the duchess said, "since you are deciding for yourself, is there anything or anyone particular you *have* decided on?"

Marianna shook her head. "There is not. I wish to go home and then see what I think next season."

"Ah, but the Mendlebans stand in the way of that. We promised them the house for the next month and so they must have it."

Marianna nodded.

"It is no great matter, though," the duchess said. "Your father said you wished to lock yourself up here and he wouldn't stand for it."

"He cannot make me go anywhere," Marianna said defiantly.

Her mother laid her hand on her daughter's arm. "We have come to a compromise that quiets your father, will be tolerable for you, and satisfies our most pressing social obligations. I will send your regrets for everything you have accepted, but for three evenings that we cannot refuse."

Marianna sighed. She'd rather not go anywhere, but she supposed she must manage three evenings before she was home again.

"One," the duchess continued, "Lady Bloomington's masque on the morrow. We grew up together in the same neighborhood and she will be incensed if we do not come. She hosts the evening every year as a snub to the patronesses and anybody not turning up is presumed to be on their side."

"She is the lady that sends trays of food and drink round the ballroom," Marianna said, as she had already been well-versed and well-warned on the dangers of Lady Bloomington's trays.

"Just so. Then, there is the party at Carlton House. It hardly need be said that sending regrets to the prince is not done."

Marianna nodded and waited to hear of the third evening she must attend. As her mother said nothing, she finally asked what it was.

"Oh, that. Just a small dinner. It is always so awkward to cancel on a small dinner."

So that was it. A masque, the prince's party at Carlton House, and a small dinner. She would manage it.

"Now, I must ask you directly, Marianna, as I do not like to be kept in the dark. Does your sudden wish to return home indicate any sort of disappointed hopes or anything untoward that might have happened?"

"Certainly not," Marianna said. She would never tell her mother of Lord Darden's ruse or her hopes that he might throw it over. It was all too stupid.

"Very well," the duchess said. "I am glad you've taken the reins from your father's hands before he ran you both into a ditch."

"You would not tell him that, though," Marianna said.

"Heavens, no," the duchess said, laughing. "I do quite like him and would prefer he remain liking *me*. And, while I do not prefer to be in the dark about things, I often think it is more comfortable for your father."

The following morning, Marianna had found her father in a state of begrudging acceptance. It was the most she could have hoped for, so she was satisfied with it. He had somehow talked himself into the idea that both Wellerston and Mayfield would remain unwed until next season and that his daughter's feelings would undergo a miraculous change regarding those two gentlemen.

Marianna was certain that, over time, he would face the reality of the situation, accept it, and be happy once more.

Now, she and her mother had arrived to the masque. Marianna had originally been meant to wear a charming costume fit for the forest faeries. She had changed her mind, though. She and Melly had gone up to the attics and searched for a mask she remembered her brother talking about and they'd finally found it. She would pair it with a light brown velvet gown and go as a fox.

It was fitting, she thought. She very much felt like a fox going to ground. Once she had fulfilled her societal duties, she would dive into the safety of her home in the countryside.

Of course, she could not ignore the idea that Lord Darden was very likely to attend the masque too. Despite telling her eyes to stop looking out for him, they had completely disobeyed and kept looking out for him.

She'd seen him when he came in with the earl and Miss Mayton. Her mother had seen him too.

"Lord Darden is looking very well as some sort of a warrior of old," the duchess said. "And Miss Mayton is looking…as unusual as I have come to expect."

Marianna had not answered and was grateful for the mask that hid her expressions. Lord Darden did look very well indeed. The leather armor of his costume made him seem very powerful. It was a stirring sight, though she was annoyed that it should be.

As for Miss Mayton, well…she was an unusual lady.

One gentleman after the next approached, all seeming to know who she was by recognizing her mother. She dutifully handed over her card but all along she could not help but look in Lord Darden's direction.

The earl had moved off and some unknown veiled lady had joined Lord Darden and Miss Mayton. Whoever the lady was, she seemed much admired. He was all smiles.

Now he was putting down his name on her card.

And now Marianna's heart sank. He'd just taken that lady in his arms and twirled her round, as if they were waltzing.

Who was she, that he would take such liberties? It spoke of an intimacy of some sort.

Marianna sighed, and then realized sighing was not very comfortable inside a mask. It was very hot. She sighed again anyway. Whoever this lady was, Marianna could not help but think that her prior speculations were coming to pass. Lord Darden would not wish to marry until some lady made him change his mind.

Or perhaps it was a different situation entirely.

Perhaps he had known her a long time. Perhaps there had been some impediment keeping them apart and Lord Darden had vowed that if he could not have her he would have nobody.

It really was likely. The lady might have been engaged or abroad or some circumstance that had suddenly changed. It would explain how Lord Darden was on his seventh season and becoming a confirmed bachelor.

Now, this lady had suddenly reappeared and he was delighted. At least, it could be so. He certainly *looked* delighted in her company.

Very suddenly, Lord Darden had looked round the ballroom. He was striding across it now. Straight to her, it seemed.

She turned away, feeling almost frozen with some feeling. A mix of feelings, really. Was he coming to her? But then, what was the point of it? She was, no doubt, just another lady he knew. That was all.

"Lady Marianna," his deep voice said behind her.

MISS MAYTON STOOD on her own near the doors to the ballroom, determined that she should not miss Mr. Brummel's arrival. Viola had gone to Lord Baderston to tell him she would waltz with Darden. The lord himself had set off to secure a dance with Lady Marianna.

Finally, there he was—the glorious Mr. Brummel. Lord Darden had been right in some respects. He wore a fine domino that seemed more fitted than the billowing capes of some other gentlemen. His hood was thrown back and he carried his half mask on a stick. He was accompanied by a gentleman she did not know and who did not wear his own domino with the same panache.

What Lord Darden had not been able to imagine was the finesse Mr. Brummel employed in whipping out a quizzing glass and surveying the crowd. He *searched* the crowd, actually.

He looked for her. He very deliberately sought her out.

Look no more, good sir.

She hurried over. "Mr. Brummel," she said. "How enchanting that we should come upon one another."

Mr. Brummel bowed. "Miss Mayton," he said. "Allow me to introduce Lord Alvanley."

"Miss Mayton," Lord Alvanley said with a smile. "I congratulate you on your costume, it is very…eye-catching."

Miss Mayton nodded. "I will be so bold as to posit that not every lady will dare to come in girlish attire, but then perhaps I flatter myself to imagine I have retained a girlish mien."

"Indeed," Mr. Brummel said.

They stood silent for a moment. Miss Mayton waited for him to ask for her card but his eyes were not even going in that direction. She was beginning to think that Mr. Brummel might be a bit shy. It would not surprise her really. He was, of course, *the* man about Town. But when such a one has been truly affected it must cause a certain bashfulness.

"Well, Miss Mayton, very pleasant to see you," Mr. Brummel said with a bow.

It was clear enough that he must be helped along. She took the opportunity of thrusting her card into Mr. Brummel's hands. "The first will do very well, Mr. Brummel."

Mr. Brummel looked…how did he look? Startled, perhaps? Or was it grateful that she'd taken pity on his painful reticence?

Whatever strong emotions that were just now coursing through him, Mr. Brummel wrote his name down.

"Gad, that's a waltz," Lord Alvanley said with a snort, seeming to find great amusement in it.

Mr. Brummel was not so callow. His face had gone distinctly pink in a blush over it. He understood her meaning. She had directed him to take the waltz so they might find themselves in one another's arms.

"Until then, Miss Mayton," he said, bowing and hurrying off with Lord Alvanley on his heels.

Poor Mr. Brummel was quite overcome by the idea. She fanned herself, as she was a bit overcome herself. In not too long a time, she would find herself in the embrace of Mr. Brummel.

As for that odious man who was trying to track her down, he could put *that* in his cigar and smoke it. She, Eloise Mayton, was poised to spin round the ballroom floor with the first gentleman of London. The one everybody admired.

Onlookers would see that there was something there. Or quite a lot there, as the case may be.

Gracious, she had not thought to go public with it so soon!

＊》》》《《《＊

MARIANNA HAD TURNED at the sound of Lord Darden's voice. He had sought her out. Why though?

Of course, though she was loathe to admit it, she knew why. She was just an acquaintance. He did not know she felt anything more than that and would assume he was doing a courtesy to take one of her dances. Or even returning the favor, as she had been so helpful in his ruse.

All of her dances were taken, but for the third. And of course, the waltz, which she would not dance. Her mother did not see anything at all wrong with the waltz, except for what people might say about it. It was perhaps safer for a lady arrived to her first season and not yet engaged to skip it altogether. Or, as her mother put it—"Tempting the *ton* to talk was very like waving beef in front of Lady Castlereagh's tiger, and was best not attempted."

Lord Darden had greeted her and the duchess. He said, "May I?" gesturing to Marianna's card.

"Not the waltz, Lord Darden, if you please," the duchess said.

"No, I hadn't thought," Lord Darden said. "I am already engaged for it and, in any case, it would not be suitable."

The duchess had nodded approvingly.

So he would dance the waltz. Marianna was certain he would dance it with the lady he'd already twirled in full view of everybody.

The waltz would, apparently, be suitable for *that* woman, whoever she was. She could only assume it meant there was some sort of attachment he would not mind advertising to all and sundry.

"Do you go to the Randalls' rout on the morrow?" Lord Darden asked.

"My daughter has decided to curtail her engagements for the rest of the season," the duchess said.

"Curtail?"

"Curtail, Lord Darden," Marianna said. "I have not found Town as engaging as I'd hoped. Therefore, I will only attend a few select engagements before returning home."

"Home? Select engagements? Which select engagements?"

Marianna was taken aback by the question, as it seemed rather bold to inquire so closely into the particulars of another's calendar.

"This event, obviously, as here we are," the duchess said. "Then there is the prince's party. And then a small dinner."

The duchess was staring at Lord Darden in some unusual fashion. Marianna could not work out what she meant by it.

"Oh, a dinner?" Lord Darden asked.

"Indeed," the duchess said. "A small dinner we should not like to miss."

The musicians had been tuning for some time and now gave

the signal that they were ready to begin.

"Well," Marianna said, "you'd best go off to your waltz, Lord Darden. Do not keep the lady waiting."

Lord Darden bowed and turned on his heel. Marianna sighed into her mask again, even though it was very hot.

As she would sit out the waltz, she was at her leisure to watch it unfold. Lord Darden approached the veiled lady he seemed so fond of and led her to the floor.

There really could not be any doubt that there was an attachment there. They were heads together talking rapidly as if there was not enough time in the world to say things to one another.

Her mother pulled on her sleeve. Marianna turned to her and found the duchess snorting with laughter.

"What is it?" Marianna asked, as so far she had not found anything the least bit amusing on this night.

The duchess could hardly catch her breath. Finally, she said, "Miss Mayton, or the milkmaid I should say, has somehow managed to wrestle Mr. Brummel into a waltz. Heavens, this is too amusing."

Marianna's eyes drifted to where her mother was looking. She'd told no tales—Mr. Brummel was leading Miss Mayton.

Goodness. The lady was looking a bit starry-eyed, while the gentleman looked positively terrified.

DARDEN HAD LEFT Lady Marianna's side exceedingly confused. She was to curtail her attendance at parties and balls? Why? She said she'd not found Town engaging. Did that mean she had no interest in him?

There was a small dinner that would be attended. Did the duchess hint that it was his dinner they would attend? The earl had not yet received a response to that invitation.

He had to find out what was meant by the season not engaging her. He could not declare himself if she'd just tried to communicate that she had no interest in him.

There'd been no mention of Mayfield or Wellerston. Was the duke's plan to see his daughter become a duchess now off?

Or worse, was it on? Had there been some agreement struck but they all had reasons not to announce it just yet?

It was a possibility. The negotiations between two dukes might be complicated. Perhaps Lady Marianna was meant to go home and live quietly in the countryside until the marriage contract was worked out to the satisfaction of all parties.

He would not stand for it! She had no business engaging herself to one of those boys.

Viola had interrupted his racing thoughts. "Darden? What has happened?"

He supposed his feelings were written all over his face. He told her what was said and his various speculations on it.

"I think you'd best move quickly then," Viola said. "You've not got many more chances. Just this evening, the prince's party, and the dinner. That is, *if* the duchess has accepted the invitation to our father's house."

Darden nodded. "First, I've got to discover how she would view a declaration coming from me."

"Rather than get right to it?" Viola asked as they spun round.

"There is the possibility that what she said just now was meant to put me off. If she does not wish to hear from me, then…"

"My dear brother, how could that be? What lady would not wish to hear from you?"

Darden smiled ruefully. "Perhaps all the world does not view me in as wonderful a light as my sisters do."

"I will not believe it," Viola said steadfastly.

"Of course you don't, you're one of the sisters that holds me in high regard, though I do little to earn your esteem."

"Nonsense, you are the dearest brother living. You've never

said a harsh word to any of us."

"I've never had need to with such jolly sisters filling up the house." Darden paused. "No, I cannot believe it," he said, just then getting a view of Miss Mayton.

It was possibly the most absurd sight he'd ever witnessed—Miss Mayton in her girlish dress swooning in Mr. Brummel's arms while he looked as if he'd seen a ghost.

"What? What is it?" Viola asked.

"It seems our own gentle governess has kidnapped Brummel for a waltz."

They turned and Viola said, "Oh yes! There they are. Our aunt is very fond of Mr. Brummel, is she not?"

"She certainly is. Very fond."

CHAPTER FOURTEEN

MARIANNA STEELED HERSELF. Lord Darden had come to collect her. Would he make comment on the lady he'd danced the waltz with?

Even now, that lady was staring at him. Or at least, in his direction, as Marianna could not see the lady's face from underneath her veil.

Who was she? What was so extraordinary about her, that she should seem to make Lord Darden throw over his idea of continuing bachelorhood?

Had they been childhood sweethearts? That certainly would account for how at ease with one another they seemed. There was something about watching them from afar that gave her the feeling of a long acquaintance.

Marianna really did not trust her feelings to hold up against hearing of this remarkable lady. If she were pressed to wish him joy, she would explode into a thousand bits.

"Lady Marianna," he said, holding out his arm.

She laid her hand upon it and it made her shiver. The manly leather armor he wore made her feel as if she were setting off with a conquering warrior.

As they waited their turn at the steps, Marianna said, "I suppose you enjoyed the waltz, Lord Darden?"

What would he say to it? Would he tell her who this veiled lady was and what their connection was? Why did she wish to know? She did not, but could not help torturing herself over it.

"Yes, the waltz, it was very good," Lord Darden said. "Now, I did wish to say something while I have the chance. As you are to curtail your season, you see."

What was it? What would he say? Oh no, Lord Darden, do not ask me to wish you joy. He'd really better not or she would give herself away with ridiculous tears and humiliate herself publicly.

"It's just this," Lord Darden said. "In the course of time, naturally, one's feelings may undergo a change. What one has held as an opinion might transform in some manner. In the course of time. One might meet with a person who makes it so. In the course of time, you understand."

And there it was—her worst fears had arrived. He was telling her of this preferred lady in a roundabout fashion.

He'd just said "the course of time" three times. So he *had* known this veiled lady for a long time. Something or some circumstance had now changed between them. Some sort of impediment had been removed.

"I simply felt that you ought to be informed of it, considering."

"Considering the ruse?" Lady Marianna said, working to keep her voice steady.

"Yes. That is it exactly. The ruse is off, it is no longer needed."

Their turn for the steps had come and Marianna put all her concentration on it. She was determined not to stumble or allow her dancing to reflect her feelings. Not a single teardrop would escape her. She had been crushed and mortified enough for one evening.

He kept staring at her! She really wished he would look elsewhere.

They completed the steps and returned to their places.

"Well?" Lord Darden said. "Will you not say what you think of it?"

It was too much. What was she supposed to say to it? Was

she to wish him joy? She would not do it. She could not do it.

"I do not have any thoughts about it, Lord Darden," she said flatly.

"No thoughts?" he asked.

"No thoughts," she said.

The rest of the dance passed in silence and Marianna willed it to end. She willed the whole evening to end and to find herself back in her bed with the covers pulled over her head.

He seemed to sense her coldness on the subject, and in fact her coldness to him. At the end of the dance, he led her back to her mother, bowed, and walked off.

Where did he walk to? Right back to the veiled lady, of course. There they were, heads together again.

Marianna was certain he'd told his lady about the ruse and her part in it. It was very likely that it had been the lady who'd insisted that he tell Marianna that the ruse was no longer necessary.

Though she'd known in her heart that Lord Darden had only used her for convenience and had no interest in her, it was a harder blow to *really* know it was so. Then a harder blow still to understand that there was a lady who was the recipient of everything she had wished for herself.

She just wanted to go home and cry into her pillow.

DARDEN HAD CALLED a meeting of the Society to Finally Chain Down Darden. He needed advice and he needed it fast.

He had thought he might press Lady Marianna into indicating whether his attentions were wanted. The only answer he'd got was no answer at all.

Rosalind breezed into the drawing room and smiled at everybody. "Conbatten sends his apologies, he's off on the queen's business again."

Everyone nodded, but for Hamill who seemed mightily perplexed to hear it. Conbatten and Hamill seemed always to be going to see the queen together on some matter or other, and so he likely wondered why he'd been left out.

Miss Mayton seemed positively delighted to hear the duke would be absent, though he could not think why.

"Now," Viola said, "our dear brother Darden set out last night to acquaint Lady Marianna with the idea that the ruse was off and to discover what she thought about it. We find ourselves running out of time, as Lady Marianna has decided to curtail her season though we do not know why. The further difficulty is in the way she answered when Darden pressed her for her feelings about this throwing over of the ruse."

"She had no thoughts," Darden said.

"No thoughts?" Beatrice said.

"No thoughts," Darden confirmed. "That was exactly what she said—'I have no thoughts.' I do not know what to make of it."

"What exactly did *you* say, though?" Cordelia asked. "Perhaps she did not understand you. When Harveston goes off on one of his literary theories, I often have no thoughts either."

"I would not characterize my theories as 'going off,' I do not think," Lord Harveston said, laughing.

"You know what Cordy means, Harveston," Juliet said. "When you start talking about dead people nobody has heard of it makes her mind go blank. Darden, how did you lead up to the question? What exactly did you say?"

"Uh, well, I said one's feelings might change over the course of time. One might transform an opinion over the course of time."

"Who is the 'one' supposed to be, though?" Juliet asked.

"Me. I was the one I was talking about," Darden said.

"You should have said you were talking about you," Baderston pointed out.

"Who else would I be talking about?" Darden asked.

"Not Mr. Brummel, I suppose," Miss Mayton said softly. "His feelings are always so steady and do not go willy-nilly changing."

Darden did his best to keep his eyes from going too wide over *that* statement.

"What else did you say, Brother?" Beatrice asked.

"Well, I told her the ruse was off," Darden said. "Then I asked her what she thought and she had no thoughts."

"And nobody has any idea why she wishes to curtail her season?" Juliet asked.

Darden shook his head. "She will only attend the prince's party and a small dinner, which may or may not be our own."

"I cannot imagine why she should curtail her season," Viola said. "Unless, perhaps, she does poorly? Could that be why she wore a full-faced mask last evening? To hide the ravages of illness?"

Van Doren, who had been fidgeting and looking toward the door since he got there said, "If she is so ill she must return home, it seems rather foolhardy to attend a masque."

"There is one possibility I'd rather not think about," Darden said. "Perhaps she has engaged herself to Wellerston or Mayfield and the negotiations will be complex. That might lead her to retire to the countryside until it's all worked out. If it's true, nobody involved will breathe a word of it until the contract is agreed upon."

"If that is the case," Juliet said, "then until something is announced there is still hope. You must corner her at the prince's party and express your real feelings. *Your* feelings, not this mysterious 'one' you talked about. Just charge in there and upset the applecart."

Van Doren snorted. "It would hardly be a Bennington plan if there were not apple carts toppled over right and left."

Beatrice laid her hand on his arm.

Van Doren was no doubt right. But then, so was Juliet. If he wished for a chance with Lady Marianna, he must be direct—a possible secret engagement to Wellerston or Mayfield be damned.

There would not be many chances—just the event at Carlton House and maybe, just maybe, his own dinner.

There was no time to lose.

He would go to the prince's party and upset the applecart.

TATTLETON HAD LOOKED round the empty drawing room with a satisfied eye. It was a quiet day in the house, the earl having gone off to his club and Miss Mayton and Lord Darden hurrying out of the house together.

Lord Darden had explained that they were off to another meeting of the society to chain him down. Why? Why was Lord Darden eager to get to one of these meetings? Was it because the ruse was off?

It ought to have made his head spin, but it seemed that his head had been spinning so fast and for so many days that it had decided to just give it up.

It had been tortuous to try to work out what connection there was between the mysterious foreign man seeking out Miss Mayton and the mysterious foreign dog who had run out of the house and disappeared.

Today, though, he found himself rather sanguine as he stared at the carpet. There was no dog to step around and all of that creature's shed hair had been swept up. It was as if the dog had never been there at all.

He wished he could say the same for the parrots, dogs, cats, and goat that still awaited him in Somerset. The only other animal that had come in and then left was that diabolical rooster. Somehow, Lady Juliet had convinced Lord Hamill they had need of one and it had relocated to that gentleman's estate.

Still, he must be grateful that at least one more creature who had wormed its way into the house had made its exit.

As he ran his forefinger along the mantel, searching for dust the maids might have missed, he heard the knocker on the front door.

He would allow Benny to answer it, as the family was not at home. Whoever it was, they had called at an inopportune time and could leave their card.

Very suddenly, the drawing room doors flew open and Benny rushed inside and closed them behind him. He leaned against them with his arms spread as if he were barring them from a housebreaker.

"What on earth?" Tattleton said, peering at Benny. The young man looked positively terrorized.

Then a terrible thought came upon him.

"It is not…it is not a mysterious foreign gentleman calling?" Tattleton asked in a whisper, the awful possibility settling on his shoulders. He'd told himself he'd tie the fellow to a chair and alert the Duke of Conbatten forthwith.

Now, though, with the very real idea of having to do just that…where did they even keep rope to tie him up with? The stables? Who would hold the fellow in a chair until the rope was fetched? He should have thought this through!

"It is the duke," Benny whispered back. "The Duke of Conbatten."

"The duke?" Tattleton said.

"He asked for you, Mr. Tattleton. He says he came especially because he knew none of the family were at home."

The duke wished to see him. His Grace wished to see him alone.

"Where is he? What have you done with him?" Tattleton asked, still trying to take in that the Duke of Conbatten was seeking him out.

"He's in the hall, sir."

"The hall! You left a duke in the hall?"

Tattleton pushed past the footman and opened the doors. "Your Grace, my apologies. Benny was a bit…startled."

The duke nodded and strolled into the drawing room. "I will not require tea or any other thing and my visit will not be long. Benny, be off with you and close the doors. If you are found listening at those doors, things will go very badly for you."

Benny's eyes were wide. He backed out of the room and closed the doors behind him.

Tattleton stood stock still. He could not imagine the purpose of His Grace's visit. He reminded himself, though, that he was the general of the duke's army. The duke had not come right out and named him thus, but here he was seeking him out which amounted to the same thing.

"Tattleton, I wish you to do me a favor. I wish you to set an extra place for the earl's dinner. The one with the Duke and Duchess of Kembleton."

"Are they to even accept the invitation, Your Grace? As far as I know it, we have not yet heard a response."

"I think the Duchess of Kembleton will see to it," the duke said.

"Oh, I see. I presume they have a houseguest that the earl and Lord Darden were not aware of? Very considerate, Your Grace, to bring it to our attention."

"No, it's nothing like that. This extra seat will be occupied by a person having nothing to do with the duke and duchess. I do not wish anyone to know of it, not even the earl. I will explain everything on the night of the dinner."

"But…but will not the earl notice that an extra place has been set?"

"Will he? I, for one, do not go round counting the plates on my table, those are my butler's arrangements. Is the earl likely to check the dining room in the hours before the guests arrive?"

"No, that is true," Tattleton admitted. "I have been long in the earl's service, he does not check on my arrangements once the seating chart has been confirmed."

"As I thought. Say nothing about this. Just have the place set and tell nobody."

"Yes, Your Grace," Tattleton said, feeling his mind begin to spin again.

"Good man," the duke said. He turned on his heel and took his leave. Tattleton stood alone in the drawing room after the doors closed.

The duke had just named him a "good man." He supposed the other butlers he knew would be green with envy when they heard of it. And they *would* hear of it.

As for the extra place set at dinner, he did not know who the extra place was to be set for, but he had a feeling it had to do with the mysterious foreign man the duke had collared outside of Rundell and Bridge. Perhaps it would even be the man himself to come and there would be a final denouement at table.

It seemed exceedingly odd though. If all was to be revealed about Miss Mayton and her murky history, it was strange that it was to be done in the presence of the Duke and Duchess of Kembleton.

Nevertheless, he would execute his part in the operation flawlessly. Horace J. Tattleton was, after all, the general of the duke's army and a good man. Much was expected of him and he would not disappoint the elevated personage of the Duke of Conbatten.

Tattleton sank down into a chair. He had begun to feel a little dizzy.

MARIANNA WAS BEING dressed for the prince's entertainment at Carlton House. She did not have the least interest in going, but go she must. Just this night, and then a small dinner with some of her parents' friends, and then she would be free of this town.

As Melly did her hair, Artemis rolled on his back and very casually gripped a throw draped over a chair between his teeth and pulled it down upon him.

"That dog has got some nerve about him," Melly said. "I never did see the like."

"Yes, he does," Marianna said, "and I hope I have some nerve about me too these days."

"Aye, it was always a mad plan to think you could be foisted on two strange gentlemen and then meant to pick one. I always said the thing was daft."

"Perhaps do not inform my father that you found his plan daft," Marianna said with a smile.

"I've never informed the duke of anything in my life, as you well know," Melly said. "I'd like to keep my position, if you don't mind."

"Well, it's done and he is disappointed, but I hope he will be in better spirits with time. I also hope he has really given up the idea, as I am certain those two gentlemen will have been invited to the prince's party. My father can sometimes be unpredictable."

"Dukes are known for their unpredictability," Melly said, with all confidence.

"Are they?" Marianna said with a laugh.

"How else can it be? Nobody can dismiss them, they're rich, and nobody ever tells them they're wrong."

"My mother does cross my father on occasion."

Melly seemed to consider the point. "Aye, she does. The duchess don't frighten off for nobody, not even the duke. Not when it comes to you, anyway."

Melly was right. Her mother had been steadfast through all of it.

"P'raps there'll be some other fella what catches your eye at the prince's house. The duchess has mentioned that viscount, Lord Darden, on occasion. What about him? Now that the two fellas that are to be dukes are off the table, I reckon any lord will do."

"I am afraid Lord Darden will not do. He is very much taken," Marianna said.

It stung to even say it aloud. She must get used to that

though.

"In any case," she continued, "I do not think Lord Darden will make an appearance at Carlton House. He does not run with the prince's crowd, nor is his father a duke. I believe that would comprise the vast majority of the guest list, so it is unlikely he received an invitation."

"What about Mr. Beau Brummel then? Everybody knows he is a crony of the prince. He'll probably be there and they say his clothes are very good."

Marianna laughed. "Goodness, now I am to wed a gentleman for his very good clothes."

Melly shrugged. "I have been looking forward to the day you hitch yourself to some lord, I won't lie about it. It'll be nice to be at the top of the heap, you see. Lady's maid to the mistress—I could say or do what I like at the servants' table and nobody will dare cross me."

Marianna fairly shuddered at what Melly might plan to say or do when nobody could cross her. She wondered what sort of example Berta, her mother's maid, had set to prompt such ideas. However, Melly looking down from the top of the heap was not an eventuality that would happen anytime soon.

"I am afraid that is not in the very near future, Melly. For now, I wish to go home. Artie will come with us and I will spoil him terribly. I will make him a comfortable bed in my room where he can sleep as much as he wishes. I will put it by the fire when it is cold outdoors. I will not even care if my bedchamber smells like my father's kennel."

"Well, that's something to look forward to," Melly said.

The duchess stuck her head in the door. "Almost ready to come down, Marianna? The duke ordered the carriage a quarter hour ago."

Melly bobbed and said, "Your Grace." She pinned the final wayward curl and stepped back.

Marianna rose. One outing tonight and then one more to go.

CHAPTER FIFTEEN

DARDEN WAS POSITIVELY speechless. He'd come downstairs to prepare to depart for Carlton House and encountered quite a picture. It had been all the more shocking for being entirely unexpected. Who could have expected the unimaginable?

He'd known something was amiss before he even saw what it was. Tattleton had met him at the bottom of the stairs. Eyes wide, he wildly gesticulated toward the drawing room doors as if there were a ghastly secret currently lurking in that room. He'd assumed it was an unexpected visitor of some sort.

Going in, he found Miss Mayton alone, anxiously fanning herself and toddling across the room.

It was not a ghastly secret or an unexpected visitor, but it was indeed ghastly. What on earth had she done?

What was she wearing? What was on her face? What in heaven's name had happened to her hair?

She was garbed in a bright green velvet gown that was far too low cut in the bodice—her person looked as if it were trying to make an escape out of it. The skirt fanned out in some manner, as if there were crinolines underneath it. She appeared an oversized parrot waddling to and fro.

If that was not bracing enough, she had gone so far as to paint her face. Or, he supposed Fleur had done it.

Whoever had done it had used quite a heavy hand! Her eyebrows were darkened, there seemed to be a thin line of coal dust under each eye, her cheeks were the color of ripe tomatoes, and her mouth lit up the room in vermillion.

Her hair was…what was it? It had started the day as a nondescript light brown with gray streaks. Now, it was as black as Cleopatra's, the crown was swept up into a bun, but the bottom half of it hung in thin strips that had recently encountered a curling tong. It was the sort of deshabille arrangement a younger lady might get up for a portrait but would never dare take out of the house!

"Ah, Lord Darden," she said, as if nothing at all was amiss.

"Miss Mayton," he said, hardly knowing what else to say.

Thankfully, the earl entered the room at that moment. The old soldier stopped short. "Miss Mayton!" he said.

"Earl," Miss Mayton said. "I see my new appearance has surprised you."

"Well, yes," the earl said. "Yes, indeed it has."

"I knew it would be so," Miss Mayton said cheerfully. "It can be challenging to adjust to a transformation, I know it very well myself. I almost did not recognize my own image in the glass when Fleur was done with me. However, I am entering a different stage of life and it suits the new era."

Darden did his best to stop any expression of disbelief. She'd looked in the glass. She'd looked and seen what he was just now viewing and thought it looked well. She was entering a new era of life—what era? Was she attempting to age backward? Or start a career on the stage?

Just then, Darden felt as if icy fingers scratched at the back of his neck. Did this paint and hair dye and odd choice of dress have anything to do with Brummel?

Darden would have found great hilarity in the situation if he were viewing it from afar. If it were not emanating from his own household.

What were they to do? They could not take the lady to Carlton House in such a state!

"My dear Miss Mayton," the earl said, "I am not sure that

rouge and such will be welcomed at Carlton House. Or at least, not so much of it."

Miss Mayton waved her fan. "You are wrong there, but of course you could not know what I have been privy to. I have received inside information about that illustrious house," she said. "Fleur knows a kitchen maid who works there and it seems the rooms are all very dark. I speculate that the prince prefers low lighting now that he has reached his middle age—he has not held up as well as one might hope."

Darden pressed his lips together. It would take more than low light to fix this. It would take a moonless midnight.

"You see?" Miss Mayton said. "My enhancements will not seem so forward, but will appear very natural in the low light of a few candles. Fleur and I experimented with it. We blew out all the candles but one in my bedchamber to see how it would be."

"Well, I am not certain that will…that will be enough," the earl said.

Tattleton appeared in the doorway and Darden could see perfectly well that he was gripping the door to stay upright. "My lord, the, the…the carriage has been brought round."

Though he spoke to the earl, their butler was entirely trans-fixed by Miss Mayton.

"We ought to be off," Miss Mayton said, fanning herself. "It begins to feel very hot in here."

Darden would like to fan himself too. "Miss Mayton, I do implore you not to depend on low light. I would even say, with a dress as vibrant as that and your rather eye-catching hair style, that perhaps restraint would best set off both of those things. It would not take Fleur even a moment to remove…your en-hancements."

"Yes, very well said, Darden," the earl said hopefully. "Exactly what I was thinking myself."

Miss Mayton let out a rather girlish giggle. "Gracious, allow a woman to come to her own womanly judgments if you please."

She swept out of the room and headed toward the carriage.

Darden and his father looked at one another.

"Perhaps a carriage wheel will fly off and we'll all be seriously injured and have to turn round and call for a doctor," Darden said.

The earl sighed. "Carriage wheels never fall apart when you want them to. Let us hope our dear Miss Mayton is right and the prince has only allowed one candle per room."

"We'll never be invited back."

"No," the earl said, "I am rather confident we will not."

MISS MAYTON WAS positively giddy. She really could not remember when last she'd felt so. It must have been when she was a very young girl.

She felt like a young girl now. Her waltz with Mr. Brummel at the masque, or as she privately thought of him, *Beau*, had been perfection. All eyes had been upon her, no doubt wondering what was between them.

When Fleur had told her of some items she might employ to better show what she felt on the inside, she was very naturally eager to go forward. She had spent the past ten years feeling invisible, and very suddenly she was blooming into a new springtime. It was unexpected, and it was thrilling.

Now, her transformation was complete. The gown was everything she'd ever dreamed of and the further enhancements to her person were striking.

She had of course known that the earl would be taken aback. It was always going to be a shock to see the butterfly emerge. He was so used to her always being the same, and now he had to get used to the new her. It would be a blow when he discovered that she was not to be long in his household, though he should have seen with his own eyes how it was between her and Beau.

She'd assuaged the earl's shock in the carriage, showing him how she looked in dim light.

She'd then catalogued all the items Fleur had used with great finesse, pointing out that a company named Pear's was to be congratulated. Their Almond Bloom had softened her complexion and then Bloom of Roses had given her cheeks their glow, as if she'd taken a turn out of doors on a crisp autumn day.

Burnt cork had been strategically used to darken her eyebrows so they might match her hair which had been, just that morning, darkened with a black walnut solution. Fleur had used a tiny brush and steady hand to line her eyes with the cork.

Lord Darden and the earl had not made comment upon her cataloguing, but then why would they? They were men and could not know what a lady's preparations actually involved.

It had not taken too long a time to arrive to Carlton House, but since then they had been in a line of carriages for the past quarter hour.

She had opened the window next to her to get some air and took to fanning herself. The weather was not as cool as she had hoped and she did not wish to perspire.

Finally, the carriage pulled to the head of the line and one of the prince's footmen in rather glorious livery opened the door and put down the steps.

He looked up and held out his hand, then staggered back, just catching himself from falling to the pavement.

As she had thought—she was set to make quite the impression.

She sailed through the doors while the earl and Lord Darden hurried after her.

Once inside, she took in the stunning opulence of the house. It was magnificent and she was dressed to match it, unlike so many of the drab ladies milling round the great hall before taking their place in the receiving line.

"Miss Mayton?"

She turned to find the Duchess of Kembleton and Lady Marianna. "Your Grace, Lady Marianna, how charming to see you here."

The duchess smiled and said, "I was thinking the very same, I had not expected to see *you* here."

"Ah well, my dear Mr. Brummel positively insisted that I be included."

Miss Mayton's eyes drifted toward the receiving line. There he was, standing next to the prince. He was looking at her. Yes, very determinedly staring.

"He has certainly seemed to notice you," the duchess said. "That is a very interesting color of fabric, Miss Mayton. I do not believe I have ever seen the like."

Miss Mayton nodded graciously. "It is named parakeet green," she said. "It is very rare."

"I imagine so," the duchess said. "Do you come unaccompanied this evening?"

"Gracious no," she said. "The earl and Lord Darden were both invited, due to my relationship with Mr. Brummel. And then Rosalind will be here somewhere, as her duke was invited."

She could not help but notice the effect on Lady Marianna to discover that Lord Darden was here. Where he was at this moment, and the earl too for that matter, she could not say. They had been right behind her, but she'd lost them somewhere.

"Well, we are always pleased to see Lord Darden, are we not, Marianna?"

Miss Mayton could not quite work out the lady's tone as she said, "Delighted." It was almost one of consternation.

It was likely nerves causing it. If a seasoned lady such as herself could be feeling her nerves, it was no surprise that Lady Marianna would feel her own.

"Ah," Miss Mayton said, "there they are. They are already in the line." She waved to them vigorously so that Lord Darden might become cognizant that Lady Marianna was here. Then she continued her wave in the direction of dear Beau. Yes, he had seen her, and the prince had noted it too.

She looked away coyly.

Her new era had begun.

✦✦✦✦

DARDEN WAS NOT certain what to do. His first instinct was to find a nearby closet, push Miss Mayton into it, lock the door, and not let her out until it was time to depart.

She had managed to find the duchess and Lady Marianna, who was looking reliably smashing. But what would the lady think upon being accosted by Miss Mayton appearing in such a state?

He could not know, but he could see well enough that the duchess was entirely amused.

Until this day, none of Miss Mayton's foibles and odd habits had troubled him very much. But if Lady Marianna was to consider attaching herself to his family, well, Miss Mayton was not making a very good case for it!

Darden looked past the receiving line to the rooms beyond. They were all lit up like blazes—where was the dim light Miss Mayton was counting on?

She was wildly waving at him like she was signaling a rescue boat from the deck of a sinking ship.

Blast it, now she was very obviously waving at Brummel, who was looking rather stern about it. Darden would very soon have to greet Brummel, Alvanley, and the prince, as he was only a few people behind. Hopefully, a person could not actually perish from embarrassment.

The prince leaned toward Brummel and said, very jovially, "Brummel, who is your fat friend?"

"Nobody of consequence," Brummel answered in a clipped tone.

Alvanley leaned round from the other side of the prince. "They waltzed at Lady Bloomington's masque," he said.

Brummel gave Alvanley a dark look; the prince snorted his

amusement.

Darden had a great wish to burst into flames and go up in a puff of smoke.

He took in a deep breath. Whatever embarrassments Miss Mayton was to offer this night, and he was certain there would be many, he'd come to upset Lady Marianna's applecart. He'd come to make himself plain to the lady and ask for her hand and that was exactly what he would do.

All the embarrassments in the world would not keep him from it.

He must just tamp out as many candles in Miss Mayton's vicinity as he could while he was working up to it.

MARIANNA FOUND HERSELF in a state of oddly conflicting emotions. She had not imagined she would encounter Lord Darden at Carlton House, but there he was. She felt anxious and annoyed and attracted and glum, all at the same time.

On top of those swirling feelings, she was not immune to the amusement her mother found in discovering Miss Mayton's rather unusual appearance. What on earth was the lady thinking?

Marianna did not know, but Miss Mayton had since set off for the receiving line.

"Gracious me," the duchess said, leaning close to her ear. "There she goes to meet the prince and her dear friend Mr. Brummel. Do you suppose Mr. Brummel *knows* how good friends they are?"

"I would not venture to guess," Marianna said noncommittally. Really, she doubted Mr. Brummel was a particular intimate of Miss Mayton's. At least, it seemed very unlikely.

"*I'll* venture a guess, and I guess no, he certainly does not. Dear Miss Mayton, I really do find her endlessly entertaining. I will venture that this is the first time she has seen fit to dye her hair and coat her face with paint. She does not recognize the pitfalls."

"The pitfalls?" Marianna asked. "You mean, that it looks so…startling?"

"That is only the most apparent pitfall. Any lady regularly using such products would not dare do it so heavily. As well, in rooms so hot, and then to add a heavy velvet dress…it cannot end well."

Marianna did not answer, but she took in the information. Her mother was an endless font of facts to file away. Marianna had already understood that such products were not entirely approved of, even if used subtly. Now she understood that heat might convince them to misbehave, perhaps in unpredictable ways.

Poor Miss Mayton. She really was a dear of a lady. Silly and strange but seeming very kind. Marianna would not like to see her land in an uncomfortable position because she'd made a small misjudgment. Or a large misjudgment, as the case was.

"Miss Mayton has made her curtsy, the prince seems a bit stunned, and now the line finally grows short," the duchess said. "Let us take our opportunity. Somewhere inside, Lord Darden will be milling around. I do like him exceedingly."

Marianna liked him exceedingly too, though she would never admit it. She had hoped that in coming to Carlton House she would only be bored. Now she was a basket of nerves and conflicting feelings.

They made their way to the line and it was not many minutes before they were greeted by the prince. Her mother had long known His Highness and he was very kind to Marianna. He congratulated the duchess on her selection of modiste to dress her charmingly elegant daughter.

Brummel nodded at the compliment, as if giving it his stamp of approval.

Marianna had allowed Melly to choose the dress, as she had not much cared what she wore. She'd found herself in a plum-colored silk with just the slightest decoration of scalloped cap sleeves.

Though she had not cared what she wore, now that it had been complimented it somehow gave her a boost of confidence. She ought to hold her head up. She ought to remember Artemis' bravery in the face of a difficulty. She had perhaps been spurned, but nobody knew it but herself. Not even the gentleman who'd done it knew it. Nobody would ever know it but herself.

She had not ever really understood the phrase "take the secret to the grave" until now. She would take this secret with her. She could not endure what would be her mother's pity or society's mockery or Lord Darden's amusement or disdain.

As well, she would marry someday. If her feelings for that man did not reach as deep as what she felt for Lord Darden, that man would never be allowed to know it. She had no intention of becoming a spinster, she wished for children and a place in society too much to consider it. So, sometime in the coming years she would wed a man she could look upon as a friend, and that must be enough.

The duchess led her into a startlingly ornate drawing room. The walls were red, and the ceiling so elaborately corniced and sporting a mammoth chandelier, that Marianna was surprised it did not fall down on their heads.

"Duchess!" a man said, approaching them. He was a short and slightly built older gentleman—very spry and very much the dandy.

"Mr. Porter," the duchess said.

"You are looking as divine as I remember you at the house party in Warwickshire," he said. "Now, as I recall you mentioned a daughter, and I see before me a lady looking equally divine— have I guessed right?"

"Indeed, Mr. Porter. May I present my daughter, Lady Marianna."

Marianna received an elegant and flourishing bow.

"Marianna," the duchess said, "Mr. Porter is responsible for much of the beauty you see around you. He is very much a man of many talents—playwright, composer, and art collector. There is little he has not had a hand in."

"The room is lovely, Mr. Porter," Marianna said. It was the expected answer and she certainly would not have given her real answer, which was the room felt too much—too decorated and heavy. It was too overwrought for her taste.

"My dear duchess, I trust in your taste implicitly. I wonder if you would indulge me. I have some ideas about the prince's music room and would hear your thoughts. It will not take but a moment if you would be so kind."

"I am flattered, Mr. Porter. Marianna, shall you like to stay behind? There are several people here that you know. Lord Darden is just over there."

"I would rather come along, if Mr. Porter will not mind it."

"Mind it? I am filled with delight!" he cried. "How kind you are to indulge an old gentleman. Very like your mother, and that is the highest compliment I can give." He held out an arm on either side and led them down a corridor to the music room he would have an opinion on.

Marianna was not particularly interested in his plans, whatever they may be, but thought it sensible not to torture herself by conversing with Lord Darden. He would be charming and wonderful to look at and she would be sad—what was the point?

In any case, Mr. Porter was a very likable fellow.

Head held high, Marianna.

CHAPTER SIXTEEN

DARDEN WATCHED LADY Marianna and the duchess being led down a corridor by Mr. Porter. Where was the old man taking them?

Probably to point out some painting he'd advised the prince to acquire. Porter was a great admirer of his own taste, and luckily for him, the prince admired his taste too.

Darden had ginned himself up to stride over to Lady Marianna and upset the applecart. He was on the verge of doing it, and now she'd disappeared.

Well, she could not stay disappeared. She must come back eventually. He would just keep his eyes on that corridor.

It was well his eyes had something to focus on, rather than Miss Mayton. Though, he could not stop himself from glancing in her direction. He had already tamped out several candles to attempt to surround her in the dimness she'd been hoping for, but as soon as he put them out a footman was there to relight them.

The room was crowded and was getting very hot and Miss Mayton was fanning herself like she wished to set sail in a brisk wind. The earl, good old soldier that he was, kept placing himself slightly in front of her, as if to block any onlooker's view.

Now, he saw Miss Mayton practically knock him aside as the prince and his friends came in from the receiving line.

Darden felt his heart speed up its pace. Was that…was that

black dye that was trickling down her neck?

He pulled out his handkerchief and attempted to waylay her, but he was not fast enough. She'd sped by him like a shot and was headed right toward Mr. Brummel.

Darden felt frozen in his tracks. What was she going to do? What was she going to say?

"Darden?" a deep voice said behind him.

He turned to find Conbatten standing there. The duke's eyes were firmly locked on Miss Mayton as she practically jogged across the room.

"Dare I inquire what has happened there?" he asked.

Darden knew very well that the duke meant what had happened to Miss Mayton. There was no getting round it, there was no excuse or story that would make what the duke was looking at sound at all reasonable.

"Uh, you might as well know. What has happened is that Miss Mayton fancies herself in love with Brummel and she has made some mad attempt to recapture her youth. That attempt is currently melting. The earl and I tried to stop her leaving the house, but as you can see, we were not successful."

"I do see."

It was a typically enigmatic comment. It was near impossible to ever guess what Conbatten was thinking. The duke was also in the habit of leaving long silences hanging in the air that made the other person feel the need to keep talking.

So he did keep talking.

"I do not really care what the prince thinks of it, not much anyway," Darden said. "As for Brummel, I most definitely do not care. But what will Lady Marianna think of a lady connected to my household appearing in public in…such an arrangement?"

With a small smile, Conbatten said, "A person unequipped to take in the Bennington family's amusing eccentricities is not a person worth your notice."

Darden did not say what he thought about that idea. It was all well and good for Conbatten to be amused by his sisters' and Miss

Mayton's various schemes over the years, but this was different. Lady Marianna was different. She was so elegant and dignified. This spectacle was in no way an endorsement for Darden's extended relations.

He and Conbatten watched in silence as Miss Mayton fluttered round Brummel. Darden could not imagine the conversation. At first, Brummel seemed polite, with a neutral expression. Then he began to appear irritated. Finally, a look of consternation overtook his features.

Whatever the conversation, it was not going well.

Brummel said something and Miss Mayton stepped back. Then she turned and hurried across the room toward the corridor.

As she passed him by, he said, "Miss Mayton?"

She said something mumbled that he did not catch in its entirety, though he was certain he heard "retiring room." He took this to mean that she would go to the ladies' retiring room.

Darden thought that would be well. It was not just her hair dye dripping now. One of her darkened eyebrows had seemed to spring a leak too and was sending gentle rivulets of black down her cheeks.

With any luck, she'd glance in the glass and then scrub everything off. They could all pretend nothing had ever happened and he could stop trying to put out candles everywhere.

"I believe Brummel has been rude to Miss Mayton," Conbatten said.

"He often is rude, in the guise of jokes," Darden answered. Just now, Brummel was whispering to Alvanley and they were laughing.

"Perhaps the joke will be on him this evening," the duke said. "I believe I will go and call in a rather large debt. One that I had been prepared to forget about, which I think he was counting on. That should wipe the smile from his face."

Conbatten set off across the room to ruin Brummel's evening. Whatever else Conbatten was, he took great care with anybody associated with him. Darden's club really ought to invite him to join the YBC sometime soon.

Darden turned and put his attention back on the corridor. Where was Lady Marianna? Should he go and look for her? She might be trapped somewhere, listening to Mr. Porter drone on about his taste in art.

It was still early, he had plenty of time, but he wanted to get to it!

MARIANNA HAD BEEN half-listening to Mr. Porter describe his ideas for the music room. Some of them were rather fanciful. He proposed lining the walls with mirrors strategically placed. That way, when the prince had in a quartet to play for a small audience, the effect would astonish. It would appear as if there were dozens of quartets, one behind the next.

Her mother found it an inspired idea and then pointed out that it would also show the audience themselves in multiples. People did so like to see their own reflection that they must be delighted to see a dozen looking back at them.

Very suddenly, the doors flew open and crashed against the walls, so perhaps it was fortunate that those walls were not yet mirrored.

Miss Mayton, who was looking askew in every possible manner, staggered into the room. "Oh dear, I am trying to find the ladies' retiring room! Where in the world is it?"

Mr. Porter stepped forward. "My dear madame," he said, "I know this house like the back of my hand. I will show the way, if the duchess and Lady Marianna would be so good as to escort you."

"Of course we will," Marianna said, hurrying forward. She could see very well that her mother had been right—the heat of the rooms had caused the applications on the lady's face to misbehave. Rather terribly. One of her cheeks was streaked with black, her under-eyes suggested she'd been in a boxing match, and her dress was stained in multiple places from the dye that had decided to decamp from her hair.

She would need quite a bit of help to put herself back together, if it were even possible to remove the stains from her dress.

The duchess took Miss Mayton by the arm. "Never fear, Miss Mayton, reinforcements have arrived. Let us follow Mr. Porter forthwith."

Miss Mayton nodded. Marianna could not work out the lady's expression. She seemed entirely devastated. Certainly she could not be actually devastated over her current mishap. It was not ideal to have one's appearance appear ridiculous, but nobody had actually died.

Goodness, the lady seemed hardly able to hold herself up. She leaned heavily on the duchess. Marianna hurried to her other side and offered her arm.

Mr. Porter led them down two corridors and stopped in front of a heavily paneled door. "Here we are, madame," he said. "I leave you in very good hands. Duchess, charmed to see you. Lady Marianna, you are a delight."

With that, the genial Mr. Porter left them.

A maid within had surely heard them speaking. She opened the door for them.

It was a charming room, long and with private apartments— some to relieve oneself and others that had a chair, a small sofa, a table hosting various helpful accoutrements, and a looking glass.

Marianna's mother led them to the very last apartment and said to the maid, "My dear, do fetch us as many handkerchiefs as you can find."

The maid looked with alarm at Miss Mayton's appearance and seemed not at all confused over what the handkerchiefs were wanted for. She hurried off and then returned with a stack of fine lawn handkerchiefs embroidered with the prince's crest. The maid quietly closed the door behind her.

All the while, Miss Mayton stared into the looking glass as if she'd seen a ghost.

The duchess dabbed at Miss Mayton's face, using one handkerchief after the next. "There now, you begin to look pulled together already."

"It was supposed to be low light and not as hot," Miss Mayton choked out.

"I'm sorry, what was supposed to be low light?" the duchess asked.

Miss Mayton sighed. "The house. You see, one of the prince's kitchen maids told my maid that it was very dark in the rooms. My maid applied my enhancements with that in mind."

Marianna's brow wrinkled. "But a kitchen maid would never be in the main rooms," she said. "Perhaps she meant the servants' quarters were dark?"

"The servants' quarters," Miss Mayton whispered. "Of course, that was what she meant."

"Very likely," the duchess said. "And you were expecting a cooler evening, I suppose."

"Very much cooler. Really, I did not think the fates would use me so badly!"

Marianna glanced at her mother, who did not seem to understand Miss Mayton any better than she herself did. She handed the duchess another handkerchief.

"Well, it's all up with me, I suppose," Miss Mayton said sadly.

"Now, Miss Mayton," the duchess said, "this has only been a minor hiccup. If anybody has even noticed, they will have forgotten it in a day or two."

"I will never forget," Miss Mayton said. "I will never forget what was said to me by Mr. Brummel!"

The duchess pressed her lips together, a sure sign of annoyance. "Was Mr. Brummel rude?"

Miss Mayton nodded.

"I am afraid Mr. Brummel often confuses 'rude' with 'wit.' I believe it will be the end of him one of these days, and I will not be sorry over it."

"What did he say, Miss Mayton?" Marianna asked. "Perhaps you only misunderstood it."

"Oh no," Miss Mayton said. "I heard him clear enough. I was flirting, in a rather charming fashion, I might add. Now, I did take him to be rather shy, so I was encouraging him on. I hinted that it might be pleasant to stroll round the garden together, in the moonlight. It would be very dim out there, you see. Which was something I'd been counting on."

The duchess nodded, though Marianna noted her eyes had gone just a bit wider. Miss Mayton had been flirting with Mr. Brummel? The age difference alone…

Marianna paused. Perhaps that was why Miss Mayton had come decorated as she had. Perhaps she had been trying to look younger?

"I take it he was not interested in a stroll in the moonlight?" the duchess asked.

"He said the idea made him wish to do a violence to himself," Miss Mayton said, sniffling.

"That is terrible!" Marianna said, forming an instant dislike for Mr. Brummel.

"That is not all," Miss Mayton said. She dabbed at her eyes, which was just smearing whatever she had used on them. "I said there was no need to consider doing a violence to oneself."

"That is not so bad," the duchess said. "In truth, it was an exceedingly courteous reply."

"And then I said, 'Mr. Brummel, consider yourself requited,' and that's when things really took a turn."

The duchess had dropped the handkerchief in her hand. She scrambled to pick it up.

"Requited?" the duchess said, no louder than a whisper.

"Well, yes, you see he did make it a point to invite me here and he did always seem so charmed to see me, and we did waltz at Lady Bloomington's masque, and I *have* retained a somewhat girlish mien, and there have been several gentlemen in my past who *did* do a violence to themselves over me, so very naturally, I was led to imagine…"

"Oh dear," the duchess said.

That was a bit of an understatement. Miss Mayton fancied herself in love with Mr. Brummel and he in love with her? And then declared herself? In a room full of people as her face and neck were dripping in black?

For all the madness in that though, Mr. Brummel could have been kinder. He should have seen that she was only a misguided matron. She was no threat to him and he *should* have been kinder.

"He said," Miss Mayton went on, "that he would never have invited me here had he known I was a lady of so little sense."

Marianna felt awful for the poor woman. Of course, she did seem to be a lady of little sense, but a person need hardly point that out.

"Miss Mayton," the duchess said, "you have made a mistake in where you have placed your affections. It is no more than that. My advice is, dispense with putting anything on your face or in your hair and simply be yourself. A fine gentleman who appreciates you for who you are will come along one of these days and Brummel will be a distant memory. In truth, you have had a lucky escape, that fellow is in debt up to his eyes and would only take from you whatever you would bring to such a union."

Miss Mayton sniffled. "He is a spendthrift, then? I hadn't known."

"And he is a terrible gambler," the duchess said.

"And a terrible person as far as I can see," Marianna added. "I imagine he will treat a wife very poorly."

"Ah yes, no doubt," the duchess said. "I've heard he has a temper."

"And then," Marianna said, wishing to encourage Miss Mayton, "he takes such pride in his appearance. I imagine he will spend every penny of a dowry on his clothes."

The duchess nodded. "He is rather ridiculous about his clothes. Good luck to any lady wishing to view herself in a looking glass—she will always find him in the way."

"Well now, I suppose I shouldn't feel so torn up over it then," Miss Mayton said. "It was just that I thought I was entering a new era. Though, I hadn't known about all his bad qualities."

"You are an original, Miss Mayton," the duchess said. "You will find your match and he will be grateful to find *you*."

"That is just what I think, Miss Mayton," Marianna said.

"Perhaps I have been saved from my own foolishness," Miss Mayton said.

"You have been saved from Brummel. However, I am afraid there is no saving this dress," the duchess said. "At least not with what we've got on hand—your maid might be able to rectify it. I think I ought to escort you home. Lady Markeley is here, she is a family friend and will not mind looking after Marianna and bringing her home later."

"That is very kind," Miss Mayton said. "I will go home and drink a large glass of brandy and go to bed. Now that I know of Mr. Brummel's bad qualities, I imagine I'll feel right as rain on the morrow."

"You will, I am sure of it," the duchess said.

"And then," Miss Mayton continued, "he will have time to reflect on what he has so casually thrown away. I would not be surprised if he is overcome with regret. Perhaps he *will* do a violence to himself. He might hang himself."

Miss Mayton seemed strangely satisfied with that idea.

"One can only hope," the duchess said, biting her lip so she would not laugh.

"I insist on coming with you," Marianna said.

"Oh!" Miss Mayton said, seeming to be caught off guard. "Wait. That would be…you see…no, you really had better not."

Marianna had no idea why Miss Mayton should hesitate over the idea, but she was determined. There was no reason to stay and torture herself over Lord Darden. This and one dinner were the last of the events of the season for her and if she could end this one early, so much the better.

"I am quite determined to see you safely to your door, Miss Mayton," Marianna said firmly.

"But what if...someone...a gentleman for instance, had something to say. To you? I would not want to be the cause of a missed chance."

"No gentleman has anything to say to me that I wish to hear."

"Now that is unfortunate," Miss Mayton murmured.

"I do insist, Mama. I propose that you go and find Mr. Porter and have the carriage called. Mr. Porter will know if there is a way for us to slip out of the house unnoticed. I will stay here with Miss Mayton. She should not be left alone at such a moment."

The duchess looked at her rather skeptically, but she nodded. "I will admit that engaging Mr. Porter is a very good idea. I'll see that it's done. Be of good cheer, Miss Mayton. The wonderful thing about awful evenings is that they do not last forever."

Miss Mayton nodded. "If only I had known of Mr. Brummel's bad qualities ahead of time. And about all the bright rooms in this house. And the heat."

"Well, do not be glum over it," the duchess said. "After all, Brummel may hang himself yet."

On that cheerful note, the duchess departed, covering her mouth to stifle her laughter.

DARDEN HAD BEEN staring at the corridor for near a half hour. Where was she?

Mr. Porter had emerged alone and Darden had a very great wish to question him about what he'd done with the duchess and Lady Marianna. He did not, though. It would be awkward for both of them if the ladies had gone to a retiring room. A gentleman never admitted that he knew that ladies did in fact have need to relieve themselves on occasion.

On the other hand, Miss Mayton had gone that way too. Did she have them waylaid somewhere? She knew what he had planned regarding Lady Marianna—why would she hold them up?

Rosalind found him and said, "Well? Have you done it? Where is she? What did she say?"

"I haven't had a chance to do it," Darden said. "Her and her mother went that way," he said gesturing toward the corridor, "and I haven't seen them since."

"Hmm. Well they have to come back eventually. Have you seen our aunt? Conbatten said she might need my assistance on some matter, though he did not say what."

"Miss Mayton went that way too," Darden said, "and you will not believe it when you see her. She has attempted to turn back the hands of time with little success."

"Ah well, she has had an extra spring in her step ever since she encountered Mr. Brummel. She says it's a new era."

Darden nodded. "Too bad Mr. Brummel has not had an extra spring in *his* step from the encounter."

"You do not think so?" Rosalind asked.

"Rosalind. Really?"

She shrugged. "Love is a funny thing, Darden. Anything can happen."

Before he could comment that she was throwing out a very wide net regarding "anything" if she thought there was any possibility of Brummel swooning over Miss Mayton, he finally saw the duchess.

But she was alone. Where was Lady Marianna?

He hurried forward, leaving Rosalind behind. "Duchess," he said. Then he found himself at a loss for words. What he wanted to say was "Where is your daughter?" But that did not sound quite right.

"Lord Darden, how propitious that I should discover you so quickly. Miss Mayton has had a little mishap with her dress, and Marianna and I are going to take her home. You will be so good as to inform the earl?"

"Leave? To take Miss Mayton home? I am sure the earl will not mind doing it. You should stay. I firmly believe that."

"I am afraid Miss Mayton requires womanly company just now," the duchess said.

"Then Rosalind can take her home. I'll fetch Rosalind to do it."

The duchess laid a hand on his arm. "Lord Darden, bide your time. Do not spook the jittery mare, if you get my meaning. By the by, I have sent the earl a note gratefully accepting his invitation to dine on behalf of myself, the duke, and my daughter. We will see you then."

"I see. Very well, Your Grace. Please give my regards to Lady Marianna."

"And Miss Mayton too, I presume," she said, smiling.

"Yes, yes, Miss Mayton too, of course."

"Excellent, now if you will have my carriage brought round, I will seek out Mr. Porter. I am quite counting on him to slip us out of the house unnoticed."

Darden nodded in acquiescence and went to do her bidding. He did not understand all of what the duchess said, but they would come to dinner.

Why was Lady Marianna taken to be a jittery mare? What did that mean? What was he meant to do about it?

Darden had no idea, but come the night of the dinner he would do something bold. He would finally get his chance to upset the applecart.

He ought to be grateful that jolly little Mr. Porter would not be there to steal her away down a corridor. And hopeful that Miss Mayton had given up trying to turn back the hands of time.

CHAPTER SEVENTEEN

IF TATTLETON HAD been dumbfounded by Miss Mayton's appearance when she left the house, he was positively bowled over at the state of her when she came back in it again.

An unknown carriage with a crest had arrived with the lady. Once she was on the pavement, the carriage window was opened and two heads, one young and one a matron, had poked their heads out and said all sorts of encouraging things to her.

Who were they? Why were they encouraging Miss Mayton? Why had the older one just said, "Chin up, Miss Mayton, and pray for a hanging!"

A hanging! Who was going to be hanged? Did the Duke of Conbatten know of this new danger?

The carriage had set off and Miss Mayton came to the door. That was when he got a closer look at her and, frankly, he wished he had not. Something had clearly happened to the face paint—it was smeared under her eyes and her eyebrows were currently one side black and the other side its usual light brown. Her dress had been positively assaulted by the hair dye she had so ill-advisedly applied.

"Good evening, Mr. Tattleton," she said, as if there was nothing at all to explain. "Please be so good as to pour me a very large brandy. Fleur can bring it up to me. This evening has rather shaken my nerves."

What had shaken her nerves, though? Why did she not come

home with the earl and Lord Darden?

"Is there anything else I can do for you, Miss Mayton? Anything that might soothe whatever has occurred?" He was hopeful she would give over some information he might pass along to the duke.

"Just the brandy, thank you Mr. Tattleton. The Duchess of Kembleton and Lady Marianna were of great assistance and demanded they be allowed to accompany me home."

With that, she set off for the stairs. As he watched her bedraggled person climb them, he pondered why the duchess and Lady Marianna had become embroiled in whatever Miss Mayton was up to.

Whatever this new outrage was, it was certain to have to do with a gentleman. After all, one did not wish a hanging on a lady. He did not think.

There were too many coincidences in this. He must think the unfortunate person that three people were hoping would be hanged was the mysterious foreign gentleman.

The Duchess of Kembleton had sent her acceptance of the dinner this very day. The Duke of Conbatten had requested that an extra chair be set at table for that dinner, which Tattleton was very afraid was for the mysterious foreign gentleman the duchess wished to hang.

What was to happen at that dinner!

Fleur tripped up the stairs from the servants' hall. "Mr. Tattleton? Benny says that Miss Mayton has returned home?"

"She has."

"So early?"

"I believe when you clap eyes on her, your wonderment over that will fly out the window. My advice, Fleur, is dispose of all that face paint and hair dye in the bin and good luck saving that dress."

"Something has happened to the parakeet green velvet? Mon Dieu. Son Coeur sera brisé."

Her heart would be broken, indeed. At the moment, Tattleton found he could not possibly care less about Miss Mayton's heart breaking over a ghastly green dress. His *mind* was breaking, and all he could hope for was to get out of this season and find a way to glue it back together again.

As the days passed by, Darden milled round the town, never really finding anywhere that would suit. The evening of the dinner grew ever closer and if he could have spun the world faster to speed it up, he would have.

He'd finally given up attempting to entertain himself at his club, or a rout, or the theater. He would not see Lady Marianna at any of those places, so there did not seem much point to it.

This evening, he would dine in. Beatrice and Van Doren were coming over from across the street and of course, they would bring Lily to entertain Tattleton. Despite the shenanigans that would go on with Benny and Johnny running the table on their own, Darden imagined that was for the best. Their butler seemed to be getting more tremulous by the day and Darden had twice walked into a room and found Tattleton staring off into space. Young Lily would soothe his rather stretched nerves.

Miss Mayton's appearance was slowly creeping back to what it had been. The face paint had been removed easily enough, but the black pigment in her hair was another matter. It had come out more in some places than others and her hair currently had the appearance of an aged and frizzed zebra.

She had, according to her, made arrangements for the removal of the stains on that alarming green velvet dress. First, she would have the bodice cut down. This, in itself, was a frightening thought. Cutting it any lower would not leave much to the imagination, even if it was a thing anybody wished to imagine. That was not all, though. For the stains hitting lower on the bodice than even she would dare to go, she would have parakeets embroidered to camouflage them. Because the dress was parakeet green.

Darden only prayed these remarkable repairs would take a very long time and not make an appearance at the dinner for Lady Marianna.

Now, they were at table for a family dinner. Benny and Johnny seemed to be less overwhelmed in taking charge and there had only been one mishap. Johnny had brought round a plate of sliced chicken with no serving forks, leaving everyone to awkwardly stab at it with their own forks.

Beatrice said, "Darden, as a family we approach this important dinner with Lady Marianna by putting our best foot forward. Juliet is even prepared to write an ode welcoming them to the house."

"That is ill-advised," Van Doren said. "Assuming you wish them to *stay* in the house."

"Perhaps we might wait on reading off any odes for another time," Darden said. Really, he would run through fire to stop Juliet from reading one of her odes. He loved his sister dearly, but there was no getting round the idea that it would be dreadful. Her odes were always dreadful.

"You will know best, Brother," Beatrice said. "We will follow your lead."

"I believe I will don my widow's weeds for the occasion," Miss Mayton said. "To indicate our seriousness of purpose."

Darden could not parse the meaning of widow's weeds to indicate a gentleman wished to propose, but it was not the parakeet green dress, so he was satisfied with the idea.

"We ought to have cards after dinner," the earl said. "Everybody likes cards."

"That might not be interesting enough, though. I know what we should do," Miss Mayton said. "After dinner, I could read the exciting conclusion of *The Crafty Convolutions of Coldwood Castle*. I could catch them up regarding what we know so far and then reveal the ending. Surely that would be diverting, they are not likely to have had such entertainment before."

They certainly were not likely to have been assaulted by one of Miss Mayton's stories. Nor did he wish them to be.

"A capital idea, Miss Mayton," the earl said. "Though, I find myself wanting to know what happens and do not like to wait!"

"I do not think we should make Father wait," Darden said hurriedly. "After all, Miss Mayton, that is the kind of story they might like to hear the whole of. At some later date."

"Very much later," Van Doren muttered, "after we are all dead."

"Now, you make a very good point, Lord Darden," Miss Mayton said, entirely immune to Van Doren's insults. "They may wish to hear it right from the beginning. Very well, I will not keep the earl in suspense. I will read the exciting conclusion tonight."

"Excellent," the earl said.

"Hooray," Van Doren said.

Van Doren might not be enthused to sit through another of Miss Mayton's dubious stories, but Darden was delighted. It was one more thing off the list of activities he would rather not have Lady Marianna and her parents staring at directly.

He was safe from Rosalind taking them on a trip through the world of music, as there was no pianoforte in the drawing room. Viola would not bring her painting supplies, so an attempted portrait was off the table. Juliet would be told to hold her ode for another day. The only outstanding matter was Cordelia. He must stop her from acting out her Desdemona dying scene and knocking over candles everywhere to enhance the drama of it.

He adored his sisters and was always entertained by their talents, such as they were. However, everything that occurred at that dinner must be absolutely normal, regular, and unsurprising. He would have a steep hill to climb with the duke and would not wish to give him any reason to march his daughter out of the house.

This dinner had been cleared and Benny was looking from the port to the earl as if waiting for instructions.

"Yes, Benny," the earl said, "you are reading my thoughts and gallop ahead of me. We will take our port into the drawing room. We have the doings at Coldwood Castle to get to, Miss Mayton has promised us an exciting conclusion!"

Settling themselves in their respective chairs in the drawing room, Darden took a large glass of port from Benny. The footman had already been given instructions to keep an eye on his glass and fill it up if it ran low. Darden had found, from plenty of prior experience, it was the only sensible way to get through one of Miss Mayton's stories.

"What we know so far," Miss Mayton said, "is that our gentle governess is in love with the duke, and she is determined to discover what it is that disturbs him so much about the nighttime. Now here we are at the last chapter, where all must be revealed."

It was midnight and the gentle governess crept down the darkened corridor and hid herself in an alcove near the duke's door, listening.

At first, all was silent. Then, she heard the telltale creak of footsteps on the ancient wood floors. The duke's door creaked open.

The gentle governess could hardly breathe. Whatever was the duke's secret, she was to find it out this night.

He stepped out into the corridor, his white nightdress billowing round his legs and his nightcap sliding off and fluttering to the carpet.

The gentle governess had not seen his legs before and she noticed they were very good.

He turned and walked past the alcove. Certainly, he must see her, and yet he did not!

He had a very blank look in his eyes, as if he saw nothing at all.

The gentle governess tiptoed behind the unseeing duke to see where he would go and what he would do.

Over the past months, so many ideas had presented themselves to her. Perhaps he had a mad wife locked up in the cellars. Perhaps he had dealings with smugglers. Perhaps he'd made a deal with the devil and had a nightly appointment.

She was prepared to face down any of those possibilities. After all, she worked hard to seem gentle but she knew that underneath that wilting appearance, she was a bit of a harridan. All governesses were.

The duke slowly descended the stairs and went toward his library.

Perhaps there was a secret book full of terrible secrets he must read every night!

Darden suppressed a sigh. He had a great wish to shake the duke awake and say, "By the by, you're mad, your gentle governess is mad, and I know perfectly well you will wed in the end, so just get on with it."

When the gentle harridan governess peered round the door-frame, she was most taken aback. The duke was not reading a book, but rather chewing on a biscuit.

Finished with it, he set it down, but he did not set it on the desk. It fell to the floor as if he were seeing surroundings that were not there.

Then, she knew. Her dear duke was a sleepwalker!

In an instant, she understood what she must do. She held her arms out and tried to adopt a blank look on her face. She bumped into the duke to wake him and then circled the room as if she was sleepwalking herself.

She heard the duke say, "What? Where am I? Gentle governess, what are you doing?"

She did not answer, as she wished to seem asleep.

"Can this be true?" the duke whispered. He raced to the gentle governess and shook her awake. "My dearest darling, you are a sleepwalker!"

The gentle governess blinked her eyes and said, "Oh dear. Now you know my very terrible nighttime secret."

"It is a secret that we share, dearest," the duke said, taking her into his arms. "I never thought to marry. I supposed a wife

must be horrified by my midnight wanderings. But you are just as bad as I am! Finally, I am free to wed—do say you will have me."

"I will," the gentle governess said. "And I will bear you many children so your stupid nephew who gets tired from breathing will never be duke."

"It is a dream come true."

And so the duke and the gentle harridan governess did wed, and they did have many children. As those children had a parent prone to sleepwalking, it surprised nobody that they inherited the habit. Nights in the duke's house were filled with wandering people bumping into each other, though the duchess herself slept soundly.

Mortimer, the duke's dolt of a nephew, was rather relieved he would not become the next duke. It seemed to him a lot of work and he was already tired all the time. He became a baronet, married a delightfully lazy lady, and happily slept half his life away.

The end.

Miss Mayton closed the book and sighed with satisfaction.

The earl said, "I never saw that coming! He was only a sleepwalker. I was certain it was something more sinister."

"Weren't we all," Van Doren muttered.

"The irony of the nephew always saying he was tired and the duke sleepwalking?" the earl said. "That's where it is very clever."

Darden did not quite see the irony, or the point of the story. Or how this Richard Roydon fellow kept getting his books published. He supposed his father's enjoyment of these stories must be enough.

Van Doren leaned his head back on his chair and muttered, "Bea, can we go home now?"

Beatrice patted his hand. "Perhaps you might go downstairs and rescue Tattleton from our daughter. If she is not asleep by now, he will be having a time of it."

Van Doren, who had been so far languishing as if he suffered from the consumption, shot out of his chair and disappeared out the door.

"What an evening, eh?" the earl said jovially.

"It was very good indeed, Papa," Beatrice said. "Now, we all turn our attention to the dinner with Lady Marianna and her parents. Darden's future hangs in the balance."

Beatrice was right. His future did hang on the dinner. All that had to happen was that his family would not trot out any of their talents for examination, Lady Marianna's father would not be affronted that a viscount wished to wed his daughter, and that Lady Marianna herself was agreeable.

That was not so much to go right, was it?

MARIANNA HAD GONE above stairs to dress for the dinner they were to attend. She did not know where they were going, particularly—just some old friends of her parents and that it would be a small affair. She had been to some dinners with her parents' friends and supposed it would be a dreary few hours of older people talking about parliament. The hostess would occasionally point out that they ought not talk politics at table and the conversation would briefly land on the theater or the weather, before circling back round to parliament.

For all that, though, it was also to be the last few hours she would be expected to smile and perform in society.

Soon enough, she would be back in the warm embrace of her childhood home.

Melly hurried in and closed the door. Leaning against it, she said, "What a palaver is going on in the library!"

"Goodness, what is it about? Has my mother bought herself more jewels my father was not aware of? It would be just like her to put them on and hope he would not notice them. Or the ensuing bill."

"It's about that dinner," Melly said. "He's just been informed of where you're going."

"Why should my father be upset by it?" Marianna paused. "Wait a moment. Where *are* we going?"

Melly looked at her, eyes wide. "So you don't know either?"

"I believe it is old friends of my parents," Marianna said. She was entirely confused.

"Ah, the duchess is a deep one, alright," Melly said. "She's kept you both in the dark and now the light's come on and the duke is having an apoplectic fit over it."

"Melly," Marianna said, almost beginning to feel afraid, "where are we going?"

Melly folded her arms. "To the Earl of Westmont's house."

"The earl? Lord Darden's father? You must be jesting."

Melly shook her head vigorously.

"Then it is my mother, she is jesting."

"If she is, the duke is not enjoyin' the jest."

Marianna knew not what to say. Or even how to feel. It was so unexpected. It was like a lightning strike on a sunny day. This evening was supposed to be so calm it would verge on boring. Now they were to go to Lord Darden's house?

No, they would not go after all. Her father would absolutely refuse and the duchess would be forced to send her last minute regrets.

But why had there ever been an invitation to dine at the earl's house? It was unaccountable.

Melly had pulled out a silk dress the color of claret. "You'll want this one, I think. Unless you have another idea."

"I do not think I want any of them," Marianna said. "You cannot imagine that my father will be induced to go to this dinner. He really does not care for Lord Darden and he's heard of Miss Mayton's appearance at the prince's party at Carlton House. Apparently, everybody is talking about her approach to Brummel and her…interesting looks. He's already heard some things about Lord Darden's sisters and their husbands. He says the whole extended family are lunatics, save for Conbatten."

Melly held the dress in her hands, seeming unsure of what to do.

There was a soft knock on the door and the duchess let herself in.

"Mama," Marianna said, in a rather scolding tone.

"I see you've heard, then?" the duchess said, laughing.

"I have, and now you've put the earl to very great trouble. He will have prepared for the evening and will not appreciate the short notice. Neither will his butler, who will have to rethink the entire table."

"Short notice?" the duchess asked.

"The short notice of us cancelling," Marianna said.

"Oh, we are not cancelling, we are going."

"Going? But Papa…"

"He put up a spectacular fight over it, the dear man, but we are going."

"How?"

The duchess shrugged. "A wife does have her weapons, Marianna. He got very red in the face and began shouting about how he would not be managed in such a manner."

"Yes, I suppose he would. I rather feel the same."

The duchess crossed the room and kissed the top of her head. "Always know I have your best interests at heart."

"I still do not see how you would have convinced my father to go," Marianna said. "Did you get him drunk?"

The duchess' peals of laughter rang through the room. "No, but that is an idea I will save for another time. I simply mentioned how it is quite the fashion for a duke and duchess to have their own bedchambers. We've never kept up with that fashion, but perhaps we ought to try it out. As it happens, your father does not think he will be able to fall asleep if I am not by his side. So, he begrudgingly goes and I have wrung out a promise that he will behave civilly."

"But Mama, *I* do not wish to go. I really do not wish to."

The duchess tipped Marianna's chin with her forefinger. "I do not know what has transpired between you and Lord Darden, other than to speculate that he's somehow made a cake of himself. Men often do, you know."

"There is really nothing to speak of," Marianna said.

"I am not convinced of it—after all, this invitation did not just invent itself out of the air. Lord Darden asked his father to host it and invite us. As far as I know, it will only be the earl's extended family and us."

Marianna felt rather stunned. Just the earl's family? And they were going? They were going to Lord Darden's house. He had arranged it. Why?

She must not get ahead of herself. It could be just more of Lord Darden's scheming to throw his sisters off.

"We will go to this dinner and see what transpires," the duchess said. "If I am wrong, I will take you home and say no more about it."

Despite wishing to keep her feelings in check, Marianna felt they were not in check at all. She felt like laughing and crying at the same time.

The duchess glanced over at her maid still holding the claret silk. "Excellent choice, Melly. Now do get my daughter dressed. We should not like to be late."

TATTLETON APPROACHED THIS dinner with the Duke and Duchess of Kembleton and their daughter with great trepidation. More than trepidation, actually. He noticed his hands shaking and he was occasionally stopped in his tracks by a fit of dizziness.

While he attempted to steady himself, Lord Darden paced in front of the drawing room windows like a caged tiger.

Miss Mayton was flouncing around in her widow's weeds again, which he supposed was an improvement. Hopefully, the guests would not notice that her hair was a collection of brown, gray, and black stripes.

The extended family had begun to arrive, the first being Lady Van Doren and her husband, but as they did not bring Lily, they did not distract him.

What nobody had noticed or mentioned was the extra place set at dinner. He did not expect any of the family to go in and look ahead of time, but what if they did? He was living in a world where anything at all might happen.

The Duke of Conbatten had not yet arrived. Would he make an announcement of some sort?

Otherwise, how was Tattleton to explain setting the extra place? The truth sounded somehow untruthful. The Duke of Conbatten told him to do it and he was to tell nobody.

Perhaps he should have confirmed what it was all about ahead of time! What if it were some sort of joke upon him? A jest played upon him on the very night that should be the pinnacle of his career. *Two* dukes were to be at table. He itched to throw that information around to the other butlers he knew.

But only if the whole thing came off. If something went awry, he would never speak of it in his lifetime.

Of course, he had never observed the Duke of Conbatten jesting with anybody so it did not seem likely he would start now. So who was to occupy that place? Would it be the mysterious foreign gentleman? If it was, why was he being brought here? Why would he be brought on the very night that they were all meant to impress Lady Marianna's parents, an illustrious duke and duchess?

The Duke of Conbatten finally arrived with Lady Rosalind on his arm. His Grace caught Tattleton's eye and discreetly nodded.

Was that confirmation of the extra place setting? He did not know!

Benny tapped him on the shoulder. "Mr. Tattleton," he whispered.

"Yes, what is it?"

"There's a fella at the back door."

"A *fella*? What do you mean, a fella?"

"He's told Cook that he comes at the invitation of the Duke of Conbatten, and it's a secret, and he's to be led straight into the dining room and be sitting there as some kind of surprise."

Tattleton staggered and Benny grasped his arm to keep him upright.

"Benny, does this 'fella' have a foreign accent?"

"Cook didn't say. All he said was the chap looked like a prosperous tradesman of some sort."

Whoever the man was, it was clear enough he was not of the *ton*. His footmen would not dare name someone a fella and a chap if he were highly placed. But a tradesman?

"It cannot be a tradesman."

"A prosperous one," Benny said, as if that would make the slightest amount of difference.

What was he to do now? The duke had asked him to set an extra place. Now a "fella" who was a prosperous tradesman had come to say he was to take the extra place with none the wiser, until they were all led into the dining room?

"Cook says he seems like he's on the up and up," Benny said.

On the up and up. How comforting that Horace J. Tattleton was about to do something outrageous on the advice of the cook. He supposed if the earl demanded an explanation, he could just explain that he'd been assured by Cook that this fella was on the up and up.

He sighed. Whatever he'd got himself into, he was in too deep to get out now.

"Show the gentleman to his place. He is firmly in the middle of the table. I do not know who he is, but he certainly does not hold rank over anybody. I am not even certain he holds rank above *me*."

"Right you are, Mr. Tattleton."

Was he right? He'd better be right.

CHAPTER EIGHTEEN

Marianna, her mother, and her father had all been got into the carriage, though the duke had dragged his feet rather terribly.

Now he satisfied himself with a gruff melody of harumphs and disgusted sighs.

The duchess patted his arm. "Come now, my darling, it is only a dinner."

"But why?" the duke said testily. "That is what I want to know."

"We have found the earl and Lord Darden very pleasant to know," the duchess said, "and apparently they feel just the same."

"I haven't found them pleasant," the duke said. "I suppose the earl is all right, but that son of his…well, to fall off one's chair while my daughter plays…I only say. And then the earl's daughters, well they are not particularly regular either! And what about that Miss Mayton? The things I hear about *that* lady."

"They are a rather spirited sort of family," the duchess said.

"Spirited? Is that what we're calling such things now?"

"Here is something that will cheer you," the duchess said. "I have discovered where Conbatten and Lady Hightower are getting that fine Tokay and have ordered you a case of it."

"The Tokay? The dry Tokay?"

"The very one," the duchess said.

"It's confirmed, is it? The order was accepted?"

"It will be on our doorstep in two days' time."

Much to Marianna's amazement, this did seem to soothe the duke. She did not suppose it would last all through dinner, but it might last the carriage ride at least.

She was glad he'd stopped questioning, as she had no answers. Why had they been invited? If it were a large dinner, it might be explainable, but a dinner with only the family was something different.

What about that lady from the masque that he'd waltzed with? The one Marianna was certain was some sort of long-lost love? There was no indication of her attending.

It was all so confusing. The only thing Marianna could absolutely decide on was to not allow her hopes to bloom. She had already dealt with her disappointment, it would be highly ridiculous to subject herself to a second go round.

She would steel herself to avoid being too struck by him, or hopeful about him. It would be a difficult evening, but she would get through it.

⇒⟫⟪⟪⟫

Darden casually pulled the curtain for the hundredth time to look for any sign of Lady Marianna. All of his family had arrived and were quietly milling round the drawing room. There was an expectant hush over them all, as if something momentous was about to occur. Even the earl seemed more on edge than was his habit.

Perhaps they would not come. The earl had assured him the duchess would manage her duke, but what if the old soldier had put his foot down at the last minute and refused to come?

If that happened, he would have no chance of seeing Lady Marianna until next season! She might be married by then. He must think there were piles of fellows haunting her neighborhood, just waiting for her return. There might be some baron or viscount lurking around who did not have the funds for Town, but had all the dashing looks and smooth manners to paper over that fact.

Rosalind laid a hand on his arm and he dropped the curtain. "She will come, Darden," his sister said kindly.

Juliet joined them. "Of course she will come. How could she fail to come?"

As he always was, Darden was bemused by his sisters' unwavering faith in him. They were the only people on earth who believed he could do no wrong, despite the recent evidence of him being very capable of it.

At that moment, they heard the distinctive sound of carriage wheels on cobblestones grow louder. And then stop.

They stared at one another. Darden used his forefinger to pull aside the curtain an inch. A well-built carriage with the duke's crest had halted and grooms raced to open the doors. It was her. She was here.

"Everyone," Darden said, as Tattleton hurried to the door, "they are here."

"The curtain is raised and the show begins," Cordelia said.

Darden hoped that was not some hint that she was prepared to entertain them after dinner with Desdemona's dramatic dying scene, but there was no time to worry about it.

Tattleton had received Lady Marianna and her parents, and now led them to the drawing room. "The Duke and Duchess of Kembleton, accompanied by their daughter, Lady Marianna Tisdale," he said in his best sonorous butler tone.

The earl went forward to the duke. "Your Grace, we welcome you to our house. Duchess, charmed to see you again. Lady Marianna, you are looking well as always."

Darden felt rooted to the spot. He had managed to get Lady Marianna here, but now what?

He forced himself forward to greet the duke. It would not do to appear a complete rube.

"Your Grace," he said, bowing.

"Lord Darden," the duke said flatly.

Conbatten stepped forward. "Duke," he said, "I wonder if I might steal you away for just a moment. I think we ought to discuss the upcoming vote."

The Duke of Kembleton nodded rather enthusiastically and Darden got the distinct idea that he'd rather talk to Conbatten than himself. The two dukes set off for a quiet corner and politics.

Rosalind said to Her Grace, "Duchess, I think you might be a great help to me if you would be so kind. There is a curio cabinet at the far end of the room and I am determined to have one very like it. Though, I find myself torn between walnut and cherry."

Marianna's mother appeared vastly amused and said, "Lead me there, Duchess, and let us thoroughly discuss this weighty matter."

As they drifted away, Darden overheard his sister say, "Do call me Rosalind. You're a duchess, I'm a duchess, and it all feels rather fraught and formal."

"Ah, the two duchesses in the same room problem, we are in danger of duchessing ourselves to death. Call me Cassandra," the duchess answered.

Rosalind and Conbatten had arranged to leave him alone with Lady Marianna and everybody else seemed to know that was the plan. They all drifted away as if they were boats being carried off on different currents. Even the earl took to examining a book on a shelf.

"Marianna…I'm sorry, *Lady* Marianna," he said. Blast, he'd been thinking of her as Marianna for so long that he'd just said it out loud.

"Lord Darden," she said.

"I am really very glad you could come. To dinner. Very glad."

"I will admit to being surprised by the invitation," Lady Marianna said. "I cannot account for it."

"You cannot?"

"I cannot. I only discovered where I was going an hour ago, as did my father. We were both very surprised, though perhaps my father most of all. I suppose this is somehow a part of the ruse to fend off your sisters?"

"The ruse? No! The ruse is off," Darden said. "The ruse has been off for quite a while. Did I not say the ruse was off?"

"I believe so, but then it might be back on again."

"No, no, the ruse has stayed off. Now, when I said how one's opinions might change over time," Darden said, beginning to get the idea that he was the most inarticulate gentleman living, "that's what I meant—the ruse was off."

"The ruse is still off," Lady Marianna said thoughtfully.

"Entirely off," Darden said.

Just then, Tattleton appeared at the door, caught the earl's eye, and nodded.

He was signaling them to go through to the dining room. Why so soon? They were just beginning to have a conversation!

And what was wrong with Tattleton? He was gripping the doorframe as if to hold himself up.

"Everyone, we can go through," the earl said loudly.

Darden put his arm out to Lady Marianna. The seating arrangements had been thought out carefully. The duchess would be to the earl's right and Lady Marianna to his left. Darden would be on the duchess' right, placing him directly across from Lady Marianna.

It was not exactly conforming to rank, but the earl's table was more narrow than most and it had been Darden's long experience that one had conversations across the table more than side by side. It would also place them looking at one another all evening.

Rosalind would be at the head of the other end with Lady Marianna's father to her right and hopefully she would keep him too entertained to notice the arrangements.

Tattleton led them forward, though he walked very slowly as if he'd suddenly aged twenty years. Darden was determined to talk to the earl about sending their butler away for a rest at the seaside. He always seemed on the verge of collapse these days.

They entered the dining room and Darden stopped short, as

did the earl. There was some gentleman sitting there already. He was seated at the middle of the table where Baderston was meant to be and an extra chair and place setting had been squeezed in. Who was he and what was he doing there?

Behind him, Conbatten said, "I pray for your indulgence everyone, but I thought to surprise the duke."

The Duke of Kembleton said, "Wagner? Is that really you?"

Wagner, whoever he was, was dressed in somber black clothes not particularly suited for the occasion. He stood and said, "Your Grace, it has been many years."

Darden had stepped back and was looking round. What on earth was going on? Conbatten had dug up an old friend of the duke's and decided to invite him without telling anyone? And why had he not been in the drawing room to be introduced to everyone? Why had he been sitting here alone? And where was he from? His accent sounded Germanic.

Whoever he was, it had somehow affected Miss Mayton. She fanned herself and then turned to leave, but Conbatten got her by the arm and said, "I do not think so, Miss Mayton."

"Wagner saved my life when I was a youth on my continental tour," the duke said. "I had been brutally attacked by thieves in Rome and he drove them off and then treated my knife wounds. He hosted me in his house for some weeks while I recovered."

Mr. Wagner nodded and said, "I was lucky to be in the right place at the right time, Your Grace."

"No, my good sir," the duke said, "I was the lucky one."

Though Darden was initially taken aback by the sudden appearance of this stranger, he began to think it rather genius. The Duke of Kembleton seemed softened at the meeting of his old rescuer.

"Gracious, Mr. Wagner," the duchess said, "the duke has often spoken of you fondly. He's told the story of your heroics to no end of people, even the prince knows of it."

"I am flattered, Your Grace."

"I suggest," Conbatten said, "that we all be seated. Then we can hear of what Mr. Wagner has been up to since his remarkable encounter with the duke."

For some reason, Conbatten still had Miss Mayton firmly by the arm and he was practically marching her to her seat. Was he holding her up or forcing her forward? She looked very pale and Darden thought maybe it was not only Tattleton who needed a rest at the seaside. Her one-sided romance with Brummel had seemed to take a toll on her.

They all found their places, which were now uneven with the addition of Mr. Wagner.

"Goodness gracious," the earl said jovially from the head of the table, "what a wonderful surprise Conbatten has arranged!"

"More surprising to some than others," Conbatten said drily, staring at Miss Mayton.

"Do tell us of your life, Mr. Wagner," the earl went on, "since that fateful day that you rescued the duke."

"And perhaps Miss Mayton might add in her own knowledge of Mr. Wagner's activities," Conbatten said with an amused smile.

Miss Mayton looked toward the door as if she might bolt for it, but Conbatten shook his head at her.

What was going on?

"Miss Mayton," the Duke of Kembleton said, "you are also acquainted with Mr. Wagner?"

"Vaguely," she murmured.

"Vaguely?" Mr. Wagner said, leaning threateningly across the table. "*Vaguely?*"

His tone was accusing, though Darden could not for the life of him imagine why.

A sudden idea occurred to him. Could this be the gentleman who'd come looking for Miss Mayton in Somerset?

He glanced at Tattleton and could see very well he was having the same idea.

Why though? What could Mr. Wagner want with Miss Mayton? Or have against her, as it was looking at the moment.

Benny was bringing round the first course while Johnny poured the wine.

Mr. Wagner said, "I have quite the unusual history, Lord Westmont. Just after assisting His Grace with his injuries and setting him on his way, I began the adventure of a lifetime. Just now, I sit across from that adventure, by way of Mrs. Eloise Wagner, née Miss Eloise Mayton, my wife. Though I have not laid eyes on her these twenty years."

A clatter of forks on plates rang out. Benny dropped the silver soup tureen and consommé ran in all directions across the carpet. Johnny appeared so stunned that he'd begun to fill Van Doren's glass but forgot to stop, and it overflowed and soaked the cloth.

"This must be a jest of some sort," Rosalind said.

"Oh yes, that is bound to be it," Juliet said. "Conbatten has arranged a joke."

Darden knit his brows. Conbatten never arranged a joke.

"It is no jest, my lady," Mr. Wagner said.

"But Mr. Wagner," Cordelia said, "we are all very well acquainted with our aunt's history—Hans, Gregorio, Phillipe, the Transylvanian count? They all died before there could be a wedding. Our dear aunt has never married."

"That is true," Viola said. "All those lovesick fellows died of love for her. There was never any mention of a Mr. Wagner who did not die."

"It's all been extremely tragic for our aunt," Juliet said.

"Tragic? A Transylvanian count? Who are these men?" Mr. Wagner demanded.

"Her lost loves, Mr. Wagner," Rosalind said, as if the poor fellow was a bit slow.

Darden was flummoxed. He'd never believed a word of Miss Mayton's stories of tragic lost love on the continent, but he'd never imagined she had a husband somewhere! It seemed the sort of thing a person would mention.

Just now, Miss Mayton's complexion had gone a deadly white and drops of perspiration appeared on her forehead. Darden noticed she was not denying she was married.

"Oh yes, I see it all now," Mr. Wagner said. "Eloise always did have some wild ideas about romance."

"There was nothing wild about my ideas!" Miss Mayton said, pretty much confirming what was becoming apparent. Mr. Wagner was her husband. Her long-lost husband, though why that should be still remained a mystery.

"But my dear Miss Mayton," the earl said, "how was it that when I wrote to you all those years ago, you were living quite alone in Rome?"

"So that's where you went, was it?" Mr. Wagner said.

"I went a lot of places," Miss Mayton muttered.

"Perhaps I can clear up a few points," Conbatten said. "Mr. Wagner is a physician. He and Miss Mayton met in Rome, married, and settled in Bonn. One day, Mr. Wagner rose and found his new wife gone, all his money gone with her, and a note that accused him of having stone for a heart."

"Certainly not," the earl murmured.

"I am afraid so," Conbatten continued. "A few weeks ago, I encountered Mr. Wagner at the doorstep of Rundell and Bridge, where Miss Mayton was making a hasty getaway from him. A rather violent getaway. Naturally, I wished to know why the lady had just thrown this gentleman to the pavement and leapt into her carriage as if she were escaping from a fire."

"Were you buying me more jewels at Rundell and Bridge, my love?" Rosalind asked.

"Naturally," Conbatten said. "Though, I will not tell you what it is until it is ready."

"He likes to surprise me," Rosalind said. "In the bath, usually."

Darden stared at Conbatten. It was all well and good that he liked to surprise his wife with jewelry in the bath, but it would be nice if he would conclude whatever ludicrous story he was determined to tell. The less Lady Marianna's father heard of it, the better, and he certainly did not need to know anything of

Conbatten's bathing habits.

"After helping Mr. Wagner to his feet," Conbatten said, "I promptly put him in my carriage. On being apprised of the idea that he was the long-lost husband of our tragic spinster here, I knew I must confirm the story before going forward."

"The duke was quite rigorous," Mr. Wagner said. "He interviewed me over a series of days—absolutely everything about my history."

"And I sent out inquiries to confirm the facts I was given," Conbatten said. "One of those facts was that Mr. Wagner was acquainted with the Duke of Kembleton, which I easily confirmed through a servant. Mr. Wagner mentioned the connection, as he'd thought of contacting the duke for help in locating his runaway bride."

"You ought to have done it, Wagner," the Duke of Kembleton said. "I would have told you to hightail it back to Bonn and consider it a lucky escape. Did you know she wears makeup and dyes her hair?"

"One time!" Miss Mayton cried.

Mr. Wagner sighed. "She's always been vain about her appearance."

"I have a girlish mien," Miss Mayton murmured.

Darden was willing everyone to stop. Just stop talking!

"Conbatten," Beatrice said, "why did you choose to reveal all this now? At this dinner?"

Now there was a good question.

"Because," Conbatten said, "the Benningtons are an interesting family. I thought Lady Marianna ought to know just how interesting."

Darden gripped his napkin. Why? There was no need for her to know how interesting. That sort of thing could come out over time. Slowly.

"I expect she will hold up very well against the shenanigans that go on in this sphere," Conbatten said. "I know I have."

Darden's sisters were all looking rather incredulous. He was feeling rather incredulous himself. He stole a glance at Lady Marianna's father—he looked dark as thunder.

"She most certainly will not be involved with any of this," the duke said.

"Now, as to anything unusual about my history, Duke, there were extenuating circumstances," Miss Mayton said. "You ought not hold it against Lord Darden. They were very extenuating circumstances."

"*Deranged* circumstances, I think you mean," Lady Marianna's father said.

"What extenuating circumstances?" Mr. Wagner asked.

"Oh, *you* know. You know very well," she said to Mr. Wagner. She turned to the earl. "Just to give you an example, Earl. As a new wife, would I not have every expectation that when my new husband comes into the breakfast room, he might say something like 'the minutes we have been parted have been agony?'"

"Well, I am sure I do not know," the earl said weakly.

"And then, what did he actually say?" Miss Mayton hurried on. "He said, 'I would like toast.'"

"I *do* like toast!" Mr. Wagner said.

"You see what he is, I really had no choice."

"Might I inquire," Mr. Wagner said, "how it is you wear the widow's weeds? Have you been telling people I am dead?"

"I only *wished* you were dead," Miss Mayton said, chin in the air.

"But Aunt, what of the gentlemen who *are* dead? Count Tulerstein and the others?" Beatrice asked. "Were none of them real?"

"Certainly they must have been, Bea," Juliet said. "I can see in my mind our poor Count Tulerstein going over the side of the Alpine cliff in his green coat after our aunt refused him."

"And Gregorio coming to despair and stabbing himself," Cordelia said, "though thank heavens our aunt was there to hear his last romantic words."

"And poor Phillipe!" Viola said. "Hanging himself in his garret because he thought our aunt did not love him."

"Let us not forget the Transylvanian count," Beatrice said. "I often have thought we do not speak of him enough. Impaled on his own flagpole after years of pining."

"They were all real, were they not, Aunt?" Juliet said.

"I said they weren't real," Van Doren said, looking positively gleeful. "I said it all along."

"They could have been real," Miss Mayton cried. "*They* knew how to act as proper gentlemen. *They* had romance in their hearts. *They* did not speak of their preference for toast."

"*They* have been a product of your wild imagination, and *they* have not been searching for you for twenty years, and *they* did not forgo informing the authorities when you robbed them blind!" Mr. Wagner shouted.

"That *is* rather romantic, Aunt," Viola said. "Twenty years shows a steadfastness of affection. He must be very loyal to put up with it."

"And he is a rather handsome fellow," Cordelia said. "A bit like how you always described Gregorio."

"And he did not tragically die, which must run in his favor," Beatrice said.

"And Mr. Wagner could have got you in terrible trouble over the money," Juliet pointed out.

Miss Mayton shrugged. "I had to live on something, naturally. Though, I would not have thought that man would have put down his beloved toast and looked for me for so long."

"Well, I did," Mr. Wagner said.

Out of the corner of his eye, Darden saw Tattleton begin to sway. Then the butler took that moment to faint dead away, falling to the carpet like an old oak in a forest.

Chaos reliably ensued.

CHAPTER NINETEEN

MARIANNA WATCHED AS the men at table jumped from their seats and ran to the stricken butler. Mr. Tattleton was not long in a faint and seemed more appalled at finding himself on the floor than concerned for how he got there.

As they helped him to his feet and the earl directed that a doctor be summoned, Marianna looked about her in utter fascination.

Was there ever such a family as this? Had there ever been such a dinner? She must think not, as surely she would have heard of it. It could not be every day that a matron is faced with the husband she left behind almost a quarter of a century ago. And, upon hearing the news, the butler of the house fell into a faint.

More importantly, the duke said he thought she'd hold up well in the family. What did he mean by that? Did he know something?

She would hold up perfectly well, she was sure. If something firm were said about it. She was done with hints. Lord Darden needed to say something firm. Soon. Right now.

As the two footmen and the earl helped the butler out of the room, the Duke of Conbatten said, "As we are down three servants and a host, I suggest Baderston and Hamill help me serve. We should be able to muddle through in some fashion."

Marianna's father rose. "Considering the circumstances, Conbatten, I believe we will take our leave. Wagner, you are welcome to come with us, I can put you up for as long as you like."

Lord Darden leapt to his feet. "Your Grace, I beg you to be seated. You must not go. I have something of great import to say."

"More to say than what's been said already?" the duke said, staring at Miss Mayton.

"Yes, Your Grace," Lord Darden said.

"I believe we've heard enough for one evening," the duke said. "If you would have our carriage called round, we will be on our way."

"Not on your life, Richard," the Duchess of Kembleton said to her duke. "Lord Darden has something to say."

Marianna felt as if the room did not have enough air. What did he wish to say? Though she had been determined to disavow any hopes that might present themselves to her mind, she found hope bursting like little bubbles as if her blood had turned to champagne.

She had been brought here, with just the family in attendance, and Lord Darden had something particular to say. Marianna had a great wish to grab him by the neckcloth and shake it out of him.

Lord Darden glanced at Miss Mayton and her recently found husband, Mr. Wagner. "You two, go to the drawing room and hash out whatever has gone on between you."

Miss Mayton looked away defiantly. "I do not see that there is anything at all to—"

"Miss Mayton," Lord Darden said, in a wonderfully decisive tone. "*Now*, if you please."

Miss Mayton sniffed, but she rose. She swept out of the room with Mr. Wagner on her heels.

Marianna's father had slowly sat down, though he did not seem at all happy to do it. She supposed he'd thought that a surprise husband and a fainting butler would be enough to get him out of the house.

Thank goodness her mother had stepped in and put a stop to that gambit. Though really, her poor father could not have wrestled her into a carriage. Not before she heard what Lord Darden would say.

Say it, say it, say it. For the love of heaven, say it, and let it be what she was hoping for.

"Lady Marianna, it was brought to my attention," Lord Darden said, "that I was not altogether clear when I said one's opinion might change over time. It was *my* opinion—I was the one I was talking about."

"Still not very clear, Darden," Lady Van Doren whispered.

"What conversation was this?" the duke asked suspiciously.

"It was at Lady Bloomington's masque," Rosalind said.

"What I meant," Lord Darden went on, "is that I thought I did not wish to marry, hence the ruse, but then I found my mind changing."

Changing over who? Changing over her, or changing over the lady he'd waltzed with at the masque? Why could he not be more specific?

"What ruse?" the duke said.

"The ruse to fool his sisters," Cordelia said. "We were trying to get him married and he wished us to think he was set on Lady Marianna since she was supposed to wed Wellerston or Mayfield. You see? We were meant to think it a hopeless case."

The duke became very red in the face. "It *is* a hopeless case! If that is what this farce of an evening is about!"

"It is exactly what it's about," Lord Darden said. "Now, Your Grace, I know you will not like it, but I have been in love with your daughter for quite some time."

"In love?" the duke sputtered. "Nonsense. No, I will not hear of it. Stop where you are, Lord Darden," the duke said.

"No, you stop where *you* are, Father," Marianna said. She turned to Lord Darden. "What about the mysterious lady? The one you waltzed with at the masque?"

"The mysterious…that was Viola."

"Lady Baderston…" Marianna said. How did she not even consider it might have been one of his sisters? She'd been so consumed with disappointment and jealousy that she could not grasp the simplest of explanations.

"Yes, it was me," Lady Baderston said. "My lord did not yet know the steps."

"I know them now, though," Lord Baderston put in.

Marianna rose. Lord Darden threw down his napkin. They met at the sideboard.

She threw her arms around his neck.

"Stop!" the duke shouted. "That is the limit! Stop this instant."

Lord Darden bent down and kissed her on the lips. Somewhere in the distance, Marianna heard her mother say, "Richard, do sit down."

"I loved you all along," he said. "I see that now."

"And I, you. How was I to know your feelings, though?"

Lord Darden laughed. "Yes, that was my fault. Never was there such an opaque declaration."

She stood on her tiptoes and kissed him again, hearing her father's groans in the background.

"So you do feel the same?" Lord Darden asked. "I wasn't certain. Really, I was doubtful, but I had to take my chance."

"All along, Darden. All along."

The earl, who had been attending to his fainting butler, reentered the dining room. He stopped and whispered, "Gracious."

"You see what has happened here, Earl," the duke said. "My daughter has been compromised by *your* son in *your* house."

"Well, I hadn't thought…right in the dining room," the earl said.

"I am not compromised, Papa," Marianna said laughing. "I am engaged."

"Not without my approval, you're not," the duke said darkly.

"I am of age and there is always Gretna Green, if I am pushed," she said, knowing how that idea would strike. She meant it, too. If her father was prepared to stand against her happiness, it was no matter. She had taken the reins of her life into her own hands. She had taken Lord Darden into her own hands. She would throw him into a carriage and drive them both to Scotland if necessary.

"Now, Richard," the duchess said, "you will not like an elopement—people will talk."

"This is all very untoward and uncomfortable," the earl said. "Somebody make up two plates and send them to the library. Conbatten, hand over two of the bottles of the dry Tokay you sent to the house and two glasses. Duke, let us repair to the library so you can clear your head and have time to think."

Much to Marianna's surprise, her father did acquiesce to the idea. She did not know if it was the draw of the dry Tokay, or her father's understanding that his defiance was a fast-sinking ship.

The earl guided the shaken duke out of the room. Lady Harveston set about making up their plates. Conbatten said, "I suppose we ought to make up our own plates too, and take them wherever we are comfortable. I presume the back of the drawing room will suit Darden and Lady Marianna."

Marianna did not know what was so particular about the back of the drawing room, but as she was prepared to follow Lord Darden anywhere, they repaired there. Of course, once she got there, she understood the duke's idea—it was delightfully dim and set apart from the rest of the room.

Their dinners were on a table in front of them but so far remained untouched. They, themselves, however, did not long remain untouched.

Touching Lord Darden felt like the most natural thing in the world, as if they had always been meant to touch.

"Do you like Town?" Darden asked, twirling a curl of her hair and kissing her neck. "You really do have the most marvelous hair."

Marianna laughed. "Thank you, and I like Town better now than I did before."

"This house is for my use year-round and will be very private now that my sisters have all married. I do not suppose my father will even come in for next season. And then the estate in Somerset, there is plenty of room for us, we might have a wing to ourselves. But I must warn you—there are an awful lot of animals wandering round."

"And Artemis would be, too."

"Ah, the dog who won't hunt. He would fit right in."

"Perhaps we ought to go back and forth," Marianna suggested, trying to keep her attention on her words and not where Darden's lips were tracing along her neck. "When we wish to be alone we will stay here, and when we wish for chaos we will go there."

"Excellent notion. I suppose my father will like the company now that Miss Mayton...well, I do not actually know what she will do."

"I wonder where they've gone," Marianna said. She had fully expected to find Miss Mayton and Mr. Wagner seated on opposite sides of the sofa when they'd come in, but there was no sign of them.

"Would it be terrible to say I would not be brokenhearted to discover they have decamped back to Bonn?"

"I have grown very fond of Miss Mayton."

Darden pulled her close. "I can only think of my fondness for you at this moment."

Time drifted on and Marianna could not really say how much had passed. She had spent so much time imagining what his hands could do and now she was beginning to find out. She would very much like to drag him into a church as soon as possible, so they might get on with it.

She had never in her life felt as if she wore too many clothes, but she did now. The silk of her dress felt positively stifling.

Marianna was vaguely aware of the activity on the other side of the room, which began to sound very jolly. Her mother, Lady Hamill, Lady Baderston, and Lady Harveston played lottery tickets to the great hilarity of them all. The lords Baderston, Hamill, and Harveston played their own game of cards. Lady Van Doren seemed much occupied by her husband and was patting him on the arm as he stared at the door. The Duke and Duchess of Conbatten sat together on a small settee, the duchess practically on his lap.

There had been no sign of her father and Marianna presumed the earl was plying him with glasses of dry Tokay to help restore his equanimity. After all, he could not put a stop to it now—she had been in Darden's arms and kissed him in a room full of people and now they were positively scandalous in a dark corner.

Very suddenly, something caught the attention of everyone at the other side of the room and it became filled with exclamations. She peered around Darden's neckcloth and saw Miss Mayton and Mr. Wagner.

"They have come back, and they are holding hands!" Marianna said. "Come, we must hear what they will say."

Darden sighed, which she found quite adorable, but he rose. He straightened her dress and held out his arm.

As they approached, Miss Mayton said, "I suppose everyone will wish to know what has happened."

"Tell us, Aunt!" Lady Hamill said. "Tell us everything."

"As you know, I was forced to leave Mr. Wagner," Miss Mayton said, "on account of his putting toast ahead of his wife."

"It was a foolish mistake," Mr. Wagner said. "I knew very well how Eloise was. When I courted her, I did all the romantic things. But then, when we were married, I thought I need not do them anymore."

"He thought that providing me a nice house and an allowance for dresses and such was in some way romantic," Miss Mayton, shaking her head in disbelief.

"Apparently, the toast was the last straw," Mr. Wagner said.

"So he's been looking for me all this time," Miss Mayton said. "Which has affected his medical practice very badly."

"Patients don't like it when their doctor is always careening across the countryside looking for a missing wife," Mr. Wagner averred.

"So here we are, come to an understanding," Miss Mayton said.

"I have sworn I will do something romantic every day," Mr. Wagner said.

"And I have agreed to wed Mr. Wagner."

"But Aunt," Lady Harveston said, "you and Mr. Wagner are already married."

"Yes, well, I feel the whole story of where he's been, and me wearing widow's weeds when he was not actually dead, might require more explanation than is convenient. So, we decided to put it out that we just met and now we are engaged. We will have a very elaborate wedding."

"Do tell us you will stay in England, Aunt," the Duchess of Conbatten said.

"Of course we will," Miss Mayton said, nodding. "Germany was so dark and cold all the time, it was not at all good for my health."

"Yes, Eloise assures me that this recent spate of rain and gray clouds is very unusual for England."

Marianna bit her lip to stop her laughter. Poor Mr. Wagner would be forever waiting for the sun to come out.

"So you will set up your practice here, Mr. Wagner?" Lady Baderston asked. "We know ever so many people we could send to you."

"I will retire from medicine," Mr. Wagner said.

"Oh, but you did say your practice in Germany had not done very well," Lady Hamill said, her brows knitting.

Marianna wondered at that herself. How on earth could a doctor with a failing practice afford to retire? But then, perhaps he had some family money squirreled away.

"Ah, well, Eloise?" Mr. Wagner asked. "You'd best tell them the rest of it."

Miss Mayton nodded. "Yes, as to the funding of a retirement.

It has been my long habit to read to the family from the books of a certain Richard Roydon."

"Oh yes, Your Grace," Lady Van Doren said to Marianna's mother, "they are ever so entertaining. We just finished *The Crafty Convolutions of Coldwood Castle.*"

"He is me," Miss Mayton said. "I am Richard Roydon."

"You never are, Aunt," Lady Hamill said.

"Oh yes, I most definitely am," Miss Mayton said. "You see, I've always known how romance should be and yet I could not have it for my own. What with having an unromantic husband too interested in his toast, you see. So one day I sat down and began to write my perfect love story. He was a tortured duke and I was a gentle governess having no idea of his desperate love for me."

"You are an author!" Cordelia said. "But Aunt, how did you manage to get it published? I'm sure Jules would like to know it— she's got heaps of odes that could be a smashing book."

"Ah yes, well," Miss Mayton said, "it was very discouraging at first. Gracious, some of the insulting letters I received back about my book, you would have thought I'd assaulted those fellows."

"She did assault them," Darden said softly.

"But then one day," Miss Mayton continued, "I received a letter from a publisher in York. He was, I will admit, rather disparaging about my talent, but he also thought a certain type of reader would like it."

"And so they have," Lady Van Doren said.

"Indeed they have," Miss Mayton said. "Thousands and thousands of times over."

Marianna leaned over and whispered in Darden's ear, "You must read me one of these books."

"I will do," he whispered, "and then you will beg that I never do so again."

"Eloise has grown rather rich on those books," Mr. Wagner said. "All because I liked my toast too much."

"How did we not guess?" Lady Hamill said in wonderment.

"I feel just the same, Jules," Lady Harveston said. "Those books are filled with romance and drama, just like the stories of Hans, Gregorio, Phillipe, and the Transylvanian count."

Darden took Marianna's hand. "Have we heard enough? That sofa back there is waiting."

"Let us not make it wait longer, then," Marianna said.

So, they tiptoed away from the crowd surrounding Miss Mayton as she regaled them with how she became Richard Roydon and how the only two people who knew the secret were herself and her publisher in York and how she was just now writing *The Mayhem and Madness of Montague Moor*. Apparently, Fleur, her lady's maid, often came upon her as she was at her work, but had been told that her mistress was writing a memoir about Hans, Gregorio, Phillipe, and the Transylvanian count.

After she and Darden returned to their private and dim corner, Marianna supposed an hour had passed, though it was rather hard to tell. Everything about Darden was fascinating—his face, his chest, his hands, his voice. He seemed to find her rather fascinating too. He could not keep his hands from her hair, or from other places she would not name.

They were entirely disheveled when the next interruption came. The earl and her father arrived to the drawing room.

Fortunately, her father was very much subdued and too entirely drunk to notice that his daughter had been manhandled for the past few hours. It would turn out that he'd drunk the two bottles of Tokay by himself, while the earl soothed him with all sorts of arrangements to the marriage contract that would be favorable to his daughter.

The footmen poured him into the carriage and Marianna found him resigned. The last thing he said before he dozed off was, "Well, Conbatten swears it will be all right."

Marianna was sure it would be all right. She was also sure no two people had made so much trouble for themselves as she and Darden had. If she had defied her father before they ever came to Town, there would never have been the idea of her wedding

Mayfield or Wellerston going round. If Darden had not been so set on avoiding a wedding, there would have been no ruse.

No matter, though. Tonight she would stay awake as long as she could so she might relive every moment of the dinner. And particularly, after the dinner in the back of the drawing room.

On the morrow, Darden would see the archbishop about a special license and the earl would set the solicitors to their work. Then, Darden would come round for her in the earl's carriage. He had his own phaeton, but the carriage was enclosed and had curtains. He said he planned to shock his coachman down to his shoes with his behavior.

Marianna was hoping she was a bit shocked too.

They would wed as quickly as humanly possible and then set off. Darden had told her they might go anywhere but she did not wish for the traipsing round a foreign country that so many ladies longed for. Once he'd described an old castle in Cornwall that he could borrow from one of his club members, the idea was set.

As the carriage trotted through the dark and quiet streets and her father snored, the duchess patted her hand.

"Well, you have steered your own ship, Marianna," the duchess said.

"Yes, I have, and I've steered it into a rather marvelous port."

The duchess laughed. "I have always liked Darden, and I am positively gleeful over his extended family. Never was there such a collection of interesting people."

Marianna nodded. It would be glorious to leap into bed with Darden. And then it would be wildly entertaining to see what his family would do next.

CHAPTER TWENTY

DARDEN GOT HIS special license easily enough, he'd known the archbishop for years. He and Marianna were wed in St. George's and the wedding breakfast was held at the Duke of Conbatten's house. It was thought that as the Duke of Kembleton was still a bit raw over the whole affair, meeting on neutral ground would be best.

Marianna's father was soothed by generous pourings of the dry Tokay and did not say anything worse than, "No turning round now, I suppose. Conbatten claims it will be all right—that's what he says, anyway."

The couple spent that first night at Conbatten's house on Grosvenor Square, the duke and Rosalind taking themselves off somewhere to be out of the way.

As soon as they were able to get everybody out of the house, including Marianna's father who got a bit weepy on the pavement and kept repeating "you'll never be a duchess," they ran up the stairs to the bedchamber they'd been given.

There, with the door shut, Darden suddenly paused. "I just thought, you will be nervous."

Marianna threw herself at him and tackled him on the bed. "I think not," she said. She was well aware of how nature would take its course and wished nature would hurry up about it.

Darden was all too willing to oblige. As the breeze fluttered the window curtains and the sun traipsed overhead across the square, she and Darden rolled around and became very well acquainted with one another. Come nightfall, Darden lit candles, hastily clothed himself, and went downstairs to find the butler.

He did indeed find him and discovered him looking in all directions but his own and refusing to meet his eye.

"We *are* married, you know," he said, laughing.

He was certain he heard the old butler mutter, "Rather *loudly* married," before directing the footmen to make up a tray and a few bottles of wine to be sent above stairs.

They spent the night talking, and then sometimes not talking, and fell asleep in the early morning hours. A tray sent up for a late breakfast woke them, and then each other's company further delayed them, and they departed for Cornwall far later than they'd planned.

It did not matter too very much, as they were to do the traveling in the Bennington style. There was no rush from one point to the next, but rather a leisurely meandering through the countryside. With all the stopping because a certain inn looked charming, and stopping for a picnic, and then stopping again for another charming inn, it was six days before they reached their destination.

Carlyon Castle was of modest size as far as castles generally go, but it was all charm and coziness. The rooms were not overlarge and the walls a heavy cold stone, but the fireplaces were enormous. When they were not otherwise occupied behind closed doors, Darden and Marianna huddled under blankets and drank hot coffees, listening to the wind whip off the sea and the waves crash on the rocky shore. Artemis had been brought with them, as Marianna was certain if he were left behind her father would pawn him off on somebody.

Artemis was very agreeable to this plan and spent the wedding trip making his way from the east side of the castle to the west, following the sun as it landed on the carpets. That, and generous helpings of Cornwall beef, satisfied his every requirement.

After a fortnight they departed, as they had promised everyone they would return in time for Miss Mayton's wedding to her husband, Mr. Wagner.

Miss Mayton and Mr. Wagner were not so highly placed as to have access to the archbishop for a special license. With the earl's help, they did the next best thing and applied for a common license. It might be guessed at, knowing Miss Mayton's romantic turn of mind, that the plans for the wedding day were elaborate.

Time helped them become even more elaborate, as everyone involved agreed that they must wait some weeks for Darden and Marianna to return to Town.

The Duke of Conbatten once more opened his house for the event, not wishing to put the earl to the trouble of it. He did not know Miss Mayton's specific plans, but as it was Miss Mayton, it was bound to be complicated, troublesome, and odd.

It was best the duke was not too well informed, as his wife, his sisters-in-law, and Miss Mayton had heads together to arrange every conceivable thing that could be arranged for a wedding. And then some things that nobody had ever arranged for a wedding.

Miss Mayton's dress was made of taffeta in a shade very close to the parakeet green. This color was rather bold, but as the appointments with the modiste went on, the color began to be subdued by a sequined and glittering net overlay that was near blinding. Finally, a cape of light silk embroidered with paste jewels went over the whole concoction.

A tiara was chosen and then thought not sufficient to suit the magnificence of the dress. A second tiara was added behind the first atop her head, the first one shorter and the second taller. Miss Mayton became very confident that the two-tiara style would soon become the fashion. Interspersed amidst the two tiaras were red rose buds blooming out of her head from every direction.

While Miss Mayton had dispensed with the face paint she'd once resorted to in pursuit of Mr. Brummel, she found she could not do without the vermilion lipstick. And some touchups to her hair. And just a hint of blush. And then the whole thing needed to be balanced out with some charcoal lining her eyes.

On the day, she glided to the top of the ballroom to meet the bishop and Mr. Wagner, a glittering ship sailing into port.

The cake designed to celebrate the nuptials was a monstrosity that had to be built in layers in the duke's dining room as it could not be carried fully assembled. Never had so much icing ever been mixed in Conbatten's kitchens and he had high hopes it never would be again.

Miss Mayton's invitations to this blessed event had shot very high and wide. Everybody she had ever heard of was invited, including the prince. The only person who had not been invited was a certain Mr. Beau Brummel.

While one as low on the societal pole as Miss Mayton might have reasonably expected half these invitations to land in the nearest bin, not so for this bride. She had proved herself endlessly entertaining, bizarre, and unpredictable. Now she'd dug up some German doctor to marry her—who would miss it?

Those few who did miss it were sorry they did, as it ended up being one of the events of the season.

Juliet read an ode dedicated to the couple named *Ode to Rekindling*.

Viola unveiled a portrait she'd painted that may or may not have depicted two people.

Rosalind played one of her travels through the world of music after having the pianoforte moved from the "family room" to the drawing room before her duke could stop her.

Cordelia acted out her Desdemona dying scene though nobody could understand how that was meant to celebrate a wedding.

Lady Rawley and her troupe performed a concocted scene from *The Taming of the Shrew*, renamed *The Taming of Who?* in which Kate turns the tables on Petruchio and entirely defeats him.

To cap off the whole affair, Miss Mayton, now Mrs. Wagner, announced that she was the famous author, Richard Roydon, and she read from *The Mayhem and Madness of Montague Moor*.

The absurdity of the wedding celebration and the reveal of Miss Mayton having written a slew of…well, nobody really knew how to characterize those books, cemented the lady as a fixture of the societal scene. She was simply too entertaining to snub. The prince liked to joke with Brummel that she was the one who got away.

As Miss Mayton had cast such a wide net with her invitations, Lord Baderston's mother came to Town for the wedding. It would turn out that the Dowager Countess of Baderston and the Earl of Westmont had been carrying on a correspondence ever since Viola had wed Baderston. They had known one another in their twenties and had since reestablished the relationship. Over time, they would wed, both of them thinking it would be very pleasant to have someone they were fond of by their side for their older years.

Juliet, very encouraged by Miss Mayton's authorial success, sent her odes to every publisher she could locate. The responses she received were not as glowing as she had assumed they'd be. After three or four times of Lord Hamill arriving home to discover his wife weeping over a scathing diatribe suggesting her odes were an insult to poets everywhere, he began taking the responses out of the post and burning them. Over time, Juliet's naturally buoyant spirits returned and she paid to have her odes put into a book, handing them out as gifts to people she favored. Very reliably, Conbatten's copy went straight into his "family room," never to be seen again.

Tattleton took some weeks to recover from the stress that had built through six long seasons. He rather enjoyed his recovery, as he was plied with all manner of things from the kitchens and young Lily was brought to see him nearly every day. When it was time for that adorable young lady to depart, she always issued the same order—"Don't die, Taddydon!"

On that sage advice, he did not die. Tattleton made a full recovery and settled into the very calm and regulated house of an earl who had no more children to settle. He became inordinately fond of the dowager countess his earl had wed, as she had taken the various animals roaming the place firmly in hand. They were all instructed on what to do and what not to do. The two parrots were forbidden to shout "Murder" and "Shut it, old man," though they did still whisper it defiantly when she was not about.

Darden and Marianna took on a rather nomadic life for the first few years of their marriage. They had a carriage built that carried every manner of comfort and were always on their way somewhere. Sometimes to Somerset, sometimes to Town, and if not those two places, they imposed on Marianna's father or one of Darden's sisters. Artemis was a genial companion, as that dog could sleep anywhere under any circumstances at any time.

Marianna's father, the duke, did finally give up his resentment of the match under the indefatigable cheerfulness of his new son-in-law. It became a little tedious to keep insulting a person who pretended he did not know he was being insulted. As well, though the duke continually protested against being managed by his duchess, he was very well managed by his duchess.

When Marianna and Darden's first baby came, they found her a sturdy traveler. Young Daisy found the carriage rumbling along soothing and the new faces to encounter very interesting. The second baby was a different matter. George was a homebody and became very temperamental on the trips. They eventually could not stand up against his wailing and settled permanently in Town, as everybody knows there is no defeating a determined and unreasonable toddler.

All settled under one roof, Benny, the earl's first footman, came in as the butler, and a matron named Mrs. Clementine came in as housekeeper.

Melly had long nursed the hope of finding herself at the top of the heap but found herself the lone lady's maid. She satisfied herself with occasionally saying something outrageous at table to see if the butler would cross her.

Richards, Darden's valet, became infatuated with Melly's daring, and they eventually married. It would have been usual for them to leave service, but there was nothing particularly usual about Darden's household so they stayed on. Years later, Darden purchased a house in Brighton and Richards and Melly relocated there to be the caretakers of it.

Mr. Wagner was as good as his word and did something romantic for his wife every day. As his wife particularly preferred public demonstrations of his devotion, these were often on display at a dinner party. Mr. Wagner would come into the drawing room after the men had their port and would loudly declare that the minutes they had been parted were an agony. This was very comfortable for his wife, though perhaps not for the other gentlemen in attendance, as their wives began to question them as to why they were not in agony too.

After six years of debate, the Duke of Conbatten was finally asked to join the Young Bucks Club. He accepted, primarily for the amusement of turning up from time to time and observing that nobody knew what to do with him.

In the fullness of time, Lord Darden and his members found they were no longer young bucks. Rather than disband the club, Darden passed it on to the new generation, providing guidance on shenanigans and tomfoolery.

In the Bennington family lore, as it was passed down from one generation to the next, the evening that Miss Mayton was surprised by the husband she'd left behind twenty years before, the butler fainted dead away, Lord Darden proposed to Lady Marianna over the shouting of her father, and Miss Mayton was revealed as the author Richard Roydon was forever known as *the dinner*.

And so, the Benningtons had very reliably created muddles wherever they went. Nobody could hold it too much against them though. After all, those muddles were always very fine.

The End

About the Author

By the time I was eleven, my Irish Nana and I had formed a book club of sorts. On a timetable only known to herself, Nana would grab her blackthorn walking stick and steam down to the local Woolworth's. There, she would buy the latest Barbara Cartland romance, hurry home to read it accompanied by viciously strong wine, (Wild Irish Rose, if you're wondering) and then pass the book on to me. Though I was not particularly interested in real boys yet, I was *very* interested in the gentlemen in those stories—daring, bold, and often enraging and unaccountable. After my Barbara Cartland phase, I went on to Georgette Heyer, Jane Austen and so many other gifted authors blessed with the ability to bring the Georgian and Regency eras to life.

I would like nothing more than to time travel back to the Regency (and time travel back to my twenties as long as we're going somewhere) to take my chances at a ball. Who would take the first? Who would escort me into supper? What sort of meaningful looks would be exchanged? I would hope, having made the trip, to encounter a gentleman who would give me a very hard time. He ought to be vexatious in the extreme, and *worth* every vexation, to make the journey worthwhile.

I most likely won't be able to work out the time travel gambit, so I will content myself with writing stories of adventure and romance in my beloved time period. There are lives to be created, marvelous gowns to wear, jewels to don, instant attractions that inevitably come with a difficulty, and hearts to break before putting them back together again. In traditional Regency fashion, my stories are clean—the action happens in a drawing room, rather than a bedroom.

As I muse over what will happen next to my H and h, and

wish I were there with them, I will occasionally remind myself that it's also nice to have a microwave, Netflix, cheese popcorn, and steaming hot showers.

Come see me on Facebook! @KateArcherAuthor